MIRACLE

Rebekah Pace

WITH STEPHEN HANSON

Copyright © 2025 by Level 4 Press, Inc.

This book is printed on acid-free paper.

Published by:
Level 4 Press, Inc.
14702 Haven Way
Jamul, CA 91935
www.level4press.com

Library of Congress Control Number: 2019943920

ISBN: 978-1-64630-793-7

Printed in the United States of America

Other books by
REBEKAH PACE

The Red Thread
All I Want For Christmas

1

An endless stream of yellow lane markers, lit up by the headlights on Frank's eighteen-wheeler, flew past as he barreled south on Iowa's Highway 169 at seventy miles per hour. Part of him—the part he usually ignored—knew he was over the speed limit. But he had been held up for over an hour by an accident on I-80, just outside Des Moines, and he wanted to make up for lost time.

He yawned as he passed another green sign designating an upcoming town. He squinted at it: WINTERSET 19 MILES.

Almost there. It was closing in on 10 p.m. and he'd been awake since 4:30 that morning. He was desperate to get off the road and into his sleeper.

He was getting old. Even five years ago he could have managed an eighteen-hour shift with no more than a few mugs of coffee. But now, after half a century of living, he got drowsy more easily and more often. His eyes darted to the empty bottle of whiskey on the seat next to him as they fluttered to a close . . .

With a jolt, he jerked his head up and instinctively pulled the steering wheel to the left, saving the truck from veering off the road. Damnit! He shook his head, slapping his face a few times.

Just nineteen more miles. You just gotta make it that far, man.

He pressed down on the gas again. A few years back, the company had installed electronic "speed limiters" that were supposed to prevent him from going too fast. Or, at least, snitch on him if he did. But Barry at the garage had come through and deactivated the one in Frank's rig. He smirked and pressed down on the pedal even harder, feeling the engine rumble.

He looked up at the wrinkled Polaroid of Nancy and Sue, which had fallen below the visor, almost out of sight. He pulled it back and gazed at it in the glow of his dashboard. It was from a few Christmases ago. Sue looked like she was still in junior high, though she wore her varsity cheerleading sweater, so she must have been older. He rubbed his eyes. Nancy had the same haircut as always, though it was a little shorter here, with her ends curling around the tops of her shoulders. She had her arm around Sue as they knelt in front of the Christmas tree wearing ugly holiday sweaters and sporting big grins, a mound of presents behind them. That was the winter Frank had won three in a row betting on the Dubuque Spartans, and he'd lavished his family with presents.

His gut clenched as he considered how different this Christmas was going to be. He instinctively reached for the whiskey, realizing from its lack of heft that it was empty. He tossed the bottle onto the floor and sighed. He was so tired . . .

He jerked awake again, pulling at the steering wheel in a panic. The truck returned to the middle of his lane. He slapped himself a few more times. He had to be getting close to Winterset by now.

In the background, Alex Meter's voice rang from the radio. He turned up the volume.

"Just let me tell ya, folks, the ol' BS Meter is going off the charts!" Meter's booming baritone was exactly how Frank thought God would sound. *"It looks like we got a new prescription from Dr. Barack Hussein Obama!"* Frank grinned. Meter always pronounced Obama's middle name with an extra dose of venom. *"This one, though, looks more like a suppository! The good Dr. Obama wants all of us Americans to bend over and take his Marxist, government-run Obamacare right*

where the sun don't shine—well, I say we bend the good doctor over and give him a taste of his own medicine!"

Frank chuckled along as Meter laughed at his own joke. *"I'm of course speaking metaphorically, folks,"* Meter went on. *"Don't want another visit from the Secret Service! Here's what you need to know about the good Dr. Obama's socialized medicine. The main question here is, who puts value on your life? For all you listeners out there, you might be thinking, well, I'm a free American, so clearly the value of my life belongs to me, and only me. And you'd be right, of course! But, you see, to a socialist nut like the current occupant of the White House, your life only has value insofar as the government says it does!"*

Asshole Obama. But even Frank's angry euphoria couldn't stop the pull of sleep, which beckoned again. His drooping eyes drifted from the road and back to the picture of Nancy and Sue.

"The value of a human life, folks," Meter continued from the radio, *"of course, comes only from God Himself. Now, the good news is that Obama and all those socialists and Marxists in his cabinet also believe this. The bad news is that, while they do in fact believe in a god, that God just so happens to be the government. The very same government that now wants to tell us what to do with our health, what medicines we can take, and what procedures we can have! And, let me tell you, folks, if your granny is sick in a nursing home, you may be thinking, 'Well, my God has told me that her life has value because she was created in His image!' But then here comes the false god of Obama's government, telling you, 'Actually, she's costing us too much money to keep alive, and, based on our Marxist doctrine, that means she don't got no value no more!' So, say goodbye to Granny, courtesy of your friendly neighborhood government!"*

Frank let the anger of Meter's words fall across him like the comfort of an old friend. One hand slipped from the wheel to his lap. The center lane marker listed across the blur of darkness and passing streetlights, floating across the windshield. Two faint lights appeared somewhere down the road, blending with the frosty white beads on Nancy's and Sue's sweaters in the picture.

From behind his closing eyes the two lights danced in the windshield as they grew closer, and brighter. He squeezed his eyes, trying to enjoy his sleep. Meter's voice became unintelligible background noise, and Frank smiled as he melted into his seat. His other hand drooped into his lap with the first. The lights were on the outside of sleep, and he knew he needn't worry about whatever they might be. Shooting stars or fireflies. Or headlights.

Headlights . . .

Frank jolted awake and, in pure reflex, grabbed the steering wheel with both hands and pulled the truck back over the center lane. At the exact same moment, the approaching car laid on its horn in a prolonged, rage-filled wail. The tires on both vehicles squealed in unison as they swerved to avoid each other.

The truck shuddered with the sudden shift back to the right lane, and Frank's hands tensed up on the steering wheel. Panic exploded in his lungs. He gasped for breath as his adrenaline slapped away his drowsiness, and he tightened his arms against the wheel and pressed down on the brake. The truck began to slow.

"*But, folks, the good Dr. Obama has no cure for America. Matter of fact, he's soon going to find that America has a cure for him!*"

Frank slapped himself for what had to be the twentieth time. That was way too close. He knew what would happen if he wrecked again.

Another sign approached: WINTERSET 10 MILES.

Don't panic, man, he coached himself. *You avoided disaster. Just stay awake the next ten miles, and you'll be fine . . .*

A piercing *bweep* sounded from somewhere on the road behind him. In the same instant, flashing red and blue lights appeared in his side mirrors.

"*Okay, okay*," Meter said, a rare softness taking hold of his rant, as if he sensed the massive pile of shit Frank had just stepped in. "*I yell and I scream about this and about that. And maybe it's because*

I'm getting old, or maybe I'm sentimental from looking at the fat ass of my HR-approved, minority quota–fulfilled Black intern, Monika, struggling to put up Christmas lights all day, but we're coming into the Christmas season and I want each and every one of my listeners to remember that life is precious. Let Christmas remind you to hold tight on to the ones you love."

Frank hit the hazard lights and slowly pulled to a stop on the shoulder. The air brakes hissed. In the side mirror, he saw the shadowy outline of the state trooper get out of his car and begin walking toward the truck.

"When you go home tonight and look at the family that surrounds you, remember that you can't put a price tag on a human life . . . no matter what those socialist monkeys try to tell you."

2

In the kitchen, Tess could hear Angela Lansbury's familiar voice wafting down from the upstairs bedroom. With her recent hearing problems, Mum always watched her reruns of *Murder, She Wrote* with the volume all the way up. Tess smiled as she added broth to the vegetables in her pot and stirred. A burner over, tea water heated in the kettle. Mum was happy, and that was all that mattered at this point.

Tess looked out the window. The BBC weatherman had predicted the possibility of an early snow to hit London but save for a few dotted crystals of frost affixed to the glass, Tess couldn't see any other signs of winter threaded between the darkness of late evening and the city lights in Chelsea.

A voice on the other end of the cordless phone she was balancing between her shoulder and her ear brought her back to the moment. With Jessica Fletcher's authoritative voice still seeping through the ceiling, she had a hard time deciphering the thick Indian accent from the person on the other end of the NHS service line. A headache was pinching at her temples, but she tried to ignore it.

"Yes, I do understand that," she spoke into the phone. "Really, I do. And I do appreciate how helpful you have been. However, this— Yes, I understand, but this . . . this goes back to my initial question. We were told the checkup does not qualify as urgent, and . . . yes . . . yes . . . yes, I understand, but my point was that, given her health and advanced age, saying it's not urgent and delaying it further is . . . yes? Yes, I can hold . . ."

The kettle reached a boil as tinny Christmas music began playing from the phone. Tess took her latest "hold" break to consider her tea options. She had a sizable collection in her cabinet, ranging from British standards such as Earl Grey to more exotic blends from India and the Far East. When Mum first moved in with her five years ago, she had attempted to get her hooked on some of the better varieties. Being American-born, though, Margaret Wilson never quite developed the proper palate for the stuff. Her six years in London with Tess's dad, Dale Johnson, had been more focused on pints than pots.

"Oh, dear, you know us—we're a bit famous for throwing it in Boston Harbor!" Mum would often say when Tess brought her a hot cup. That hadn't stopped her from coming to London for college and marrying an Englishman, but after their divorce she'd been quick to return to America, leaving five-year-old Tess to be raised by Dale. Tess had a happy enough childhood in London, living above Dad's pub. She supposed that Dale fit into the category of a serial monogamist with commitment problems, in that he had a series of relationships, each lasting roughly five years. Fortunately, all of Dad's "female friends" were nice enough, and Tess was able to pretend that she was lucky in that she had many mothers, not just one. But as Dale grew older, his life became centered around the regulars at the pub and his daughter, which Tess found she preferred. When he died of a heart attack, she took over running the pub without ever really deciding that was what she wanted to do with her life. She found that all too often, life happens to us, rather than us controlling it.

"Tess, Tess, honey!" Her mum's words sliced through Angela Lansbury and the "on hold" music from the phone.

"Coming, Mum!" she called upstairs. She had two cups of tea—some of her most decorative porcelain—spaced symmetrically on the tray, alongside bowls of sugar, milk, and honey, though her mother rarely, if ever, added any of those. Keeping the phone propped between her ear and shoulder, she scooped up a stack of clean clothes, hooking the hangers on one arm, and managed to get a proper hold of the tea tray. She carefully made her way upstairs to her mother's bedroom.

Inside she scanned for a sufficient place to set the tray. The room, to her chagrin, had grown overrun with pill bottles, adult nappies, NHS pamphlets, and various other medical paraphernalia. Taking care not to drop the phone or the clothes, she awkwardly swept a few empty pill bottles from the top of the bedside dresser and laid the tea tray down there.

At her ear, the orchestral version of "Good King Wenceslas" came to an abrupt stop. "Your call is highly important to us," an automated voice said. "We thank you for your patience, and we will be with you shortly." The music resumed.

From her chair, Tess's mother began a sudden, violent coughing fit into her sleeve. Tess dropped the phone and the clothes and rushed over. But Mum waved her away. Tess cleared her throat.

"Tea, Mum?" she asked. Her mother gave her an all-too-familiar look of guilt and mild embarrassment. At the same moment, Tess noticed the foul odor seeping through the room.

"Bathroom," her mother said. In her midwestern American accent, the word came out with a casual abruptness.

"Ah, no worries about that. We'll get you taken care of." Tess retrieved her mother's walker and helped her up from the easy chair. This was the third time this week that Mum hadn't made it to the toilet.

"Okay, up you go," Tess said. She guided her mother across the room to the small en suite bathroom next to her bed. "I can manage it from here," Mum said as she took hold of the handicap rails that had only recently been installed next to the toilet.

"Are you sure?" Tess asked.

"I do still have some modesty left, dear." Her mother shot her a wrinkled smile, which Tess returned.

"Well, then, I'll be just outside the door, if you need something." Tess picked up the phone from the bedroom floor and brought it to her ear again. "Jingle Bells." Then a different smell hit her nostrils, wafting from downstairs and cutting through the unpleasant bathroom stench. Something burning.

"Oh, bollocks!" Tess swore.

"What is it?" her mother asked through the door.

"Oh, just some soup I left on the stove. I'll be right back, Mum."

She zipped down the stairs and into the kitchen. The soup had boiled to the point of spilling over the sides of the pot—the pot that was, in hindsight, a bit too small—and into the oversized flame from the stove with venomous hisses of heat and burning fat. Tess waved her hands over the billows of smoke and steam and turned the flame to low. The soup appeared to have been spared the worst of it, at least the part that had managed to stay in the pot. She stirred it a few times with the wooden spoon, taking a moment to catch her breath.

3

Angie saw Dawn at the other end of the marketplace well before Dawn saw her. Dawn, the only white face in a sea of dark skin.

Angie raised her sunglasses, watching Dawn scan the cheap tourist trinkets while the broken English of the eager hawkers flew about her as they tried to lure in the gullible American. She rolled her eyes. Who was the "exotic" one now? Angie of course blended into the crowd, with her yellow sundress and sandals and her dark, braided hair pulled up in a tight bun. She could be one of the local women who threaded the narrow pathways through the market booths, carrying their wares in boxes bunched on their heads while keeping a vigilant eye on the children who bounced around their feet. Except she didn't have any wares, or any children. Didn't want any, for that matter.

Ten days back in Haiti and Angie had all but forgotten about her life as a medical office manager in Berkeley, falling into the grooves of life and energy that buzzed from every corner of Port-au-Prince, that cascaded down from the vibrant Caribbean sky, filtered through the palm trees that shimmered overhead in the warm breeze, and echoed in the calls of the Mèl Dyab birds fluttering between the palm fronds. She'd settled into the flow more easily than she'd expected. Not her mind, so much, but deep in her skin—in her feet, her fingers, her toes, as the humid air breathed a "welcome home" even as it pulled sweat from her pores.

It was a relief to turn away from the anxieties she had forged back in Berkeley. The mortgage, the gas bill, the black mold that she suspected was growing in the water stains in their basement. Returning to Port-au-Prince, those thoughts faded away as her hips fell back into the thumping rhythm of life on the Haitian streets and as her heart returned to the deep familiarity of her childhood home. Home, with the memory of her mama's thick legs as the two of them danced through the outdoor marketplaces, listening to the comforting patter of the barkers offering her candy and handmade dolls.

Home, as her mama had told her, "is where your bones been carved to fit in without no trouble. Like a shoe been worn so long it knows how your feet is shaped."

Across the market, Dawn was engaged with an older woman in a green and red karabela dress and a yellow headscarf who offered her a Vodou love doll that looked to be crafted from fake feathers, straw, and synthetic yarn. It was the kind of thing you could buy at the airport, and this one looked like cheap crap imported from China. But Dawn, true to form, handed over a wad of money from her purse and took the fake Vodou trinket in return.

Angie leaned against a palm tree and rubbed her shoulder, the bare skin slick with sweat. Behind her, she heard a sharp whistle and the rumbling of a small engine. Reflexively, she pulled her body away from the sound just as a man on a motor scooter blazed past carrying a box of bananas on his head. The people of the market parted for him, flowing in a human wave to clear his path without even looking up from their booths or their wares or their children. Except for Dawn. Still working her new Vodou toy over with her eyes as if it were a mysterious archeological artifact, she didn't notice the motor scooter until its driver had to pump his brakes in front of her and offer an angry curse in Creole—twice. With deer-like eyes,

Dawn looked around and finally took a few clumsy steps into the dirt clearing to her left. The driver carried on with only a brief head shake at the silly white lady blocking his path.

Poor Dawn. But still, Angie chuckled from behind her sealed lips. The previous night's fight had left an aftertaste of bitterness toward Dawn that soured her thoughts.

The irony was that the Haiti trip had been Dawn's idea in the first place. "Let's get away from Berkeley," she had told Angie. "We can visit your family down there, you can show me around Port-au-Prince, all the places you remember growing up."

Angie had been skeptical, and rightfully so. Early in the four years they had been together, Angie had learned that Dawn's good intentions often jumped well ahead of any practical planning. In the weeks leading up to the trip, Angie was left to navigate the issues of flight bookings, car rentals, visas, and so on while Dawn waxed poetically about the wonders of what she called Haiti's "exotic" culture. Angie was used to white American liberals turning into bourgeois do-gooders while discussing her country of birth, but Angie had thought Dawn would be better than that.

She'd thought wrong. Throughout the week, Dawn's overly appreciative comments on Haitian street art, food, and patois began to grate more and more on Angie's nerves. Not least of all because every example of Haitian culture that Dawn celebrated came with an unspoken addendum of how "sorry" the nice white lady felt for the poor, pathetic Haitians.

But what forced things closer to the breaking point the previous night had been the school.

"Did you see those poor Haitian kids across the street?" Dawn had asked. They were staying in a hotel rather than with Angie's parents, because while Papa loved her and had mostly accepted her lifestyle, he couldn't quite bring himself to let her sleep under his roof with her girlfriend. Their hotel room happened to overlook a school, and the sounds of young children playing on the bare asphalt turf were audible throughout the day.

"Poor?" By that point, Angie couldn't help herself.

"They're all so cute," Dawn said with a meek expression of childish innocence, so very Dawn-like. "I wish we could take all of them home with us."

Angie knew she shouldn't respond, even as her mouth opened and her voice rose in a caustic monotone. "What's wrong with their lives here?"

Dawn was still looking out the window, oblivious to her partner's threatening tone. "I'd just like to adopt one or two of them. Take them back to California with us. We could expand our family and give them a good life. Wouldn't it be wonderful?"

Angie closed the book she was reading with a loud thump. "You didn't answer my question," she said. "What's wrong with their lives here? And, for that matter, what's wrong with our life now?"

Dawn turned to her, eyes wide. "You never think about expanding our family?"

This was an obvious deflection. "I'm satisfied with what we have," Angie said. "Aren't you?"

Dawn briefly recoiled. "I mean, of course, I'm happy with just the two of us. But . . . I don't want to dismiss the possibility of having children. I mean, we have the cats . . ."

"*You* have the cats," Angie said. She hadn't realized Dawn viewed her pets as practice children, but that was what she was saying.

Dawn dropped her eyes out the window again. "But these kids here, they're so adorable, and I feel so bad for them."

"Bad?" Angie's voice rose louder than she intended.

"I mean," Dawn said, "I've been watching the orphanage since we've gotten here, and the kids look so happy despite their circumstances, I just think if we were able to bring one home with us and give them a better life . . ."

Angie had a million thoughts at once. "Home?" she said,

bewildered. "What circumstances? And . . . wait a minute, what do you mean orphanage?"

"The orphanage across the street," Dawn said. "What did you think I was talking about?"

Angie was flabbergasted, and it took her a second to find the words to respond. "That's a school. You think any building with a bunch of Haitian children is automatically an orphanage? You're acting like these Haitian kids are sad puppies just waiting for you, the nice white lady, to come and rescue them. They have families of their own! They're happy here! Don't start fantasizing about using them to screw up what we have together!" Angie's voice was a tightly constrained shout. "You see shirtless black kids playing in the dirt, you only see the dirt, the bare feet, the shirtless backs. You don't see the games they're playing! You don't hear their laughter, see their joy!"

"I'm just saying—" Dawn started, but Angie cut her off.

"Plus, don't just drop some shit about adopting kids on me in the middle of what's supposed to be our vacation! I'm trying to relax, not have a panic attack!"

Dawn abruptly rose from her chair and retreated into the bathroom. Running away from her problems like always. Within a minute Angie heard the bath water begin to run.

They hadn't talked about it since.

That was why she'd let Dawn come to the market alone. Angie had wanted to sleep in that morning, but Dawn had insisted on doing some last-minute shopping, despite Angie's repeated warnings that traffic to the airport would be awful. And now here she was, with her petite body, freckles, and hair cut in a choppy bob—looking completely out of place as she dragged her small suitcase behind her through the market. She wore a big straw sun hat and a pale-blue tank top—the one Angie had gotten her the previous Christmas to blend in with the softer colors of their Northern California home. It stood out in the tropical brilliance of Haiti.

From her perch next to the palm tree, Angie allowed herself to sink into the comfort of not being the outsider of the two of them, for a change, before waving her sweaty arm in Dawn's direction.

Dawn didn't notice it.

Am I just another black face to her here? Angie thought. *Another Haitian in a sea of so many?*

But then Dawn broke into a broad, goofy smile of recognition and waved back.

"Took you long enough," Angie said. Dawn marched over and pulled her in for an awkward hug with the hand that wasn't gripping her suitcase. She was drenched with sweat and had red blotches across her skin from the sun. "I thought maybe you forgot you have to catch a flight."

"I pack light," Dawn said as though that explained things. "Carry-on only." She was clutching the fake Vodou doll in the hand draped over Angie's shoulder, and against her skin, Angie could tell it wasn't Haitian-made. It was too soft and too synthetic, nothing like the natural beads and handmade rope her mama used to thread into her hair as a little girl.

"I thought this would look good on the mantle." Dawn held the doll up into the light.

Angie bit back her critique. "I suppose it would."

"Assuming it doesn't bring a curse to our house or something!" Dawn let out a giddy laugh.

Angie had expected a comment like that and smiled along. "You've been living with a real, live Haitian lady for three years now," she said, keeping her tone light and soft. "If you was going to be cursed, it'd done happen by now."

"'You was'?" Dawn teased. "'It'd done'?" Her smile was wider, but it looked strained. "Am I talking to the Haitian Angie or the Berkeley Angie?"

"They's one and the same, babe!" Angie replied in her exaggerated Haitian accent, the caricature of a patois that Dawn got such a kick out of when they were in bed together, with the lights turned low, asking for a tour of all the dirty Creole words. She loved how her body sounded when described in a thick, foreign tongue. As the outsider in Berkeley, Angie was willing to play along, but here in her native land, she felt a coil of unease twisting down her stomach and across her damp skin. In her peripheral vision, she saw the blurry forms of the locals streaming around her, and she imagined their eyes cast toward her in judgment.

"Sorry if I was a bit short-tempered last night," Angie said. "I guess it's just stress from all the traveling."

"No worries." Dawn offered a light smile instead of an apology, which Angie begrudgingly accepted. "Believe me, I know all about the stress of visiting family."

Angie laughed. "Yeah, you have a lot more to complain about on that front than I do!"

"I've got oceans more I could tell you. But you're . . ." Dawn trailed off. Her eyes shifted to the side with a tinge of sadness that spiraled away in the warm tropical breeze.

"You're the only family I need," Angie finished. Dawn smiled and nodded, saying nothing else.

Angie licked at a drip of salty sweat that had slipped between her lips and felt Dawn's eyes watching her mouth. As Dawn leaned in for a kiss, Angie ignored how the scents of Dawn's perfume, body wash, and lotion clashed against the smells of Haiti that blew around them. She slipped her arms around Dawn's shoulders and brought her face toward her white lady's.

An affronted snort fractured the kiss before it even began. Angie and Dawn jerked their faces back in a mirrored reflex. Next to them, an older Haitian woman was glaring as she passed. The woman muttered something in thick Creole that Angie couldn't hear. But she could guess easily enough.

She'd had her sexual awakening in Haiti and heard everything that gets muttered under the breath to people like her. Or, sometimes, shouted through snarled lips.

"Well," Dawn began. She had dropped her gaze to the ground. "I guess I should head off to the airport now." The soft, innocent curvature of her face had fallen into a pained frown. At once, the distance that had spawned between the women since arriving in Haiti was bridged in mutual solidarity. Angie thought of the horror stories Dawn had told her about growing up gay under the righteous fury of her drunk of a father in middle-of-nowhere Iowa.

Dawn was many things. But an out-of-touch Berkeley lady she was not. She was a refugee too.

"Here," Angie said. "Let me take your suitcase."

Angie disentangled her arms from Dawn's and took the suitcase's handle, leaving Dawn holding nothing but the fake Vodou trinket.

"Oh," Dawn said. "You don't need to. I'm just going to catch a cab from here."

"*We're* going to catch a cab," Angie said.

"You're coming to the airport with me now?" Dawn's muscle-memory frown was lifting.

"Of course," Angie said. "What kind of girlfriend would I be if I didn't see my American lady off at the gate? Besides, airport good-byes are so much more romantic, don't you think?"

"Yes, I suppose so." Dawn brushed her sweaty hair from her face. "I wish I didn't have to go back early. But I have those gigs at the university this week. I'm already booked three nights at the coffee house. I can't miss them. We need the money."

Dawn's singing career was in that chasm where she was well-known enough, at least in the San Francisco area, for performing to take up most of her time and energy with none left over for any other "real" career, but not yet well-known enough to command the fees and fame that would be her hoped-for reward.

"I know," Angie said, nodding. "And I'll be home in time for Christmas. But for now, if you're going to catch your flight, we need to leave."

"Aw, I wanted to buy a few more souvenirs." Dawn glanced down at her watch. "We still have some time before I have to be at the check-in."

"Honey," Angie said with a laugh, "I think I'm a bit more acquainted with Port-au-Prince traffic than you are."

While Dawn's attention was arrested by another trinket booth nearby, Angie shuffled over to the street to hail a taxi. Over the next hour, she resisted the urge to give her partner a smug look as they sat together in the back seat of the cab.

"This traffic's pretty bad, alright," Dawn said.

Angie simply nodded. "Yup."

The cab made its slow but steady way down the Boulevard du 15 Octobre, which would, at some point, carry it to the Avenue Toussaint Louverture, and then on to Toussaint Louverture International Airport. The streets were packed full of traffic, both vehicular and human.

The cab hit a bump and Dawn yelped. Outside her door, two loud motor scooters buzzed past in the narrow gap between their cab and the car next to them. Dawn recoiled slightly. Then their driver slammed on the brakes and honked furiously at two shirtless teens who darted across the road in front of the cab. The boys cast threatening glares but kept walking. Angie heard Dawn gulp.

"These houses are lovely," Dawn said a few moments later, her voice sounding meek and resigned. She was looking out her window at the hills, which burst with color. Thousands of small houses painted in blues, purples, pinks, and oranges were laid out in layers that molded to the natural contours of the island's curvature as if they had sprung out of the Earth itself alongside the trees. The foliage, forged by the equatorial sun into a lively shade of emerald, was far richer than the deeper greens of Northern California. The tropical birds passing overhead carried bright colors undreamed of by the pigeons of Berkeley.

This undeniable beauty contrasted so cruelly with the other side of Angie's homeland: the endless slums, the brutal poverty, the social decay. It was this tragic dichotomy of Haiti that threatened any attempt by Angie of accepting the country fully into her heart.

Dawn wasn't wrong that things could be better, she was just wrong in her white savior mentality.

"Yes." Angie felt guilty at her feelings of triumph over being right about the traffic. "Growing up here I always thought these houses on the hills mimicked the ocean waves just offshore. Right where the island's flora meets the yellow sand of the beaches and the blue water of the sea."

Dawn nodded. "I'll have to write a song about it," she said. "To raise awareness."

Angie folded her lips. "Right. Awareness."

Dawn didn't say anything else for a time, instead leaning her shoulder against her door and casting her gaze out the window. Angie gave her hand a little squeeze, and Dawn, shaken from her reverie, cast her partner a warm but spacey smile and squeezed gently in return. Over the sound of the car horns and busted mufflers, Dawn began to sing a soft, melodious folk song, somewhere between a whisper and a hum. Angie, though she couldn't decipher them by ear, knew the lyrics by heart.

To Canaan's land she's on her way.
Where the soul never dies.
Her darkest night will turn to day.
Where the soul never dies.

It was a song Dawn sang from time to time, whenever she withdrew into the magical world she had constructed in her head to survive her dismal youth, the lost years trying to find herself as a newly outed lesbian in the conservative American Bible Belt. Retreating from harm and pain and fear into some strange and ascetic sky.

Lifted on wings of song, Angie thought. *If only you'd think to take me with you.*

4

Jim leaned against the beige and brown wall of his trailer, which, despite its coloring, stood out like a sore thumb in the flat desert. But Creech Air Force Base was crammed in the middle-of-nowhere, Nevada, so Jim figured any building would look out of place. When he had first gotten there, a JO doing the newbie in-doc said that they were at a point where the Mojave and Great Basin deserts converged, and the scenery showed it. Aside from the brown mountains off in the distance, the land around him was as flat and boring as Iowa. Except with less corn and more rocks.

Jim squinted at the trailer wall to get away from the glare, Cooper standing by his side. Cooper and Jim were both first lieutenants, though Cooper was technically the senior officer of the two by four months because he was in AFROTC during college, so he was able to skip Officer Training School. But they'd been together through Initial Flight Training in Pueblo, Undergraduate RPA Training at Randolf, and five months of Formal Training Unit training here at Creech.

"You ever wonder if we get invisible when we stand next to the trailer like this?" Cooper asked. He had annoyingly taken his smoke break at the same time as Jim's dip break.

Jim rolled his eyes. "What?" He spit a tobacco-rich loogy into his empty Pepsi can.

"They painted the trailer in the same color as our uniforms,"

Cooper said. He gestured to the yellow-brown camouflage of their trailer with his non-cigarette hand and then the uniforms they both wore.

Yeah, I had thought that, Jim said to himself. But out loud he said, "You're an idiot."

"Screw you," Cooper said in a bored tone. Then, in the same tone, "There's another one of the new Reapers." He pointed across the road to where a group of Air Force ground crewmen pulled a new model Reaper drone along the runway into one of the base's massive hangars.

"It looks about the same," Jim said.

"On the outside, yeah. But you know firsthand how much better all the new high-tech shit is," Cooper said.

Jim did, and it was actually quite exciting to be flying the new model, but he wasn't about to show it. "All I care about is that they can blow shit up."

Cooper took a drag off his cigarette. "What was that shit you told us when you got here? When you saw the Reapers for the first time?"

"I said a lot of shit."

"About the lizard or something?"

Jim grunted. He'd have preferred to have his break in peace. "Yeah," he began, pushing the wad of tobacco deeper into his gums with his tongue. "When I was a kid, my school went on a field trip to the zoo. I was screwing around the whole time, not paying attention, but I remember in the reptile house, there was this dark glass cage with no light except for this purple UV shit. Inside was some kind of blind salamander. That's what it said on the sign. They said the salamander had lived so long in dark caves that after millions of years it had lost its eyes entirely. It just sat on a rock in the purple light, staring at nothing, with smooth, gray skin where its eyes should have been."

Cooper snorted through his cigarette smoke, and Jim continued. "I mean, these Reapers didn't look like much when we were in RPA out at Randolph. I never was around airplanes much. These drones looked the same as any old planes, at least at first. But then I noticed the window in the front. Or, I guess, the fact that there's no window there. I said, 'The things look blind and eyeless.' Like that lizard."

"Nerd," Cooper scoffed. Jim grunted and took another wad of tobacco in his mouth.

A car pulled up between the drone and the trailer. Major Udall leaned out the window and started talking to a doughy-faced enlisted kid. The radio was blaring out of the car's speakers, drowning out their conversation. Jim instantly recognized the familiar voice of Alex Meter.

"*Well, that's just stupid!*" Meter howled, his tone high-pitched and mocking. Jim guessed he was responding to some dipshit caller. "*You're darn right there's times when killing's 'in God's plan.' Hell, there's times when outright murder is in God's plan! Lives are not all worth the same, buddy! We don't spend trillions of dollars on the greatest military force the planet has ever known so that we can just stare at those shiny weapons! We do it so we can take out the enemy before they take out ten of us! Even Monika would know that, and she's just our latest Black quota hire. Next caller!*"

Udall pulled away before Jim could hear what the next caller had to say. It didn't matter much—one of the other grunts would have Meter blaring in the mess hall at some point. And having Udall too close always made Jim nervous. Udall was career Air Force all the way, going back two generations, and with the Air Force Academy ring to prove his commitment.

"Hey, man, you see those faggots out past the gate?"

"Code pink again, right?" Jim pinched a glob of spit off his lips into his can.

"How the hell should I know? It's the MPs' problem. But I was going to tell you, when I passed them this morning I did see some hippie chick with her tits out."

Jim glanced over to the eastern entrance of the base. Past the fencing, the small crowd of protesters was gathered where they normally were. A few cars filled with base security stared them down with what Jim figured was the MPs' usual "bored asshole" look. At that distance, the protesters weren't much more than blurs, so Jim couldn't tell if any of the women were topless. He could make out three large signs held up by a row of about a half-dozen protestors facing the base.

STOP DRONING AFGHANISTAN!!!

And:

DRONE PILOTS: LISTEN TO YOUR CONSCIENCE! REFUSE TO FLY!

And:

WHOSE LIVES MATTER TO YOU?

Jim turned back to Cooper. "Was she trying to make some kind of statement, having her tits out, or was she just tryin' to cool off?"

Cooper shrugged. "Hell if I know."

From the fence, a commotion rang out. It looked like a few of the MPs had gotten out of their cars and were trying to arrest one of the protestors. A woman. She was shouting but he couldn't make out what she said. Jim found himself transfixed, watching her struggling against the MP as he grabbed her arms and forced them behind her back.

She managed to break one of her arms free and raise it into the air. The remaining protestors let out a cheer, and Jim suddenly felt some part of himself let out a silent cheer along with them. Almost rooting for the woman, even though he couldn't see her face. Or hear her voice. Or know her name.

Then the MP grabbed her arm again and she disappeared into the back seat of one of the base police cars.

Jim scooped out his wad and flung it into the garbage by the door to the trailer, tossed his can in after it, opened the door, and stepped inside. It took his eyes a moment to adjust to the low lighting. The other pilots, all fresh into their twenties like him, were sitting in a row of leather chairs, dressed in standard Air Force flight suits. None of them paid him any attention as he walked over to a chair near the corner of the room where Bradley was reclining with his feet in the air and his eyes only half-focused on the screen. Jim rapped on his shoulder.

"Alright, dipshit, move over. I'm back."

Bradley muttered an annoyed grunt and slowly made his way to his feet. "Whatever, I gotta take a piss anyway."

Jim smirked as he settled into the leather chair and leaned back into the headrest, grateful that the Air Force had splurged on more comfortable seats at Creech than most military bases got. His station included a keyboard, a standard aircraft joystick for his right hand, and a throttle for his left hand. Six large screens arranged in two rows of three each gave him visuals and instrument readouts. Overall, the effect was very much like being in an actual aircraft cockpit, or at least a high-quality aircraft simulator. With its current configuration, one screen showed a complicated 2D map of relevant targets. Another held coordinates, while a third beamed out various pieces of intel. But the real star of the show was the large screen in the middle of the display, set to a smooth HD image of a rocky landscape from a high angle. The image didn't look too different from the surrounding Nevada desert. But this scene lay on the other side of the world. The small town of Khewa, near Jalalabad, in Northeastern Afghanistan. That's where his Reaper drone was currently flying, sending him real-time footage through complex satellite feeds.

The image made it seem like the drone was stationary. Jim knew it wasn't—the Reapers couldn't hover in place like a helicopter. But they could hit a standard loiter speed, and their onboard cameras had a special technology that allowed them to home in on a single spot and make small adjustments to keep it in frame as long as possible. Tiny movements appeared at the edges of the screen, where the background of the desert scene shifted slightly every few seconds as the camera made the adjustments, but the center of the camera feed held steady. It was focused on a concrete, single-story building planted in the middle of the Afghan wilderness. As out of place on the rocky ground as Jim's trailer.

When Jim had first reported to Creech a year ago, the image was black and white, with the main computer capabilities dedicated to providing contrast between moving bodies and their background rather than giving a full range of color. But in the last month, they'd deployed a new batch of Reaper drones fitted with high-tech cameras that had color plus even better definition. Since getting the new shit, Jim had been able to get high-def close-ups of anyone on the ground in Afghanistan. Not just indistinct faces, but details on clothing and facial features, and even individual hairs. Plus, Jim could zoom into ultra-high-def from over a mile away. Most of the time his drone wasn't close enough to the target to draw anyone's attention, and whoever he was watching just went about their lives without noticing.

The new cameras offered a better range of image options too. He still had the standard HD daylight camera, of course, but with just a few clicks he could switch over to a "shortwave infrared sensor" camera or "laser designator" camera. Jim had gotten a thorough rundown of the science behind all of that at basic training, but in his day-to-day work, he had taken to thinking of the different visuals as the "wacky color" camera and the "holy shit! Everything's green!" camera.

Jim's drone was cruising at an altitude of about a mile, with its camera trained on a location a mile out to the side. It was early morning in Afghanistan, and the sun was just breaking over the mountains. Jim could see the scene as clearly as if he were sitting on top of his old water tower back in Iowa, drinking beers and gawking at cars going by below.

Scales across the top and left side of the screen let him calibrate the camera's focus. Tabs across the edges of the screen gave him control over image quality and the camera's zoom function. Coordinates, altitude, airspeed, and a lot of additional values that were only important when things were going to shit with the equipment were also displayed at the screen's edges. But the center of the image was the star of the show. There, trained directly on the concrete building in the middle of nowhere on the other side of the world, were the circular target sights.

Within a few seconds of sitting down, Jim saw a person appear on screen, walking along the dirt road in front of the concrete house. Jim leaned forward to get a closer look, before remembering he could zoom in with the new camera. The figure stopped being just a black smudge and began to come into focus. It was a man, a Jihad-Johnny. He was tall, wearing white and brown robes. He had a long, scraggly beard and a white turban swirling around his head. Jim zoomed in even closer, and he could make out individual strands of the man's beard as it blew in the mountain breeze. He watched the man pause for a few seconds before he walked out of frame. Jim reached for his joystick to refocus the camera to find him again, but just then a large US Army transport vehicle rolled by.

"Late," Jim muttered. That unit was supposed to be patrolling the area, and he was supposed to provide air cover in case they got into trouble. But none of the soldiers ever looked anything other than bored, and Jim had a hard time forcing himself to care.

Another man appeared in frame, another Jihad-Johnny, towel-head and beard and all. Most of the potential targets had become Jihad-Johnny to the crew. Sitting in a trailer for eight hours looking at drone feeds was dull as shit most of the time. Jim had taken to filling in the blanks around the human forms that crept across the Afghan mountains on his monitors. The lady wearing about seventy layers of burka was diddling her dentist and trying to keep her husband from finding out. The kid kicking the ball was a secret agent trying to infiltrate the Taliban's kindergarten unit. And so on and so on.

This old guy here was the starting quarterback for Afghan Central High before he blew out his knee from a dirty hit by their archrivals at Iraqi Tech, Jim decided. He had a walking stick, but he seemed familiar enough with the rocky terrain that he passed through the frame quicker than Jim expected. This time, Jim made no attempt to refocus the camera to find him again.

He leaned his head back in the chair and yawned. He had been promised imminent intelligence on a new strike for the past several days, but so far nothing had come in. He had spent the better part of the past week sitting on his ass and watching the random comings and goings of some of the 30,000 residents of Khewa, plus various convoys of some of the 100,000 US military personnel stationed in Afghanistan.

Keep your eyes open for anything unusual, and we'll get the intelligence in ASAP, his commanding officer had told him.

"Hey, Bradley! Check this out, Bradley!" Cooper's Georgia drawl came from two seats down. Bradley was fresh out of the FTU, though he'd done his training at March AFB. Jim couldn't figure out how a screw up like Bradley could constantly be getting the lucky breaks that kept him out of trouble. He briefly glanced across the room, where his colleagues had converged in front of Cooper's console. Cooper had aimed his crosshairs directly on a small caravan of four camels, carrying packs of tents and household items for a family of nomads walking alongside them on the dusty roads around Khewa. The group let out a laugh.

"Dude, draw a dick!" Bradley said with a snort.

"No, dude, maybe you could blow the top off that girl in the back," Jason offered. He was from the Northwest originally—Washington state, Jim was pretty sure—and had been at March with Bradley. "I bet she's hot."

"You can tell?" Bradley asked.

"I mean, under the burka, she's probably hot enough." The way Jason was always going on about hot chicks made it obvious he'd never had an actual girlfriend. Not that Jim was one to talk.

"Dude, you really need to get laid." Cooper said.

Jim longed to be back in his trailer, playing Call of Duty, instead of dealing with these idiots.

Before his attention could drift too far away, he heard the dreaded sound of the trailer door bursting open and the grating voice of his CO barking his name.

"Wilson!" Jim immediately straightened his shoulders and drew his head up to attention. Around the trailer, the other junior officers grew hushed at their stations. "New intelligence just in," Major Udall said. "They have credible reports of an IED being planted on Khewa highway. They've identified three targets, currently awaiting authorization for a strike."

Jim nodded as the excitement in the room began to build. The screen on his left came to life, displaying a series of coordinates detailing the target's location. The screen on his right displayed a 2D topographic map of Afghanistan, with a clear route already lined up to guide him to the target. He redirected the drone's camera from the empty roadside, and the central monitor became a wide shot of the Afghan mountains occasionally breaking through white and gray clouds.

Taking hold of the joysticks, Jim pulled the drone from its holding pattern and followed the route on the right screen to the target. The altimeter told him the drone was cruising at 15,786 feet. High enough to avoid unwanted detection from the ground, but close enough to zoom in on anyone below. And low enough for a missile strike.

Over the next few minutes, the drone's main camera was grayed out by the cloud cover over the mountains, while the 2D map showed his drone icon moving along the predetermined course line to the final target, denoted with a red dot. When he was close enough, Jim began the drone's descent to just below the cloud cover. For a few seconds, his main screen remained in the foggy white of early morning mountain clouds. Then the drone broke free, and Jim had a clear view. He zoomed the camera closer to the ground, training the central target reticle on the cheap foreign car parked haphazardly on the side of the Khewa highway, a major (relatively speaking) thoroughfare through the area that was often used by US and allied forces. Three Jihad-Johnnys stood nearby, working around something on the road. A package.

He flipped his headset to the command channel. The computerized voice blared through the speakers from who-knows-where in the chain of command. "Possible targets approaching highway," the voice said in a monotone.

"Pilot copies." Jim instinctively used his "official" voice, which he had come to realize was something of an imitation—or mockery—of his father's when he chewed Jim out, deep with a layer of raspy gravel like he had been smoking a pack a day for forty years.

Jim didn't spend a lot of time thinking about his father. When he'd seen Jim off to basic training two years ago, his father's disappointment was as evident as the fact he was drunk. Not that either of those things were new. His dad's love of whiskey wasn't a secret, and Jim couldn't recall ever making his dad proud. But Jim had stopped caring what his dad thought during his junior year of high school, after he'd overheard him asking his sister for money. What kind of a man can't support his own family? A man who drinks too much and makes poor decisions, that's who. Right then and there, Jim's perception of his father had shifted, and he'd promised himself he'd land a solid career with steady pay. And he had. In so doing, he'd also lost touch with his dad. He didn't have a personal problem with the man, exactly. If he was asked, he'd confirm that, of course, he loved him. But somehow, it was always a relief to find an excuse for not going home. And there was always a good excuse. Eventually, his mother stopped trying to get him back for a visit, or at least stopped trying very hard.

Everyone else had left their stations and crowded around him. Udall was clearly annoyed by this, but when it came time for a strike, no one would pay attention if he told them to get back to work.

On the screen, the three men continued to work on their package at the side of the highway.

In his headset, the computerized voice clicked back to life. "Black car parked at side of target highway. Targets one, two, and three."

"Pilot copies," Jim said.

"Targets one, two, and three have exited at side of highway by side of black car. Confirm targets at side of highway."

On screen, one of the men raised his head. Jim could see his long black beard flapping in the breeze as he looked up.

"Pilot confirms. Targets one, two, and three by side of highway."

"Shit," Bradley said from behind him. "Asshole gets three targets. What the hell am I gonna do with that?"

"Shut the hell up," Udall said.

As far as Jim could tell, the three men were alone in the mountainous landscape. The nearest village was miles away and there was no traffic on the highway. *Just the wind, guys*, he thought. *Nothing else around. Go about your business. Nothing to worry about . . . nothing at all . . .*

Blackbeard took one last cautious glance around him and resumed focus on the package.

"Pilot," the computerized voice continued. "Confirm checklist."

"Pilot confirms checklist." Jim began to rattle off the protocols for the pre-strike checklist from the laminated sheet, although he had memorized the checklist long ago.

"Check out that fat asshole on the right!" Jason said. Jim assumed he was gesturing to the one having obvious trouble kneeling.

"I don't think they got Planet Fitness over there at the Taliban," Bradley said.

"Maybe he should declare jihad on carbs," Cooper said.

"Shut the hell up," Udall said again, with minimal conviction.

Jim completed the pre-strike checklist. A click rang out on the other side of his headset as the line went silent for a second. He sucked in a sharp breath of anticipation. His pulse drummed in his ears. Whoever was gripping his seat from behind began to clutch it even tighter. The room was silent. The seconds stretched into minutes. The air grew dense.

"Pilot, you are cleared to engage black car at your discretion."

Jim's hands, steady as ever, clutched his joystick.

"Pilot confirms. Launching rifle in three . . . two . . . one." If he left a slightly longer pause before the "one" for dramatic effect, he doubted anyone could blame him. Eyes and sights locked on the screen, he pulled the trigger. Immediately, the screen lit up with a countdown to impact.

The two less-heavy Jihad-Johnnys had gotten to their feet. As Jim waited, he imagined the younger man smiling with the kind of pride folks like Jim tended to save for scoring a three-pointer on the court. On the screen, the older man's silhouette patted the younger man's shoulder, in congratulations.

And then . . .

The younger man's head jolted up. It was a slight movement, and someone with fewer hours watching drone footage might have missed it. Jim tried to imagine what the young man heard. He had never actually witnessed a missile strike in person. All he had to go by were years of action movies stuck in his head. The slight, high-pitched whistling of an incoming missile, getting louder and louder as it cut through the air. The roar of its boosters. The flapping sound of every bird in the area taking flight at once.

Jim bit his lip. The young man looked like he was listening for a second, then he shouted to his compatriots before turning and fleeing. The second man quickly joined him. The fat man, still struggling to his knees, tried to lunge away in a panic and toppled over.

But Jim knew how fast the missile flew. By the time they heard the sound it was already too late. He watched the countdown click toward zero. The two men had just managed to make it to the black car. "Impact in three . . . two . . . one," he said.

The car and all three men disappeared in a fireball of smoke, debris, and dust. A white shock wave radiated with fury across the shattered remains of the highway and surrounding wilderness. Cooper, Bradley, Jason, and the rest erupted into cheers, and Jim reclined into his leather seat. The screen showed only the expanding cloud of smoke and dust from the missile blast. There weren't any bodies to gawk at. Whatever was left of them was no bigger than the pebbles flying in all directions.

Before Jim got to Creech, he didn't know how he'd feel about the "killing" aspect of the job. He hadn't been worried so much as curious. His dad had taken him hunting a few times, on a sober kick when Jim was about twelve, and Jim had bagged on old buck and a handful of geese. But killing people was something else entirely. So all through training, he'd pondered the reality of pulling the trigger on another person. Even one on the other side of the world. When he finally got his first strike—a Taliban ammo dump out in the mountains with a few guards surrounding it—he was surprised to feel . . . well, nothing. The entire setup of the command center seemed designed to keep him detached from his actions. The comfy leather chair, the high-tech screen—it felt like playing a shitty video game. The people he saw through his drone camera were little more than black and gray smudges even before they got blown to shit.

And when he had picked up some collateral damage? When there were a few civilians outside the epicenter of the blast but close enough to get killed by the shock wave? Well, even then they didn't look like much. Just the same black and gray smudges, only now lying motionless on the ground. Might as well be nothing more than cartoon characters, for all Jim could get from them.

And if some tiny voice in his brain tried to make him stop and think about what had just happened, even for a second? Well, then the jokes and insults from his comrades pulled him back to reality quick.

Jim swung his head around and blew imaginary smoke off his finger in an imitation of a gun. Major Udall nodded. "Good work, we'll get specs ASAP. Keep an eye on the corridor for any potential retaliation." And with that, he was gone.

"Nice shot, man!" Jason said. "All three in the bull's-eye!"

"Marines are gonna be pissed at what you did to the highway when they pass through," Bradley added.

"Who gives a shit!" Cooper whooped. "If they don't like it, they can try their luck with the IEDs! We just saved their lives, and they can go on pretending they're the ones with the big dicks if they want!"

Jim swiveled his chair around and cast a smug look at Bradley. "Count it! That's three!"

Bradley scowled. "Looks to me like our killer-boy here musta sucked someone's dick in the chain of command if he keeps gettin' multiple targets."

"Cry some more," Jim said. "If you need help getting going, I think Jason's got the running tally."

Jason rubbed his head. "Well, you and Coop were tied, so this'll put you up by three."

Jim cocked his fingers like a pistol. "Plus, it's December if I'm not mistaken. You know what that means?"

To make up for the fact that the stakes of their "combat" experience didn't quite reach the heights of danger as their compatriots stationed on the ground in Afghanistan and Iraq, the man with the lowest tally of confirmed targets had to buy a case of beer for the man with the highest. Jim winked at Bradley. "And, who has the lowest tally again?"

Bradley continued sulking. "Whatever, faggot, I'm glad I'm not sucking anyone's dick."

Jim grinned again and flopped back into his chair. On the screen, the explosion had dissolved into a murky cloud of dust and smoke. Only the charred landscape, blast crater, and twisted and burned metal of the destroyed car suggested what had just happened. Jim's shoulders drooped, the excitement of the strike already past. The next day or so would involve little more than staring at empty Afghan landscapes and villages, with a few breaks outside in the Nevada sun.

Not too bad, all things considering. But, yeah, he would definitely rather play Call of Duty.

Since that wasn't an option, Jim thought he might try to find Marcus once his patrol started. They'd been friends since high school where they played on the football team together—well, warmed the bench—and sported the same lousy grades. They both left home for Iowa State and then enlisted in the military right out of college. While Jim chose the Air Force, Marcus the Psycho had gone into the Marines. As luck would have it, his unit was stationed in Afghanistan, right in the vicinity of Khewa. Jim hadn't yet managed to find him out of the sea of Marines and soldiers that passed across his screen, but the knowledge that his old friend was out there made Jim feel a little less lonely in the desert.

Someone switched on the trailer's out-of-date clock radio. Alex Meter's animated voice burst forth.

"So, how much is a human life worth? Scientists tell us that the elements in a human body are worth a bit under $5. From my perspective, the value of one of those rag-head terrorists over in Afghanistan is about the cost of a bullet, so $5 is not too far off. But for God-fearing decent folks like you and me, I tell you that the value of a human life is priceless, and no murder board of doctors should be deciding whether it's cost-effective to keep me alive."

Jim leaned back and let Meter keep him company for the next several hours until his next break.

5

"You sure you don't need a hand, Papa?"

Angie's father brushed her offer away with a blunt wave of his cane. "Child, you've been too long gone up there in the States. You think I gotta have a guiding hand to walk my own streets?"

Angie, dutifully chided, sat back and watched as Augustin Altidor, white-haired and burdened with arthritis but still strong in core and character, maneuvered his way through the narrow shelves of the family *famasi* and market shop toward the front register.

The morning rush was over. The businessmen had already retreated back to their offices, and the store's main customers at this time of day were middle-aged mothers wearing blue and pink and orange dresses, with their hair done up in intricate vertical patterns. A few young boys skulked between the shelves. Angie's father would periodically deter them from shoplifting with the same authoritative glare she had endured during her own childhood.

"Just trying to help," Angie said. Her dad had always had an independent streak, but Angie knew the day would come when he could no longer maintain the shop without assistance.

Just then her mother bustled in from the back room with a tray of hot ginger tea. "Child," she said in her native hum, "if *I* can't convince your father to take a helping hand every now and then, I don't know what hope you have." Papa gave a half-chuckle, half-grunt from behind the counter as he took his tea. "I used to think I married a mule," her mother continued, "until I realized that you can actually persuade a mule with a carrot."

Angie reached for her cup with an appreciative nod.

"Good to be speaking Creole again," her father said bluntly, and Angie's sip of tea turned into a pained gulp.

"You hush, now!" her mother chided. "Don't make our baby think she's a burden!"

"It's no burden," her father said, though his expression indicated the opposite. "I'm happy to speak English with Angie's . . . uh, with Dawn. I'm just saying it's nice to be speaking our language again."

Angie smiled politely. While Dawn was there, her parents had exercised their English skills even when talking between themselves. But Dawn had left three days ago, and Angie had switched from the hotel room to her childhood home, and it was now both comforting and stressful to be conversing with her parents in Creole.

"It's good to practice English, regardless," her mother said.

"Oh, I keep meaning to tell you that your English is very good!" Angie said, relieved at the opportunity to turn the conversation positive. "Both of you."

"I've been watching YouTube videos," Mama said with a grin.

Papa scowled. "Internet. Bah! At least our girl is talking like a full-blood Haitian again."

"Hush, now!" her mother chided again.

Angie took another awkward sip. "Sorry," she said. "I guess my Creole got a bit rusty in the States."

"You always sound like an angel to me!" Mama beamed. "Plus, I like your new American accent!"

"Keep talking like a Hollywood lady and I can tell folks we got a movie star for a daughter," her father added.

Angie rolled her eyes. When she moved to America to get a degree in public health from UC Berkeley, her father had taken to

referring to anywhere in California as "Hollywood," and Angie had
given up trying to correct him. Her mother gave him a gentle slap
on the arm.

Angie gulped down the last of her tea, a bit too quickly, then
lifted herself from her stool. "The tea was lovely, Mama," she said.
She leaned in to kiss her mother on the cheek. "I want to take a walk
before the streets get too crowded, so I'll see you later."

"Streets are always crowded," her father mumbled. But he was
distracted by another suspicious youth who had wandered in, shirtless and with an oversized canvas bag.

Her mother squeezed her hand. "Oh, let me walk with you for
a bit, dear! I was going to make some pol an sòs around seven, so I
have to go to the grocery store anyway."

"Sure," Angie said.

"Hey! Vòlè!" her father shouted at one of the youths who had
pocketed a bag of chips. "Your mama teach you to steal, tèt zozo?!"
He rose from his chair and waved his cane threateningly, and Angie
took that opportunity to slip out the front door, with her mother
buzzing along at her side.

Outside, the day was warm but with a well-calibrated Caribbean
breeze sweeping away whatever lingering humidity may have turned
the elements unpleasant. Along the street, rows of palm trees stood
guard in front of pink and purple walls adorned with intricate graffiti and street art. People zipped past on scooters, mopeds, and on foot.

"Where did you want to walk to?" her mother asked.

"Oh, I don't know," Angie said. "When Dawn was here, we saw
all the main sights. But I was acting like a tour guide. It'll be nice just
to wander around a bit." Angie missed Dawn, of course, but also felt
relief in being unburdened from her duties as "cultural ambassador"
for Haiti.

"A walk always does one good!" her mother said. "And I'll bet it's
nice to be back in the 'real' sun we have down here!"

Angie laughed. "No doubt. It's nice to feel the warmth of the Caribbean and the extra hours of tropical sunlight again." She relaxed her shoulders as the breeze of her homeland washed against her skin.

"You and Dawn are such a nice couple," her mother said. "I'm just so happy that you can be together up there in California. I pray that down here in Haiti we can catch up so you two can make a life together here."

"I mean . . ." Angie had a hard time believing that would ever happen. Haiti was a long way from the freedom she had discovered in and around Berkeley. She and Dawn first met at the White Horse Bar in Oakland during a karaoke night. She was amazed to find a bar openly focused on catering to an LGBTQ clientele, and even more surprised when she learned that the bar first opened in 1933. *Maybe by 2033, Haiti would catch up with California*, she thought.

"I just want this place to feel like home for you again."

Angie grabbed her mom's hand and squeezed. They walked in silence until the grocery store came into sight. Her mother kissed her on the cheek as she turned toward the door. "Have fun on your walk, dear! Try to be safe. Remember to be back for dinner by seven!"

"I will, Mama," Angie said.

"And Angelique . . ."

"Yes, Mama?"

"Welcome home!"

Angie smiled back as her mother disappeared into the store. Then she turned toward the crowded market square in front of her and tried to force a feeling of "home" into her overwhelmed brain. She wandered over to the Marche en Fer. During the happy days of her childhood, she had wandered through the thick clusters of multicolored market stalls of the Iron Market while clutching her mama's hand. She remembered that unique feeling of fear and exhilaration that came with looking up past her mama's dress at the frenzy of the marketplace.

I should have taken Dawn here, she thought. But then she was saddened by the realization that Dawn wouldn't have been able to tell the difference between this and those tourist traps closer to the airport.

Angie turned the corner and was met with a booth selling art: Afro-futurism, graffiti, caricatures, and abstract expressionism that mirrored the tropical colors all around. Nearby, two men argued as they attempted to assemble a few booths for an upcoming Christmas market, a large Santa statue—black-skinned, of course, since this was Haiti not Berkeley—looming over them. A line of young mothers strode past her with bushels of produce balancing atop their heads and infants in cloth bundles wrapped across their backs.

Next to the Christmas market, a group of teenage boys was playing an impromptu game of *fútbol* in a vacant lot, dancing between the broken bottles and rusty bits of metal. The goalkeeper shouted "Ha! Masisi!" at his friends as she passed. Even though the slur couldn't be meant for her, Angie abruptly cringed at the Creole for "faggot." Teenage boys were the same everywhere.

She caught sight of a large building that rose two stories above every other building on the block. Next to it, the shouts of schoolchildren poured through the chain-link fence separating the asphalt playground from the sidewalk. The kids wore uniforms, some better maintained than others. A couple groups of children tossed balls back and forth, while others ran around chasing each other in what looked like a complex game of tag. They were changing the rules on a whim and officiating based on emotion rather than any set rules.

If only those helicopter parents back in Berkeley could see this, Angie thought with a chuckle. She had grown used to sanitized playgrounds full of soft, rounded edges, gentle plastic, and ground protected with comfortable foam. The sight of kids running around without any care on hard, cracked asphalt, carrying sharpened sticks and with only a rusty jungle gym to climb on almost sent her California self into a panic. But at least she knew this was a school and not an orphanage. How could Dawn have been so blind about that? Angie's own school had been much like this one, even though her parents had gotten her into one of the more prestigious Catholic schools for the kids of a higher class.

A pair of young mothers approached, one pushing a double stroller and the other carrying an infant on her back. As they passed, the baby raised her hand and gave Angie a clumsy wave. Angie gawked for a second, then offered a delayed wave back. But the baby's attention had moved on to something else.

Across the busy street, another Christmas booth began playing a traditional Haitian Christmas carol. Dawn would have complained about the discrepancy between the Christmas season and the hot weather, just like she did every year during Christmas in California. But Dawn was from a brutal climate in the American Midwest, where the holidays were accompanied by snow and cold. For Angie, the warm breeze sifting through sun-fanned palm leaves was just the kind of thing that spelled out the Christmas season.

Christmas in Berkeley was always an intimate affair, a small plastic tree perched on their corner coffee table, a string of lights, a glass of wine on Christmas Eve. Just the two of them. Just how Angie wanted it. And until a few days ago, just how she'd thought Dawn had wanted it.

Another shout drew her attention back to the school playground. From the main doors, the headmistress was projecting her voice across the schoolyard and letting the kids know it was time to come in, while the teachers tried to corral the rambunctious kids back inside.

A cluster of schoolchildren dispersed in front of Angie, revealing a low area of mulch and grass shaded by an overhanging tree. Sitting by herself in that shady grove was a girl no older than six, dressed in a neat and orderly school uniform, her hair kept tight in pigtail braids. She had her eyes cast down into a book, and she was sounding out unfamiliar words and drawing a finger across the pages as she went.

The girl paid no mind to her loud peers streaming past her. As the last few groups of students finally made their way back into the school, the headmistress approached the young girl with a sympathetic hand, clearly reluctant to disrupt her self-imposed reading exercise. The girl looked up from her book, and for a second Angie saw her eyes, clear and piercing, full of innocence and curiosity. The girl placed a marker on the page she had been reading, slipped the book into her old but sturdy bag, and rose.

She was so different from the rest. Just like Angie had been at that age. How many recesses had she spent sitting alone under the broad reach of the elephant-ear tree behind her school? How many hours lost in her own world, oblivious to the silly games being played by her classmates, running around in a frenzy and engaging in play fights that would turn into real fights later in life? Her own strong, bright eyes scanning the world around her for something to come along commensurate with herself . . .

And then the girl was gone, disappearing into the building, and the schoolyard fell silent against the noise from the surrounding streets. Angie shook her head, coming back to reality. If she wasn't careful, Dawn was going to convince her to adopt some Haitian kids after all.

A sudden surge of caws and shrill shrieks echoed down from the air above her. Angie looked up. A swarm of pigeons and crows, brightly colored tropical specimens, and bland brown sparrows were all mingling together and fleeing their perches. Their calls rained down in such a frenzy that she cringed. Then, just as quickly as it had started, the great avian mass departed, and the bird sound faded away.

Angie began walking down the street. Beneath the car horns and rusty chugs of out-of-date mufflers, she became aware of something else. A low rumbling sound, like distant rolling thunder, was coming from everywhere and nowhere, or perhaps seeping up through the ground itself.

"You hear a train?" a man sitting on the sidewalk said to his companion.

Without warning, Angie's feet were ripped out from under her, the ground that had just been solid turning into the thinnest rubber trying to hold back a tidal wave. Thunder erupted, not from the clouds but from the ground itself. All the sounds of the city became mute against whatever terrible thing was breaking out of the earth to collide with them in an elemental fury. Before Angie could try to understand this, the thunder was joined by the crashing of walls and trees being cast aside like papers blowing in the wind. Windows shattered, and the initial shocked silence around her morphed into a wild cacophony of screams. Angie blinked, and suddenly her field of vision was filled with panicked people trying to run, falling, trying again, then either crab walking or giving up and curling into a fetal position.

The earth beneath all of them lifted, fell, then lifted again with no respite or mercy, obliterating the already cracked pavement and hurling dust and rocks into the air. The ground was trying to shake Angie off, fling her into the sky. Her knees hurt, and she realized she had fallen on them. A palm tree crashed down next to her. A geyser of foaming water rained down a short distance away, and somehow in the chaos her brain managed to deduce a water main must have ruptured. Power lines cracked in whips of sharp reports and bursting sparks. The raging ground dislodged a chunk of pavement and shot it into her face. She clutched her forehead and curled up into a ball, pain and terror directing her body to make itself small.

Through her clutched fingers, and a thick screen of smoke and dust, Angie could see the school across from her. At that moment, the bricks and plaster of the outer façade of the building gave way. The windows shattered, and the stained concrete above the front door split in an ugly gash. Angie got one seemingly impossible glimpse inside: the exposed classrooms were filled with screaming children, some still sitting at their desks, some crouched underneath. Then the entire front of the schoolhouse tipped and tipped and collapsed, sending a terrible expulsion of brick and dust in every direction.

For the briefest of intervals, the furious Earth paused its onslaught, just enough for Angie to see one last horror through the darkening dust and smoke. Under twisted pipes and smashed plaster, an adult and child knelt in an almost prayer-like pose. The adult, the same schoolteacher who had been the last to usher her flock of children back to their courses and the supposed safety inside their building, had her head lowered and her arms wrapped around a young child. Angie met the girl's terrified eyes, the same piercing, intelligent, innocent eyes she had seen only moments before, the ones that gazed into her book under the cradling shade of the tree while her classmates played around her, oblivious to them as she crafted a world for only herself.

But as the girl screamed, that world came crashing down. The ceiling above the two gave way, and the black cloud of dust and smoke overtook them, choking Angie's vision, blinding her, strangling her, becoming the only world there was.

6

Tess watched the snow slowly accumulating on the other side of the kitchen window as she sipped her tea. The voice seeping through the ceiling broke her vague feeling of relaxation. She winced. Jeter or Beater, or whatever that American conservative ponce was called, was going on an angry and offensive tangent about something or other.

Mum had asked Tess to find the station for her on the fancy satellite radio she had gotten a few Christmases back. "Really, Mum," Tess had protested. "You can get radio channels from all over the world, on any topic you like, and you want to listen to that?"

"Oh, dear," her mother had said. "You're right, of course. It's just that your father loved to listen to him, and hearing it now helps me go to sleep. A comfort in my old age, I guess."

"My father?" Tess had asked. "Dale?"

"What's that? Oh, no, not your father. Frank." Mum's second husband, with whom she'd had three more children in America. Tess had never really gotten to know Elizabeth, Frank Jr., and Dawn very well, living an ocean apart. But when Frank Sr. had died six years ago, none of them had been willing to take Mum in, so Tess had brought her back to London to live with her above the pub. Only Elizabeth had come to visit, and only on business trips when she popped in for an hour or two between brokering deals.

Tess attempted to block out the caustic stream of bloviation seeping through the ceiling as she sipped her tea. When she heard "Obama" and "Kenya," she gave up and retreated to the living room to watch the BBC. The room was small but comfortable. An over-stuffed lavender paisley-print couch dominated one wall, with two matching hassocks providing a place to rest tired feet. The couch was bracketed by small end tables purchased with utility in mind, each with enough room for a mug of tea and topped by a lamp bright enough to allow aging eyes to read comfortably. The coffee table was a bit small for the length of the couch, but that left enough room to comfortably get past the hassocks. An old console featuring an ancient television, a record player, a radio, and storage for vinyl records covered much of the wall across from the couch. A bay window overlooked the street in front of the pub.

Tess relaxed into the couch cushions. She hadn't realized until just then how stiff she had become. But that's what working full time and caregiving full time will do to a person. She loosened her shoulders and let her spine sink into the soft fabric.

Then, from the room above: "*The ground beneath our feet is shifting! Shifting right now, even as you listen to this! Obama and his commie pals . . .*"

Oh, bollocks, Tess almost said out loud. *I'd love to see that bellend even explain what a communist is.*

Most days when she had to listen to that rubbish from her mum's radio, she came tantalizingly close to barging in and shutting it off. Mum wouldn't put up much of a fight. But she always stopped herself when she remembered this was her mum's only taste of native Iowa in London. Still, with each ethnic slur and aggressive pronunciation of the "Hussein" in Obama's name, Tess found her better angels getting quieter and quieter.

Tess quickly fumbled for the remote and increased the volume of the BBC. The calming Oxbridge accent of the newscaster drowned out the grating howl of the dreadful American above. Tess tried to relax again as she sipped her tea and listened to the refined, if dull, recounting of the day's political stories.

"*. . . shared a tense exchange with the Prime Minister, renewing accusations against the Conservative government of surreptitious plans to privatise certain NHS services. The Prime Minister denounced such accusations in the strongest possible terms. Though when reached for comment, he could not account for certain . . .*"

Tess had just settled into a light doze when she heard her mother's bedroom door creak open and Mum's soft but deliberate footsteps move across the ceiling above and make their way to the stairs leading down to the parlor. Tess shook herself out of her reverie and rose from the couch. She was surprised to see her mother beginning a determined and steady descent down the stairwell, gripping the railing tightly.

"Mum!" Tess said, still in a half-standing position over the couch. "What are you doing? Do you need help?"

"Oh, I'm fine, dear. I can manage the stairs."

Tess hovered in an unpleasant limbo. "I can see that, but . . . Mum, you haven't left your room in—"

"You worry too much." Her mother gave her a smile, and Tess found herself with nothing left to say. Mum managed to reach the bottom of the stairs, transferred herself to a walker that had sat there unused for six weeks, and slowly but confidently made her way to join her daughter on the couch.

"Please sit down, Mum," Tess said. "I thought you were asleep. I hope the sound from the telly didn't wake you."

Her mother waved her hand in a kind dismissal. She oriented the walker perpendicular to the couch and slowly lowered herself onto the cushion. Tess remained standing. "Can I get you some tea? Coffee?"

"I'm fine, dear."

Tess sunk back down next to her mother. "I must say, Mum, it's quite good to see you up and about like this! After talking to the NHS helpline, I was worried we weren't going to get too much assistance there, so this is good news!"

Her mother nodded, staring at something in front of her and smiling warmly. Tess allowed the tension of the previous moment to subside and began to relax into the couch cushions again. They sat in silence for a few moments like that, Tess unable to think of anything meaningful to say. But it was her mother who broke the impasse. As the newscaster droned on about unimportant political frustrations, Mum turned and, in one gentle and deliberate motion, brought her wrinkled hand against Tess's cheek. She patted a few times, and despite the silence, Tess felt her mother speaking to her in a subtle language that could only be deciphered mother to daughter.

I love you, Mum told her through that simple touch. *I want to thank you. For all of this.*

Tears welled up in Tess's eyes. But rather than let them fall, she returned her mother's smile and brought her own hand against the one cupping her cheek. Her mother nodded, and they returned to watching television.

"The snow is lovely tonight, isn't it, dear?" her mother said. Tess's gaze went to the parlor window, where the snow was accumulating in the deepening London night.

Tess nodded. Mum wasn't normally this lucid. Might this be a Christmas season miracle?

As if to serve as an answer—though of what kind Tess didn't know—a lorry or bus, a large one by the sound, plowed down the road outside.

"I . . . just came down . . ." her mother began. She seemed to struggle with her words, like she was swimming through quicksand. "I . . . wanted to tell you . . ."

The BBC newscast cut abruptly from its ad break and a "Breaking News" image jumped across the screen, catching Tess's attention. Behind the news anchor was a crude image, taken from a mobile phone or cheap camera, of a chaotic cluster of rubble and debris in what looked like a city center.

"We interrupt our regularly scheduled news broadcast with a BBC breaking news alert. The BBC has confirmed reports of a 'significant' earthquake having just struck the Caribbean nation of Haiti. According to initial reports, the earthquake's epicenter was located within the Haitian capital of Port-au-Prince. No seismic readings have been released, but seismologists have indicated that the earthquake was of a 'severe' magnitude."

Different footage filled the screen, showing a room shaking violently, its walls cracking as furniture and shelves fell onto the floor. The window nearby splintered, and the video's audio blared with shouts of panic in an unfamiliar language. The image turned into an indecipherable blur as the unknown citizen journalist abandoned any effort to capture the scene.

"Oh, dear," Tess said. "How horrible. As if Haiti doesn't have enough to worry about. And so close to Christmas too!"

The news anchor returned to the screen with a grim face. *"We don't yet have an exact number of casualties, but we are being warned to expect a devastating number, perhaps in the tens of thousands."*

The broadcast cut to an image of young Haitian schoolchildren crying and bloodied amidst the devastation. Tess turned away.

"How dreadful, indeed. I wish there was something we could do, but . . . Mum?"

Her mother's head was slumped to the side, her eyes glassy and vacant, her mouth agape.

"Mum? Mum!" Tess shook her mother's shoulder. Her body was limp. "Mum! Mum! Oh, help! Help!"

She didn't know who she was calling out to in the empty room. She looked up and caught sight once more of the snow falling gently against the window. Whatever horrors lay in both the broader world and this parlor, tranquility still reigned just outside that window.

From upstairs, the voice of the American right-wing shock jock called out, "*Ladies and gentlemen, life will pull the rug out from under us when we least expect it, a fact my thunder-thighed black intern wouldn't know anything about thanks to equal opportunity blah blah blah. But if you want to know what your life is worth . . .*"

Tess swallowed, took a breath, and grabbed her phone to call an ambulance.

7

"Impact in three . . . two . . ."

It was 2 a.m. in Afghanistan, and Jim's camera was on night vision mode, which made the Afghan landscape light up in neon green. When he was bored, Jim liked to imagine he was looking at some strange alien planet. But at that moment he wasn't bored. He was hyper focused on the countdown to the missile strike displayed on the screen.

The targets—four of them—had pulled up to a parking garage in an old pickup. The drone was circling around at angels fifteen above the town, and the glowing targets looked more electricity than man. But Jim had seen their movements well enough. Four men, in the middle of a small town at two in the morning, setting up what looked like a package. Didn't need to be in the CIA to figure that shit out.

"One . . ."

White and yellow light erased everything else as the Hellfire missile exploded the parking garage. As the flare of bright light receded, it illuminated the now-shattered city block. A good chunk of the Khewa street had been dragged to hell along with the pickup truck full of terrorists.

"Shit," Cooper said. Jim recognized the vague concern in his voice and knew it would soon pass. "You nail any civilians there too?"

"They don't count toward the final tally!" Bradley shouted. "Only initial targets!"

On the screen, a few rattled civilians staggered out of the damaged buildings nearby. They were little more than green blurs, stumbling slowly and aimlessly, as if drunk. Or sleepwalking. Standard post-traumatic shock, the automated bodily movements when the world turns upside down without warning and any higher-level control over the body goes bye-bye. Most would incur severe hearing loss from the damage to their eardrums, maybe permanently. In the earlier days, Jim felt sorry for them. Or, at least, he told himself he should feel sorry for them. But it was hard to conjure any empathy for a green smudge taking up less than an inch of a computer screen.

The Marines arrived a moment later with a squadron of Afghan Army personnel in tow. Jim leaned back and watched. The Marines began to sift through the wreckage, looking for bodies they could ID as an intended target for whichever higher-ups wanted that on record. Though Marcus had let slip that they'd sometimes just bullshit an ID with a body blown up beyond recognition, and no one really seemed to care.

Jim tried to spot Marcus among the Marines. It was pointless, he knew. Hell, Jim could barely tell the green blobs of the US personnel from the green blobs of the Afghans, let alone one Marine from another. On an earlier video call, Marcus said he would throw up a shocker when he knew a drone was watching them to let Jim know who he was. None of the Marines here bothered.

Jim yawned. The order for the targets had come in just an hour ago. He wouldn't have much to do for the rest of his lengthy shift. Behind him, Bradley was still pissed off that Jim had climbed yet higher above him on the kill-count tally. Jim raised his index finger in a "number one" gesture, and Bradley flipped him off. Jim grinned, moving his hand like a pistol and blowing the imaginary smoke in Bradley's direction.

Before he could mock Bradley further, something on the screen caught his attention: a person crawling from a pile of rubble where the parking garage and adjacent buildings once stood. The cluster of Marines and Afghan Army were either doing nothing or screwing around and didn't seem to notice.

At first, the figure blended in with the other shell-shocked civilians wandering out of frame. But Jim had been watching drone strikes long enough to notice the subtle differences separating civilians from the "bad guys." This new guy didn't move with the zombie-like trauma of someone whose world just blew up with no warning. Though he was only an inch-tall blotch of green, he moved deliberately. The man—and it was a man; Jim could see the outline of his beard even from 15,000 feet—scuttled away from the blast zone in a straight line. Jim imagined him focusing on a single destination, aware of the enemy troops and aware of what would happen if they saw him.

Without thinking, Jim flipped the camera to infrared mode. The black and green of the night vision flicked over to a rainbow blend of hues that showed heat and body temperature. Human bodies appeared as smudges of red and orange, while the background city blocks were shifting to green and blue as the heat from the blast dissipated into the atmosphere. The man who had just emerged from the rubble strode across Jim's screen as a confident blob of pumpkin.

Hmmm. Jim rubbed his eyes for a second and flipped back to night vision. He caught the last trails of the man's outline as he passed behind a building and out of sight.

On the other side of the screen, the Marines stood around with their thumbs up their asses.

Well, well, well, Jim thought. *The Marines are useless once again. Looks like it's up to the airmen to keep track of things around here.*

Jim reoriented the coordinates on the drone camera to where the man would come out on the other side of the alley. Sure enough, within a minute Jim caught sight of him. He was alone. Jim leaned toward the screen and squinted. He was not being paid to identify potential terrorists, only blow them up. But since he started watching shit in Afghanistan, he had a pretty good feel for who was a good guy and who was a bad guy. And this particular dude fell through his "terrorist" checklist and hit every mark.

And if this was one of the four original targets, they'd dock him a point in his tally.

Jim's drone was in a holding pattern circling around the area at cruising speed, which gave him enough space to keep the camera focused on the man from a distance. The man clearly moved like someone attempting to stay hidden. Jim only lost track of him twice, and both times he quickly found him again lumbering down an open street or making a wrong turn down one alley and needing to circle back around to another.

After half an hour, the man ended up in the wealthy corner of the town. Nowhere in Afghanistan really compared to upscale neighborhoods in the US, but upscale compared to Jim's shitty small-town Iowa home? Sure.

On the screen, the man staggered down a street. He stopped in front of a few houses like he was looking for one in particular.

So, Mr. Terrorist here has got himself some rich friends?

Mr. Terrorist did. He finally recognized a house and started pounding his fist against the door. For a moment, nothing happened.

Uh-oh, Mr. Terrorist. Looks like no one's home. What are you gonna do now?

But at last, the door opened. It looked like the man was trying to say something to whoever was in the doorway, but Jim's view was blocked. He cursed and checked the drone's altitude. It was still around 15,000 feet. He could bring it closer to the ground, but the lower he got the bigger the risk that Mr. Terrorist would notice it. The Reapers were quiet compared to most aircraft, but below 10,000 feet people on the ground could hear them. Especially if they're circling around a set location. Still, Jim sensed a serious conversation brewing in the doorway. His imagination had already conjured dozens of scenarios where new terrorist plots were hatched. He bit his lip and slowly brought the drone down a few thousand feet.

If the man noticed the sound, his body language on the monitor didn't show it. Gradually, the image got clearer. The night vision camera revealed a few more stark details in its green tinge. Jim could see the whisps of the man's beard, his wrinkled robe, the turban haphazardly tied around his head. And finally, the camera angle shifted enough for Jim to see past Mr. Terrorist and into the doorway of the house. Right to the person facing him down.

The person was a woman. A young woman, maybe even a teenager. The high-tech camera was able to pick up a surprising number of details. Jim could clearly make out her traditional headscarf. Her face looked smooth and feminine. She was tall—almost as tall as the man standing across from her in the doorway. Her green-tinged shoulders were raised in what looked like quiet defiance. And across her face, Jim thought he could make out a forceful glare.

She reminded him of someone—he was struck by an image of piercing green eyes. And not just because of the night vision camera. Jim racked his brain and landed on vague recollections of a famous picture of an Afghan girl on a magazine cover. A young woman, her head framed in a traditional scarf, staring down the viewer, just as this young woman in the doorway was staring down her visitor.

Jim began to envision this girl with bright green eyes as well. In his mind he saw traces of dark hair spiraling from underneath her scarf. Smooth skin, a few acne scars, and some moles here and there for beauty marks. He imagined her painting her nails and washing her hair with fruit-scented conditioner, even though it would spend most of the day hidden beneath a scarf.

As the girl in Jim's imagination and the green smudge on the screen became indistinguishable from each other, Jim watched her hold eye contact with the man at her doorstep. She had an unflinching, fiery intensity. Was she Pashtun? Jim knew little about the ethnic groups of Afghanistan, but he had picked up a few identifying markers here and there. As he squinted to soak in every detail, he realized that his nose was only a few inches away from the screen and his eyes were beginning to hurt with how hard he was straining them.

The man at the doorway continued speaking to her in what looked like quiet desperation. The girl, however, did not show any sign of fear. At most, she looked annoyed at this interruption of her night.

Then another man came up from behind her and ushered the girl back inside. Her father, most likely. He started yelling at the man in the doorway with aggressive hand gestures. Mr. Terrorist pleaded his case, but the girl's father merely gestured outward from the doorway—to somewhere, anywhere, away from their house, Jim surmised—and finally slammed the door in the man's face.

The terrorist fled down another nearby block of houses. Jim followed him with the drone as best he could. After shuffling across several blocks, the man came to a stop on a corner between two run-down houses. A few minutes later, a car rounded the corner and slowed in front of him. The man hopped in and the car sped off. Jim attempted to follow it, but the car disappeared behind a building and off Jim's screen.

Jim sat back. How did the car know where to pick up Mr. Terrorist? Did the man he had spoken to at the house give him viable info? If so, why did he turn him away? And who even was that guy?

Or his daughter, for that matter?

Jim tried to retrace the drone's steps back to the house. He eventually found what he thought was the right block of houses—larger than any in the surrounding areas of the town—but they all looked the same.

In the end, it wasn't the exact characteristics of the house or specific coordinates that identified the correct location. It was a second-story balcony. He brought his face close to the screen once more, trying to verify that he was indeed seeing what he was seeing.

The young woman sat on the balcony, more relaxed than she had stood in the front doorway. She was reclined on what may have been a lawn chair or even a bean bag on the ledge outside her window. Jim zoomed closer. The green robes that wrapped around her body didn't look like traditional Afghan robes that women wore outside. These were less bulky and more intimate. A nightgown? The girl's leg stretched in front of her, lighter and paler than the rest of her. Jim sucked in a sudden gulp of air. Her leg was bare, the naked skin running all the way up to her thigh. He was no prude in his home country but watching Afghanistan every day had taught him about the much, much stricter standards of decency and modesty there.

Especially for women and girls.

The young woman had something propped in her lap. A book? Jim zoomed the camera yet closer. Yes, it was definitely a book of some kind. A diary? The woman began writing in it, and Jim nodded to no one. A diary. He had never kept a diary, but he imagined a black leather-bound book, its pages edged in gold. Something better crafted—and more expensive—than what he would have assumed you could find in a shithole like Afghanistan. The kind of journal sold in countless American bookstores that Jim never went to. Her face had a quiet, thoughtful intensity as she moved her pen across the pages. Every now and then she paused to consider something, or drift on a particularly interesting daydream, before returning to her work.

"What are you writing?" Jim mumbled as if she could hear him from half a world away.

Separated from her by thousands of miles, he watched as she scribbled and thought and yawned in her sleeplessness. She showed no signs of fear or distress from the strange man who had recently plagued her doorstep, or the violent missile strike that had only a short time ago rattled her town. Jim felt himself relaxing, imagining himself next to her, feeling the wind blowing through the night, watching the moon framed by the Afghan landscape, watching her closer and closer . . .

"Jim!"

In a surge of confused panic, Jim mashed random buttons on his keyboard. After blinking a few times, he saw he had abruptly pulled the camera away from the girl, and his night vision was now trained on the empty Afghan mountains.

"Sir?!" Jim said, forcing himself into stringent attention within his chair.

"I'm not the major, idiot." It was Jason. "But you see this?"

Jim looked over. Jason and the rest of the group had gathered around the shitty TV in the corner of the trailer. Before Jim got up to join them, he cast a brief glance back at his screen in some fool's hope that the young woman would still be there.

Of course, she wasn't.

The TV screen was filled with images of rubble and debris across a dilapidated city street.

"You managed another strike without me?" Jim asked, before he realized that wasn't possible. He was looking at a television, not a drone screen. This was a news broadcast.

"It's not Afghanistan, idiot," Bradley said, not taking his eyes off the TV. "It's Haiti. Big, humongous earthquake."

"Haiti?" Jim had grown up with a map of the world on his bedroom wall, and an image of the nation that shared its island with the Dominican Republic smack in the middle between Florida and South America popped into his mind. "When was this?"

"Just now," Jason said. "I think. They don't know much, but they're saying thousands could be dead. Tens of thousands."

"Ah, man," Jim said. "That's hosed."

"Uh, yeah man, hosed," Bradley said, as if he had a more insightful comment he was holding back. Asshole.

"I think they've already authorized some of the UAVs to divert from Afghanistan to go help the rescue mission down there." Like Jason could know that if the earthquake had only just happened. Jim would have heard the order if Udall had announced it to the trailer. But it did sound plausible.

"Okay," Jim said. He didn't know what else to say. The news broadcast kept a helicopter shot focused on a city of rubble. Small dots streamed through broken streets—people, Jim abruptly realized. Hundreds of people, stained in blood and dust and stumbling across piles of what were once buildings. Their clumsy, jerking movements were the same as those he had just seen from the civilian survivors of his drone strike. All the way down to the uneven path they walked and their slow, almost random speed. From above they always looked like sleepwalkers. Here, they could be zombies.

Jim had long ago learned how to feel nothing when looking at scenes like this. But this moment was different. He thought of the strange Afghan girl he had just watched, perched on her balcony in the moonlight, dyed emerald green by his drone's night vision lens. He saw the eyes he had half-seen and half-imagined become stupefied by the trauma of a blast. He saw the hands that had written in the diary covered in dust and blood and shaking with a pain that her body registered before her brain. He saw her stumbling through the destroyed streets of Haiti without any purpose or destination.

A sick feeling started in his stomach and rose into his throat and across his body as the newscast went on.

8

A minuscule part of Angie's brain that was still somehow rational told her it had only been a moment or two since the world was last stable. But the rest of her brain—the part that kept her hands clutched around her head as if it would fly away—told her that this stable world might only have been a dream and the current chaos was all that had ever been.

She managed, with great effort, to dislodge one hand from her head and drop it to the ground. She fingered the pavement and found it cracked, painted with dust and debris and far more fragile than it had been that morning.

But it was no longer shaking.

She opened her eyes. At first, she saw nothing but a grotesque brown and gray haze.

I'm blind, she thought.

But the dust and smoke began to dissipate, just enough for her to see the silhouetted outlines of what was left of the city around her. The buildings that had only a moment ago lined the street had been replaced with a dense cluster of rubble, piled haphazardly against upturned palm trees and smashed power lines. Shattered pipes spewed fans of water into the sky. The water fell back to the ground in a cruel imitation of rain, mixing with the dirt and disemboweled innards of the buildings to form a sickly, ominous brown muck that had already begun flooding the streets. A siren rang out from somewhere in the distance.

Angie managed to catch her balance and stand on uneasy and boneless legs, like a newborn foal trying to take its first steps. She touched her head and noticed a smear of blood coating her fingers. Tentatively, she brought her hand back to her forehead and winced with a sudden shock of pain from what felt like a nasty gash on her temple. Looking down, she saw her white sundress stained with a thick layer of dust and mud and her own blood.

High-pitched wails caught her attention, and she began to consider how many people might be buried alive under the tons of broken concrete and steel. But that thought proved too ghastly for her fragile state, and she shook it off.

Some of the shouts were futile attempts to get help for the injured. As if the cruel world that had just inflicted this upon them would immediately realize its error and, out of remorse, conjure from thin air a state-of-the-art emergency response within the wreckage of their third-world island nation.

Angie took a few tentative steps. Her legs, though jellified by panic and shock, did not seem injured. A wave of dizziness hit, and she thrust her hands out in front of her, searching for something solid to grab and steady herself. She latched onto an upright metal pole and was hit with the realization that this pole, alongside a row of others like it, was what remained of the metal fence that had ringed the campus of the elementary school. A prolonged, wailing scream, resonating up and down in pitch but drawn from an inexhaustible oxygen supply, rang from the school. Though she couldn't say how, Angie knew immediately that a young child was making this sound.

She propelled herself into the ruin of the schoolyard, which was a mess of wayward bricks, shattered glass, and shrapnel of concrete and rebar. The school's roof and front façade had been torn apart like the flimsiest of parchment paper, exposing the classrooms like a form of crude viscera. The screaming continued, banshee-like, and Angie grabbed hold of the sound as if it were a siren song that would guide her to her destination.

She climbed atop a pile of rubble where the school's main entrance had stood. It occurred to her, in the rational part of her mind still sending out warnings, that a snapped electrical wire could pose the risk of electrocution. But the screaming of the young child continued, and against her better judgment, she clumsily entered the school.

The main corridor was blocked by several feet of what used to make up the ceilings and walls, painted with a cloud of white dust. It looked like something ancient and buried, a long-lost tragedy that had played out in the distant past, and she was a modern-day interloper finally opening its secrets to the sunlight after millennia underground.

You know those are the bodies of the children, her rational monologue offered as she climbed the pile. Indeed, within the debris and dust lay tiny hands and feet and remnants of torsos, all buried under rubble and caked with dust, none showing any signs of movement. Her inner voice was calm and strangely detached from the reality of the situation around her. *There will be time for horror later.*

After reaching the top, Angie fell onto her butt and slid the rest of the way into the front corridor. She followed the screaming to what she assumed was once a hallway entrance, where a large slab of concrete weighed atop a kneeling figure. It looked like an apparition of the Virgin Mary, complete with a ghostly white gossamer of dust. Angie navigated the uneven floor as she made her way to the figure. Looking closer, she realized it was one of the school's teachers. The same one, in fact, she had just seen shielding the little girl who loved to read, as the school fell on top of them.

The woman was propped up on her knees, her head bowed and her arms clutching something unseen under the rubble. Over the dust on her face ran streams of dark blood that had flowed from her catastrophic head injuries. She showed no signs of life.

Angie began digging into the debris. Within a few seconds she saw the source of the screams. A tuft of black hair, somehow still neatly bound in its braids, and a child's school uniform writhed under one of the larger slabs of concrete. The little girl was caked with dust and blood, but alive.

"Help!" Angie shouted reflexively. "Help! Help!" But she knew her calls were futile.

She looked back down at the girl, whose head was trapped at an awkward angle that must have been putting pressure on her lungs. And yet, those lungs somehow found air enough to continue screaming.

"Hey, um, little girl . . ." Angie said. "It's okay . . . It's okay. We'll get you out of here soon enough. It's okay." The girl continued screaming, and Angie realized she had been speaking English, so she tried again. Fragments of Haitian Creole, proper French, and English floated around her addled mind. "Ti fi . . . li nan oke . . . uh . . ." The girl wailed on.

Angie had to do something. She wasn't sure she could lift the large piece of concrete holding the girl down, but she gripped it anyway. She tightened her back and drew the full force of her arms and torso upward like a human lever. The slab rose a few inches, but Angie could go no farther and collapsed. The slab crashed back down. The girl's screams intensified.

Angie picked herself up and regripped the slab. This time, she attempted to pivot the mass vertically, opening enough of a hole for the girl to squeeze through. Angie had no idea how injured she was—if she could move under her own power. But the girl's perpetual howling suggested she still had some life left in her. So Angie tensed up her back and shoulders once more and pulled with all her strength.

The slab moved several more inches. It might be enough.

"Can you . . . can you climb out?" Angie asked in her best Creole. It was hard to speak under the strain of holding the heavy slab back.

The girl just kept screaming.

You're stronger than this, Angie chastised herself. *You moved all the cinderblocks to the backyard when Dawn wanted to renovate the garden. You can do this.*

Huffing in as much of a breath as she could, Angie gripped the slab again and gave one final, desperate heave to pull it away from the girl. The slab moved a few more inches and the pile of rubble underneath it gave way, freeing the girl from the slab while throwing Angie backward onto a hard mound of bricks.

Angie shouted a profanity that she hoped the girl couldn't understand and scrabbled back to her feet. The girl was still curled in a crude fetal position within the arms of her dead teacher.

"C'mon, c'mon now . . . dear," she attempted. "We have to get out of here."

The girl's screaming continued unabated.

"Are you injured?" Angie asked. No reply. With still-shaking hands, she reached down and took the girl's fragile hand. She didn't resist.

"You just let me know if I'm hurting you," Angie said.

With one fluid motion, she pulled the girl's body out of the teacher's protective embrace. The girl flailed a bit but then clutched Angie's hand. Her screaming stopped.

"Oh . . . okay, then," Angie said.

She maneuvered them out of the ruins of the school and back to the outside world. The girl made no sound but seemed to quietly speak to Angie through her tight, quivering grip, which communicated both terror and absolute trust.

Angie got them past the schoolyard, doing the best she could to shield the girl's eyes—and her own—from the bodies of her classmates and teachers. On the other side of the fence, Angie stepped onto the street and surveyed the damage. She had been hoping to see the flashing lights of an emergency crew, an ambulance, police car,

fire truck, anything. Some authority figure into whose more competent hands she could give the child without any guilt, and then go off
to deal with the incalculable things she needed to deal with. But the
street was just as chaotic as it had been before she entered the school.

A woman walked past them just then, and Angie darted in her
direction, thrusting the little girl up to her face. "Uh, excuse me.
Can you help plea—"

But the woman was sobbing and muttering incoherently from
under a frosting of dust and blood. Angie picked up vague references
to both Jesus and the Vodou gods, as if in the woman's trauma she
had forgotten any distinction between the two. Still chattering her
syncretic prayers, the woman continued down the street without noticing Angie or the girl.

Take her to Mama and Papa, Angie thought. *They'll know what to
do. If they're still alive.*

She banished that final thought and took off in the direction of
her parents' house. They passed two men moving a group of wound-
ed people using a big sheet that had been turned into a makeshift
stretcher. A tap-tap car was valiantly trying to manage the shattered
and debris-ridden street. People on foot staggered at a slow, mechan-
ical pace that hardly looked human. They skirted the dead, which
lay in vast numbers, bloodied and shattered limbs sticking out of
the rubble as if they had been components of the foundations of the
buildings.

"It's okay," Angie muttered to the girl still clutching her hand,
chanting it in a kind of mantra. "It's okay."

She was suddenly struck by the absurdity of her situation. She,
who was perfectly happy with her safe, kid-less life in Berkeley, was
wandering the decimated streets of her native city, responsible for
the safety of a young child. How did she wind up here?

9

Throughout the morning, Tess paced what felt like the length of the Thames back and forth along the hospital waiting room, trying to restrain herself from looking at the clock on the wall above the nurse's station. The clock seemed to have noticed this and elected to punish her by running even slower.

She had tried to reach her half-siblings while she waited for word of their mother's condition from anyone wearing scrubs, but all three calls went straight to voicemail. It was only early evening in America, so Elizabeth was probably at a dinner meeting, Frank was probably driving, and Dawn, well, Dawn was so flighty. A whimsical folk singer, she was no doubt prone to leaving her phone on tables in cafés or on shelves at bookstores after her performances, or letting the charge die without even realizing it. Tess didn't bother leaving messages. This was the kind of news best delivered in person.

Eventually, a man who looked a bit too young to be a physician had emerged through the sliding doors.

"We need to run a few tests to determine her level of neurological functioning," he'd said. "We were able to get her stabilized, but it may take some time before we know the extent of the damage to her brain. We are awaiting availability for a CT scan before we can proceed."

Tess did not recall hearing the word "stroke," but it was implied. She'd managed to get some sleep on one of those two-seater chairs in the waiting room, the kind with no armrest between the seats. Now she was massaging her neck, trying to lessen the inevitable crook that had set in overnight. She wondered when the doctor would appear again and if it would be the same one as before, given it was 9 a.m. the following day. Surely there had been a shift change at some point.

As it was still way too early to try reaching her half-siblings again, Tess went off in search of a cup of tea.

After what felt like several years, the clock finally ticked past noon, and if 7 a.m. was too early for Elizabeth, Tess no longer cared. They had a semblance of a family relationship, and this was important. Tess tapped "Elizabeth" on her phone's screen and listened for the dial tone to switch from the British to the American line. It rang several times, then went to voicemail again.

"You have reached the voice message service of Elizabeth Lancer, Merger and Acquisition Analyst with Blarney, Thompson, and Grant. I am away from my phone, but if you leave your name and number, I will get back to you presently." Bollocks. She must be getting ready for work or already on her commute. Tess reluctantly left a message.

"Hi Elizabeth, it's Tess calling. From London. Sorry to call so early, it's just something's happened with Mum. If you can call me at your closest convenience, that would . . . that would be best, I think."

There, that wasn't so bad. She hadn't delivered bad news over the phone, she'd just asked to be called back.

She decided to give Frank a little more time to wake up—he was acerbic at the best of times, and 6 a.m. was probably not his favorite hour—and debated whether it was totally inappropriate to try Dawn in California. It would be even earlier for her, around four in the morning. Tess figured there was a possibility she hadn't even gone to bed yet. Dawn had come to London many years ago, when she was in her twenties, and stayed with Tess under the guise of visiting family, though it was obviously more about the free lodging.

Dawn's proclivity to stay awake most of the night then sleep for most of the day hadn't made for a lot of meaningful family time.

She hesitantly tapped "Dawn" on her mobile and hoped for the best. The tone rang out a few times, and Tess was about to resign herself to more clock-watching when, after the fifth ring, the line clicked, and Dawn's voice wafted through her phone. "Hello?"

"Hello, Dawn?"

There was a pause, and then, "Yes?"

"Hello, it's Tess. From London."

"Oh . . . oh, yes, Tess, sorry I didn't recognize your voice at first."

"No worries, love." Tess's voice was raspy and alien to her own ears, like something marinated in whiskey and left to ferment in a dark, dusty place. "I apologize for calling. I assume it's quite early where you are."

"Oh, that's not a problem." Dawn sounded like she was stifling a yawn. "Jet lag. My sleep schedule's all messed up, so I was awake anyway."

"Oh, I see," Tess said in as charming a tone as she could manage. "Were you on holiday?"

"Haiti," Dawn said.

A flash of something dark and sinister crossed Tess's mind, but the specifics were lost in the trauma of the past several hours. "Haiti?" she echoed.

"Yeah, I was there with Angie, visiting her parents. You've met Angie, right?"

The closest Tess had come to meeting Angie was in belated Christmas cards to Mum, which Dawn knew full well. "Listen, Dawn, the reason I called you . . . I'm afraid there's bad news."

"Bad news?"

"Yes. I'm at the hospital now. Mum has had a medical emergency."

"Oh, no! What happened?"

Tess swallowed, struggling with how to convey what was

happening. "I think . . . well, the doctors don't quite know yet. They're doing tests, but I'm afraid it doesn't look good. They think that it might have been a stroke."

As the words left her mouth, she glanced up at the television on the opposite wall of the waiting area where the BBC was broadcasting grainy aerial footage of a city in ruins. Smoke rose from destroyed buildings, surrounded by rubble and debris. Streets and sidewalks were cracked, and cars lay crushed under fallen houses or wrecked into destroyed lampposts and overturned buses. Though the audio was muted, the chyron at the bottom of the screen spelled out the situation clearly enough.

HAITI DEVASTATED BY MASSIVE EARTHQUAKE

Tess stared at the television in horror. This was why Haiti had struck a chord. These same images—or ones just like them—had been on their screen at home when Mum lost consciousness. A few seconds lapsed before she realized Dawn was talking to her.

". . . Tess? I said, how bad is it?"

"Bad," Tess blurted out. She swallowed to collect herself. "What I meant to say is, I'm afraid I don't think she's in great shape."

"Oh." Dawn's voice was falling, as if uncertain how to proceed. "Do . . . you think I should come out there?"

"Well," Tess began. A sudden urgency had charged through the conversation. She felt a nervous need to be as efficient as possible with her information. She turned away from the TV. "I mean, I would say yes. Unfortunately. I mean, it's up to you, of course. I know it is a bit of a journey, from California to here. And you having just gotten back from Haiti . . ."

Tess's voice died in her throat, but Dawn's lack of a reaction made one thing clear: the poor thing didn't know yet. At least she got out of Haiti in time. Just in time for this to happen, of course.

"I-I-I . . ." Dawn was stuttering on the other end of the line. With every syllable, she sounded more and more like a scared child awaiting chastisement. "I will certainly try. I mean, I have to look at my money situation. The trip to Haiti took up a bit of our savings . . . but . . . I mean . . . if you say it looks bad . . ."

"To clarify, love, I haven't gotten official word from the doctors yet," Tess said. They were certainly taking their sweet time on that front. "So I don't really know what to tell you at this point, other than it does not look good. It's up to you, of course. But, if I were you, I would come out. If you can, I mean."

Dawn let out a prolonged sigh that turned into something of a whine. "I'll have to call Angie; she should be up now. She's spending a few more days in Haiti with her parents."

"I have to go now," Tess said. Only after she hung up did the devastating significance of Dawn's last sentence register.

"Oh, my dear God," she said aloud. A passing nurse sent a strange glance in her direction before continuing to a restricted area.

Tess thought about calling Dawn back. What a conversation that would be: *Sorry to bother you again, love, but here's some more news: In addition to your mother suffering what was a severe stroke, the country you were just in has been destroyed by an earthquake, and your girlfriend could very well be dead. Alright then, Merry Christmas!*

She looked down and saw that her fingers had already moved into place above the contact labeled "Frank" on her mobile screen. Might as well get it over with. She tapped it and drew her ear once more to the sound of the British signal giving way to the American one.

She'd avoided breaking the Haiti news to Dawn, but she knew Dawn couldn't be trusted to tell Frank about their mother.

But instead of Frank, a woman's voice came on the line. "Hello?"

Ah, yes, this number was the landline. Tess wasn't sure if they even had mobile phones in whatever red-state rubbish heap Frank lived in. Remembering her manners, she quickly swallowed the bitter thought.

"Yes, hello . . . er . . ." What was Frank's wife's name again? "Is Frank there?"

The woman audibly sighed on the other end of the line. "Can

I take a message?" Her voice had the singsongy quality evocative of rural America, with a slight Southern twinge, halfway between Scarlett O'Hara and a Bible Belt televangelist. Sweet on the surface but hiding deep caverns of judgment and prejudice that could rear themselves out of the darkness at any moment.

"Yes, this is Tess, calling from London."

"Tess?" the woman said. "Oh, Tess! This is Nancy. How are you?"

"Nancy!" Tess said with a bit too much enthusiasm. "Er, I apologize for ringing you so early. I imagine it must be some dreadful hour where you are."

"Oh, it's not a problem, dear," Nancy said with a melodic, conversational tone that still made Tess feel vaguely uncomfortable. "I was up anyway. Frank had to haul outta here before sunrise. He tends to wake me up on his early morning shifts."

Tess's eyes drifted back toward the television, where the troubling images were still flashing across the screen. "So," she said, "Frank's not there now?"

"I'm afraid not, hon," Nancy said. "He's taking a shipment of somethin' or other across the state. We're in Iowa, you know. It's flat but big. He's staying at a motel overnight and should be back tomorrow. You could try him on his cell phone, but he tends to just throw the thing in the back seat when he's drivin' and ignore it."

Nancy paused with a quick breath in. Tess thought she heard the potential gravity of the situation finally make its way past Nancy's middle-American niceties. "Is everything okay there?" Nancy asked.

Tess considered breaking the news directly to Nancy and letting her tell Frank. But that would be the coward's way out. "If you speak to Frank between now and whenever he gets back, could you just ask him to call me? He has my number, right?"

"I think so," Nancy said. "But, if not, it's written down here, somewhere. I'm sure I can dig it up." She paused again, and Tess bit her lip. "I hope everything's alright!"

"I don't want to panic anyone," Tess said, as a nurse's voice broke through the hospital intercom to page a doctor with what sounded like a long Indian name. Tess pressed down on her free ear with her fingers. "He . . . he should call me as soon as possible, though. Yes, tell him to call me right away, if you can."

"I will certainly do that." Tess picked up a slight downward shift in Nancy's tone, like her initial Southern charm had devolved into xenophobic suspicion of the strange woman with a foreign accent calling her out of the blue. *Still*, Tess thought to herself, *not as bad as Frank.*

"It's about his mother," Tess blurted out. "Just, he should call me as soon as possible."

"His mother? Oh, okay, I will let him know." A tentative Dolly Parton cadence had returned to Nancy's voice, but Tess was still eager to get off the line.

"I'd love to chat longer," Tess lied, "but I have a few more calls I need to make. And I assume that you would enjoy a tea or coffee at your hour, so I will let you get to that. Frank can call me at his convenience, I'll have my phone on." And be up anyway. "But it was lovely to talk with you!"

"Yes," Nancy said. "Lovely to talk with you as well. I'll send your message to Frank."

"Alright, thank you, ta-ta!"

She realized she was pacing again—had been the whole conversation with Nancy. She sank onto the two-seater chair she'd spent the night on and took in her surroundings. The waiting room matched her mood. A few other nervous-looking relatives were strewn about, pacing like she'd just been or allowing themselves to rest, only to jerk their heads in sharp alert like meerkats as soon as they drifted off. A dreadfully dressed man, who Tess assumed to be some kind of vagrant, was slumped over in a seat across the room from her, either napping or passed out. Down the hall, a young couple tried in vain to calm a crying toddler.

And then there was the BBC broadcast, still covering the

developing story in Haiti, complete with more footage of destroyed buildings and bloodied Haitians. Tess noticed her jaw clenching and her shoulders trying to retreat to the top of her head.

"I should have told Dawn about Haiti," she said aloud.

"What was dat, love?" a Jamaican accent sounded from nearby, and Tess startled. She looked up to find a nurse standing only a few feet away, chart in hand and staring at her through glasses perched on the tip of her nose.

"Noth—nothing, so sorry," Tess managed. "Just talking to myself."

"Mmhmm," was all the nurse said before walking away to deal with whatever.

Tess dropped her forehead to her palm and tried to count the tiles on the floor. She rubbed her eyes, somehow both more tired and more restless than she had ever been.

She was the one who had grown up without a mother, or with a series of temporary mothers, while Mum raised three other children a continent away. And yet when it counted, she was the only one willing to take that aging mother in, to reverse parenting roles even though she'd gotten the short end of that stick decades ago. She was saddled with the stress of caring for an ailing parent *for six years*, and now in Mum's twilight, two of her offspring couldn't even be bothered to be available and the third acted more like a child than an adult.

Tess quashed the rant in her head before it could grow any bigger, as she always did. She loved Mum, and she willingly signed on for this. She could handle what was happening. What was coming.

From somewhere far away, almost lost among the dry voices over the hospital intercom, the screaming children, and the shouts from emergency personnel . . . in hardly more than a whisper . . . Tess heard that special benediction her mother had given her right before everything went to hell: "I wanted to thank you, for everything."

For everything.

10

As morning arrived in Afghanistan, the green-eyed girl's house again showed signs of life. At first, there was only a hint of movement behind one of the windows, so slight Jim couldn't tell if it was real or he had imagined it. But eventually the front door opened and two figures emerged. Jim dragged his head from the back of his chair and immediately zoomed in on the doorway, so quickly he almost overcompensated the camera angle and lost the house entirely.

With the benefit of the high-tech daylight HD camera, Jim could see the figures much more clearly. The older man who had kicked the suspicious figure off the property the previous night was dressed in a modern "western" outfit, sporting a tie and khaki slacks. Behind him was the girl. She wore what looked like a standard school uniform: a loosely fitted white headscarf; long, grey coats; and pants that flowed past her ankles. They stood by the doorway for a moment, talking.

Jim brought his face so close to the screen his nose was almost touching it, trying to pick out every detail. The girl was carrying a neatly packed stack of books. Schoolbooks, he assumed. He squinted. Was that a black diary sitting atop the pile? A leather-bound diary, with gold-edged pages, that she had been writing in last night, perched on the balcony, under the light of the moon?

The pair finished their conversation, and the man—her

father?—began heading for a beige two-door coupe parked in the driveway. The girl drew a hand across her face, and Jim imagined her gracefully brushing a few wayward strands of hair back under her scarf. As she approached the car, Jim thought he saw her shoulders tighten, and she raised her face from the ground up toward the sky. Jim's screen began to center on her, and Jim realized he was moving his joystick to focus the camera's target directly on her face. It was only a pale gray fraction of an inch, but Jim could imagine her piercing green eyes looking into the sky.

Looking at him.

He jerked back. Did she see his drone circling above her? The drone wasn't nearly as big as a passenger plane, and at 15,000 feet it would be almost invisible. Plus, the air was hazy, and the glare from the morning light should give him even more cover. But the girl stood there nonetheless, gazing up, like she was looking for something.

An electric panic buzzed in Jim's chest, and his stomach clenched. Shame washed through him. He felt exposed and guilty. His mind flashed to a painful memory of the time his mom caught him jerking off to porn on her computer when he was fourteen. Her mouth had silently opened and closed like a bass out of water, then she'd turned from the room and closed the door behind her. He'd been mortified. She never spoke about it, but the next time he checked, her computer password was changed.

The girl scanned the sky for a few more seconds, but her father said something that pulled her focus back to the car. She opened the passenger door and stepped in. Her father cast a few suspicious looks to his left and right before climbing into the driver's seat.

As the car pulled out of the driveway, Jim glanced back at the house. He waited a beat to see if anyone else would come out, then followed the car. It crawled through the poorly paved roads and after a few minutes pulled up to a newish-looking building, surrounded by a large crowd of young women and girls. They were all wearing the same modest but official school uniforms.

His green-eyed girl got out of the car and exchanged a few words with her dad. Her mouth pulled tight and narrow, and her jaw jutted in what looked like anger. Was it related to the events of the night before, or just the usual gripes teenagers have with their parents?

The girl turned and joined her fellow students entering the school, while her father pulled out and drove back to the main road. Jim kept the camera trained on the school's entrance, watching even after the girl disappeared inside amid a sea of girls all more or less indistinguishable from the back.

He glanced up at the icon in the corner of his screen. The footage was being recorded, as it always was. Not that Jim was off task. On the contrary, after reporting to his superiors how the mysterious survivor of the drone strike had gone to a house after his friends got blown to shit, they had dryly instructed him to "keep an eye on it" before disappearing back into whichever high places they went to before ordering a strike. So he was told to follow the man and girl. And so far, the girl had been more interesting. But now she was gone from sight.

Jim sighed and rubbed his eyes. He broke the camera away from the school to follow the man again. The car drifted through the streets of the town, dodging mule carts and pedestrians, until it eventually pulled onto the main highway. It left Khewa heading south and drove for an hour, weaving along the mountainous highway to Jalalabad, with Jim dutifully following along. When it arrived in the city, the car pulled up to a large academic-looking campus. Nangahar University? Jim tried to remember the limited lectures he had gotten on the schools and hospitals and other administrative spots in Jalalabad. The car pulled into a parking lot, and the man got out and entered the nearest building.

Jim cursed himself for the hour he had just wasted. Not that his superiors would care, of course, but he was gripped by an urge to get back to Khewa. Without a car to slowly tail, it only took him a few minutes to retraced his drone's "steps" from the larger city back through the isolated mountain passes and into the small town. Not much of particular interest was happening—the markets were beginning to fill up with farmers and artisans drawing their mules and horses. The drone attack survivor was still hiding out there somewhere, plotting who knew what.

Jim took a sip of coffee and grimaced—it had long ago grown cold—then glanced up at the time. His mouth was already watering in anticipation of his next dip, but his shift didn't end for an hour. He figured he'd kill the time checking a few of the so-called "hotspots" in town—areas where terrorists and their sympathizers were known to congregate, usually parking garages, abandoned warehouses, and mosques—on the off chance he'd see something suspicious go down.

But as his camera panned over to a street where insurgents had been spotted before, he caught sight of the school where his green-eyed girl had been dropped off. He stopped the camera and zoomed closer. No one was outside anymore. The windows were closed, and no one appeared in any of them to lean out into the open air with a book and exposed skin.

Jim glanced back up at the recording icon in the corner of the screen and rubbed his eyes in an attempt at self-discipline. He took another sip of cold coffee and resumed aiming for the hotspots. But the image of the school windows stayed in his mind over the next hour, as he sat in his comfortable leather seat and watched from the other side of the world.

11

A ngie squeezed her phone against one ear while plugging the other with a finger, trying to hear Dawn's voice through the terrible connection and over the low rumble of another military convoy droning past outside.

"I'm sorry," Angie said. "You're breaking up again."

"... mother in London ... in the hospital, according to Tess ..." The connection faded in and out, and Angie rubbed the growing throb underneath the bandage affixed to her temple.

Over the past three days Angie's waking life had become a blur of wails, dust, and the hovering stench of dead bodies. Her thoughts were as vaporous as the clouds of dust that still didn't seem to have settled since the earthquake, or the slow whirlpools of vultures and other scavenging birds that every hour descended in greater numbers. She had vague memories of pulling the little girl from the ruins of her school, but whatever positive emotions she had felt then were now lost to the horror of reality that numbed all else. She felt unmoored, adrift, nothing more than a hollow outline of a person.

On their walk to Mama and Papa's house following the quake, Angie had tried to figure out where the girl lived, her parents' names, or any other identifying information. But after her shrieking had stopped, the girl had gone mute. The only answers Angie got to her questions were pursed lips and wide, fearful eyes. Angie gave the third-degree a rest for a while, and when she tried again, the girl finally uttered three soft syllables.

"Love-e-lee," she said.

"Lovelie," Angie repeated. She'd had several classmates named Lovelie during her primary through secondary years. "Is that your name?"

The girl slowly nodded.

"Well, Lovelie, I'm Angie," she started, but she had no idea how to interact with the child beyond introductions. She felt her lips twist against her empty thoughts and floundered for something more to say. She landed on, "That's a very pretty name."

The girl just looked down at the ground.

Angie had wept when she and Lovelie had made it back to her parents' house and discovered they had survived. Their famasi and market shop and the attached house had withstood the worst of the shaking, though the front window was shattered and much of the cheap plastering had fallen from the walls.

"Oh, Lovelie!" Angie's mother had exclaimed after she introduced the little girl. "Such a fitting name for such a lovely girl!" The earth-quake had triggered a dormant maternal instinct in Celeste Altidor, who was more drawn to the young child than her grown daughter. "Yes, so lovely."

As one of the few standing houses in the area, Angie's parents had volunteered their home as a makeshift shelter for neighbors. They had quickly run through their famaci's stock of bandages, aspirin, and other first-aid supplies, giving them away to those in need rather than selling them. How could they put a fair price on such supplies when the need was so great? Angie had heard rumors of international relief organizations trickling into Port-au-Prince but hadn't seen hide nor hair of them. As far as she was concerned, rescue efforts could most aptly be described as haphazard and absentee.

Lovelie had remained adhered to Angie's side and came with her as Angie ventured out to explore the endless blocks of destruction.

The wailing bodies of the injured still lay in incalculable numbers on every corner, their cries for help slowly descending into moans against the realization that none was coming. Mothers cradled the bodies of their crushed children, so soaked in blood, dirt, and dust that they didn't even look human. And that was the living. Corpses were even more prevalent, growing bloated and distorted with the cruel process of decomposition. Unyielding swarms of flies enclosed each corpse, leaving clusters of maggots writhing and crawling, shaking the loosened skin in a crude imitation of breathing. Before the vomit could take hold of her throat, before her lingering sanity was swept away against the terror, Angie would drop her eyes to her side and see, once again, the sad but stoic face of the little girl. The pigtails, so lovingly crafted by a mother, still held their shape despite the violence they had been subject to. The wide, soft amber eyes. The quivering nostrils and tight lips.

Lovelie, Angie would think. *So lovely.*

And this would carry her through the destruction from one minute to the next, until she returned home to the sanctuary of her parents' shop and house.

She had longed to call Dawn and tell her she was okay, but cell service had been totally knocked out. UN crews had finally restored a degree of service in some parts of town, which let Angie get through to California. She had hoped for a better connection, to be able to talk to her girlfriend and find comfort there, but instead she was confronted with static and further emotional chaos.

". . . mother's sick . . . in London. I . . . know how bad . . ." Dawn said in fragments, "but Tess . . . half-sister, said . . . I should go visit . . . but with you there . . ."

Even though Angie couldn't make out all the details, she got the gist. "Don't you worry about me. Me and the folks are okay. I'm working on getting us out of here. The US embassy is swamped, but I managed to get through to someone. I'll see what happens. If you need to go to London to be with your mother, go."

". . . feel guilty . . ." Angie could hear Dawn's voice drifting into the faux-whimsy of a small child trying to make believe she didn't have to worry about life's troubles.

"Like I said," Angie went on, stuck being the adult as always. "Don't worry about me or any of us here. The house survived, and we've got supplies from the relief workers. I'll get me and my folks out of here ASAP. Go to London to be with your family. I'll update you whenever I can."

"Okay," Dawn's voice crackled. ". . . love you."

"Love you too," Angie said. The line clicked, and Angie wasn't sure if the connection died or if Dawn had fled the conversation.

Angie slipped her phone back into her pocket and dropped her eyes to Lovelie, who was sitting at a card table, sipping a juice box. The girl was silent as always. While she hadn't left Angie's side since the earthquake destroyed her school, she had also barely spoken, offering only a few brief, babbled syllables.

Angie was overcome with a stab of longing for Dawn. Sure, she was sometimes child-like herself, but she'd know what to do with Lovelie, how to interact.

"So, Lovelie," Angie said, leaning down to the girl, who looked up with her innocent eyes but did not take the juice box's straw out of her mouth. They were very lucky Papa's shop had been fully stocked when the quake hit. "Do you want to go see Mama Celeste?"

Lovelie tightened her lips around the straw.

"What about the other kids, do you want to play with them?"

It was either yesterday or the day before, she had come around yet another grisly street corner and looked down to her side for the reassurance of Lovelie's innocence and calm, when she saw not one childish face, but several. Two boys and one girl, all around Lovelie's age, all looking up at her with unhampered expectancy.

She had no idea where they'd come from and started to wonder where their parents were—until a glance at the rotting bodies sticking out of the fallen buildings on all sides gave her the answer.

Angie roamed around the city all day like that, with an ever-growing tail of children streaming behind her. She searched for relief workers, emergency personnel, police, parents, anyone who would be more equipped to take care of the children than she was. But all she found was the same ruined city, the same wailing of the injured, the same dead bodies half-buried in rubble, and the same blank, zombified look of survivors who, like her, seemed to be wandering from one destroyed block to another with no rhyme or reason other than to hold off the anguish.

And so, Angie ended up back at her parent's house with a group of more than a dozen children.

"My, my, you poor dears!" her mother gushed. She opened her grandmotherly arms and let the children flock into her embrace. "Don't you sweeties worry no more. Mama Celeste's going to take care of you."

Angie wished a brood of children could help soothe her pain like they seemed to do for her mother's. She watched them play in the hot sun, chasing each other, giggling, and occasionally breaking into fights that were then interrupted by more play.

None of them asked where their parents were. At least they figured that out themselves.

In front of her, two of the older kids had gotten into a fight. "Matant Angie!" a tall, skinny boy shouted in Creole. "He stole my plane!" Emmanuel pointed at an equally scrawny but shorter boy, holding a dirty toy airplane with a broken wing.

"You had your turn!" Evans shouted back. "It's my turn!"

"There's only a few toys here," Angie said through gritted teeth. "You really need to learn how to share . . ."

The boys looked at her blankly, then went back to shoving each other, sending the already-broken toy plane crashing to the ground.

Angie couldn't believe Dawn wanted to adopt some of these ruffians.

She looked for an escape from the situation, and her eyes fell back to her original charge. "So, Lovelie. Do you want to go look for your parents again?"

Lovelie said nothing but dutifully rose from her chair and took Angie's hand while keeping her juice held firm in the other.

"Matant Angie, wait for meeeee!" another child's voice shrieked behind her. Angie froze in her tracks and clenched her eyes shut. Crap . . .

When she opened them again, a gaggle of a dozen children was stumbling into line behind her, including Emmanuel and Evans, who were continuing their fight over the toy plane as they bounced alongside their peers.

Angie's eyes darted around, trying to figure out how to ditch the posse, when she saw her mother coming out of the house. "Look, kids! Who do we have here? Would you kids like to spend the day with Mama Celeste again? Mama!"

Angie waved at her mother, who gave the kids a warm smile. "My sweeties!" she said, approaching. "So good to see you frolicking in the sunshine." Then she swiveled her good cheer to Angie. "Dear, would you mind watching the children for a time? I must help your father into that awful makeshift toilet they set up behind the house. The stress of all this made him constipated, and with his bad hip I need to make sure he doesn't fall in!"

"Well . . ." Angie began, but she knew it was hopeless.

"Thanks, dear!" Her mother waved at the children. "Goodbye, my babies! Have fun with your Matant Angie!"

And with that, she disappeared back into the house.

Angie led her cluster of parentless children through the ruined streets of Port-au-Prince. Lovelie, as always, walked by her side, clutching her hand with a small, desperate intensity, while the other kids followed behind, staying organized in something resembling a line.

As they walked, a cloak of foreboding began to weigh Angie

down. It wasn't just fear that another earthquake would hit—that was ever present. It was something more sinister. Throughout this entire ordeal, she had kept a firm faith in the goodness of the people of her native city—that they would rise to the occasion and their mutual bond as Haitians would lead them to help one another. But block after block, she instead saw more signs of violence and conflict than solidarity and compassion. The few people out on the streets were looting damaged storefronts rather than offering help.

It was becoming clear that her devastated city, already filled with crime and poverty, and now with no real police or military presence to keep law and order, may not be the safest place.

Which meant it was not a great time to get lost, but somehow Angie did.

"Um, does anyone remember where your school was?" she asked. She didn't know if they'd all gone to the same school, but given it was in the neighborhood, it seemed likely. Behind her, the children continued noisily playing and fighting, not paying her any attention. Angie peered down at Lovelie, who stared at her with wide, expectant eyes. Angie attempted a smile to reassure her but couldn't quite get her lips to work.

She led her crew down an unfamiliar block, searching for something recognizable. Across from them, two young men dug through a pile of garbage. One wore a uniform of some kind. A sanitation worker?

Angie heard her voice call out before she could think over the situation. "Excuse me!" she shouted. "Do you know where a school is? Was? I have these children, and . . ."

She trailed off when the men raised their heads like wolves scenting prey in the air. Both of their faces were gaunt and bloodied.

"Yo!" one man shouted at her. "You got money? You wanna help a brother out?"

"What?" Angie was already backing away. "No, no, I'm sorry."

"Lying bitch!" The man suddenly withdrew a hatchet from behind the garbage and raised it menacingly.

Bile surged up Angie's throat. She ran for the next block, dragging Lovelie along with her, hoping the rest of the kids were smart enough to follow quickly.

"Get the hell back here!" the man yelled. Angie glanced back, fearing he would give chase, but he had a pronounced limp and merely swung his hatchet around in the air. Right as Angie rounded the corner, an older woman with a shopping cart filled with items that looked salvaged from the rubble approached the men. Before Angie could shout any kind of warning, the wolves set upon their new prey.

Angie heard the old woman scream but didn't turn back. She pulled the kids down the street until her legs gave out, then plopped down on the curb, Lovelie beside her, and tried to catch her breath. The children immediately went back to fidgeting and fighting as if they hadn't just been present for a murder.

I can't do this, Jesus. But what choice did she have?

Angie took stock of their surroundings. Down the street was a large building, still partially intact, surrounded by a campus and fencing. Not the school, of course, but perhaps a government building of some kind? Angie noticed a group of men walking toward them on the opposite side of the street. The nearest man sported tattoos of skulls, daggers, blood drops, and barbed wire across his bare chest and arms. He glowered at Angie as they strode passed, and she ducked her head, but she tracked their movements out of the corner of her eye. When they were near the corner, Angie jumped up, yanking Lovelie to her feet, too, and led their group toward the complex.

The fencing separating it from the street was in tatters, but that was to be expected after the quake. So were the bodies strewn on the ground around it. Except . . . these bodies seemed different. They weren't partially hidden underneath rubble or other fallen debris, as most of the other victims were. In fact, they did not appear to have met their ends during the earthquake or its immediate aftermath at all. As Angie approached, she noticed with increasing alarm that most of them lay in pools of blood that were still red and thickening in the sun, pouring from savage stab wounds and contusions. Many of the bodies wore uniforms indicative of police.

Or prison guards.

It was then that she saw the sign outside the building:

PÉNITENCIER NATIONAL DE PORT-AU-PRINCE

12

Frank watched the snowy streets of London pass through the window of the taxi. His eyes were drooping but also twitching from all the coffee he drank during the eight-hour flight. The coffee made him anxious while the fatigue sapped his ability to think clearly. Not a great combo. A whiskey would smooth things out, but he was in a cab, not a bar.

Before arriving at Heathrow, Frank's passport had only ever seen action on a few long-haul shipments to Canada, which was basically just an extension of America. But London truly felt like a foreign land. The fact that everything completely refused to look American was intensely unsettling. The houses were crammed into every tiny city block, and the narrow streets twisted at absurdly winding angles. It couldn't be further from the smooth lines of Iowa's neighborhoods and open roads. Frank's tension only eased when the cab passed the recognizable symbols of a McDonald's or KFC.

"Here we are, sir." The cabbie had stopped in front of a three-story building with a large burgundy awning ringing the ground level and a sign depicting a smiling bird-like creature with a huge beak and top hat. The building was old brick, with bay windows on the first two floors, dormers on the third floor, and a grey slate roof.

"Uh, what's that?"

"The pub 'ere—The Happy Hangman. This is the address you gave me."

"Oh, uh, yeah." Frank struggled to remember the instructions Tess had given him over the phone. Or, rather, the instructions Tess had given Nancy and Nancy had written down for him. Tess lived in a neighborhood called Chelsea—it figured it would have a Clinton vibe—and The Happy Hangman did sound familiar. "I'm actually going to an apartment . . . or flat, maybe, you call it . . . over the, uh, pub." He didn't know why they couldn't just call it a bar like it was supposed to be called. And an apartment. The British had stupid words for everything: pub, flat, loo. The latter he'd picked up just an hour ago at the airport, mistakenly thinking someone was trying to call him Lou. "Very good, sir," the cabbie said, nodding. "Do you need help with your bags?"

"Uh, no, no, I'm good, thanks."

Frank spent about a minute fiddling around with the ridiculous money he'd extracted from an ATM at the airport until the numbers on the bills matched the meter. He dragged his bulging suitcase through the dirty London snow and up to the big wooden door of what he assumed was the bar his mother's first husband had managed. Dale Johnson. He'd never met him, but he knew Tess had taken over running the place after Dale died. It was dark inside, but he saw an old but clean oak floor, wood-paneled walls, a carved-wood bar that was actually pretty awesome, a bunch of tables with upside-down chairs atop them, and the decorations on the walls seemed to be celebrating the neighborhood a little too enthusiastically, with signs and banners reading Chelsea FC all over the place.

Frank spotted a more normal-looking door to the right of the bar's windows and made his way to it. It was burgundy like the awning but didn't seem directly connected to the business. Frank hoped it led to Tess's apartment upstairs. He mashed his palm against a button next to the door, and after a few seconds, it buzzed open without any word.

Frank grumbled as he lugged his suitcase into the narrow corridor and up the stairs, which spat him out in a dark, overcrowded

kitchen. The cabinets were some kind of dark wood, and the coun-
tertops were covered with tins and baskets. The drainer beside the
sink was filled with a mound of clean dishes, and a kettle sat on the
range, which was on. But the kitchen was empty. Frank had spent
much of the too-long flight from O'Hare rehearsing his speech in
his head. And he'd spent even more time imagining Tess's shocked,
British stiff upper lip melting in guilt as she took in his words. Yet
she was nowhere to be seen. What kind of hospitality was this, not
even being present to welcome a guest?

He stormed out of the kitchen, down a short corridor that led to
a sparsely decorated living room, but the person sprawled in a beige
armchair was not his older half-sister. Instead, Dawn sat there with
the same deer-in-the-headlights expression she always had whenever she wanted someone else to handle a problem for her. Seeing
her hippie dress and unkempt, California liberal hair in that stupid,
cramped British house only made Frank angrier.

It took Dawn a few seconds to notice him, and she brightened.
"Oh, Frank, you're here! How was your fli—"

"Ten days ago?" Frank shouted, all the venom he'd been saving
for Tess unleashed on his younger sister instead. "Mom's been in a
coma for two weeks and you didn't think to call me until last night?"

Dawn's face fell. "Last night?"

"Or whenever! Three days ago! I don't . . ." Frank had hoped
his anger would clear up his brain fog, but no luck. Both had been
flaring since that asshole cop pulled him over outside Winterset and
ruined his life. The now-familiar tremor overtook his right hand,
which he shoved in his pocket. "You know what I mean!"

Dawn folded her hands across her stomach and peeled her eyes
away to the window. She was no doubt hoping some glimpse of
liberal California sunshine would sweep in and save her. Not this
time, little sis.

"She's been sick a long time," Dawn finally said. She had scooch-
ed back into her chair, and one hand was twirling her hair, a habit

she had pulled with their father when he was rightfully on her case about her dumb bullshit.

"A coma's not 'sick.' A coma's a hell of a lot more than just 'sick'! Sick is a cold! Sick is the flu! A coma is . . . a coma's like . . . a coma's more than sick!"

"Tess called when it first happened and said Mom was not doing well at all," Dawn said. "That's why I decided to come over. You could have come over then." She dropped her gaze down to the floor. "I mean, believe me, I've been dealing with my own stuff, and I still flew here days ago."

"Well, if the bitch had mentioned anything about THE FUCKING COMA, I would have come over!"

"Don't call her a bitch." Dawn's voice rose slightly, but her eyes didn't leave their spot on the floor. "She's our sister."

"Half-sister."

"That's right, Frank. Half-sister." Frank's head jumped to his left, just in time to catch Tess emerging through a doorway in the corridor that he'd failed to notice earlier, clad in a bathrobe and drying her hair with a towel.

"Oh, hi, Tess,'" Frank said, letting her pass. "I didn't realize . . ."

"So, how was the flight?" Tess kept her expression neutral instead of reacting to Frank's outburst. "Exhausting, I should think. Would you like to get a shower?"

"Yes," Frank said. "No. I mean, in a little while. First, I want to hear about Mom."

"Well, put your bag in the guest room upstairs and then sit down," Tess said, pointing toward a narrow staircase. "That's where Mom's been living. Dawn's staying in there now, so you'll need to sleep on the couch out here, but you can use the bottom drawer in the dresser upstairs and there's some space in the closet."

"I . . . well . . . okay." Frank dragged his suitcase up the steep stairwell. The closet in the pathetically small bedroom was already overflowing with suitcases and clothing. "Is everything in this country three sizes too small?" he muttered under his breath as he tried to force his suitcase into the front of the closet.

"Can I get you a cup of tea?" Tess called from downstairs. "Coffee?"

Frank managed to close the closet door with his suitcase inside, then returned downstairs where he collapsed onto the couch. With his anger drained, the full weight of his drowsiness came over him in a sudden thud and weighed down his entire body.

"Can I make a cup of coffee?" Frank asked. "I've been flying all night."

"I'll pour you one," Tess said. She vanished into the kitchen and returned with three cups on a silver tray. She set it on the coffee table and handed Frank a mug of coffee. The other cups were filled with a paler liquid. Why did the British insist on drinking tea when it was so boring?

"Okay," Frank said. "So, Mom's been in a coma for more than a week. How much longer do they think?"

Tess paused, mug in hand. A brief look passed between her and Dawn, and Dawn accepted her tea with a clear look of apprehension. Tired as he was, Frank could feel the room's mood shift. He took a sip of the black coffee, tasting nothing but its bitterness—wishing it wasn't inappropriate to ask for a whiskey at this hour—and waited for someone to answer him.

"Well," Tess began. "Today will be her sixth day on the Liverpool Care Pathway, so it shouldn't be much longer."

"It's all very natural," Dawn said. Her voice was abnormally chirpy. It was grating. "The way things are meant to be."

Frank took another sip of his coffee and passed his eyes back and forth between Tess and Dawn. He didn't know Tess other than as a name, and she felt strange and foreign to him. And if he looked too long at her, a strange guilt settled over him, though he couldn't identify the specific reason for that feeling. His feelings for Dawn were confused as well. On the one hand, she'd been banished from the family, or exiled herself—he still wasn't sure of the exact circumstances surrounding her leaving. He knew that if his father was around, just talking to her was potentially an issue. But his father wasn't here, and growing up, Frank's relationship with Dawn had been as strong and loving as a boy with his pet puppy. And those feelings were still around as well.

"So, not much longer," he said. "Good. Real good. I mean, a coma and all can be serious. I was freaking out all the way here. I mean, I guess there's different types of comas. Shouldn't we be there? I mean, we should be there when she wakes up."

Tess and Dawn exchanged another look, and Dawn drew her cup close to her chest, like she was drawing safety from its warmth.

"She's not going to wake up, Frank," Tess said calmly. "The Liverpool Care Pathway is used by NICE—"

"That's Britain's National Institute for Health and Clinical Excellence," Dawn cut in sleepily.

"Yes, that's right." Tess had taken a seat on the couch beside Frank and sipped her tea with a slow and methodical rhythm. "The National Institute for Health and Clinical Excellence runs a program called the Liverpool Care Pathway, which is used when a patient is approaching the end of life. After consultation by the entire medical team, who all must agree the patient is terminal and there's no way to reverse that status, the patient is put on the pathway. The team then assesses what sort of palliative care is appropriate and whether medications and unnecessary treatments should be ceased."

Frank's third sip of coffee died in his mouth. What on earth was she going on about? None of those words made any sense.

"She's been on the pathway for almost a week," Tess continued. "And it shouldn't be much longer."

Frank set his cup down on the end table next to him and smiled his most annoyingly genuine smile at his half-sister. "Would you be so kind as to explain what this Liverpool bullshit actually means? I mean, in reality. Not in government bureaucrat speak?" Fake politeness had always driven him crazy when his father used it on him, and it was a favorite, and effective, technique of Alex Meter's when dealing with self-righteous Dems.

But Tess didn't bite. "It's actually quite straightforward," she said, her voice level and smooth. "Mum is in what's known as palliative care. That means the doctors believe there is no realistic hope of recovery. Under the Liverpool Care Pathway, the medical staff in hospital began the process of ending her life support and managing her pain. That means discontinuing all fluids and food, and only medicating with a morphine drip to manage pain."

Frank pressed his lips together. He couldn't be hearing this correctly. No food? No water? A series of images ran through his mind. Starving infants in front of African huts, their bellies distended. Jewish Holocaust survivors, standing like Halloween skeletons. Men fighting over a thimbleful of water in the movie *Mutiny on the Bounty*. He had to be misunderstanding. "Wait, 'ending her life support'?"

"Yes," Tess said. Her tone hadn't changed, and the angry ball in Frank's gut gained new life. "Her feeding tube was removed, among other things. Artificial life preservation has been stopped. The hospital will make sure she's in no pain as she approaches the end of her life."

"It's the standard protocol here," Dawn added. "The best end-of-life care for someone in Mom's condition."

Frank was so stunned he didn't speak for a few seconds, his eyes darting back and forth between Tess and Dawn. "Wait," he said. "Did I just hear you say that the hospital is going to murder Mom, and you two haven't done anything about it?"

Dawn slumped lower into her chair, and Tess merely took another sip of her tea. Her expression was firm as she said, "It's not murder."

"Starving someone to death sounds a hell of a lot like murder to me!" Frank shouted.

"It's a recognized protocol by the NHS here in England."

"NHS? As in Nobody Here Survives?"

"It's their National Health Service," Dawn chimed in, her voice mouse-like. "I've already met with some of the doctors and case-workers. They all seem very nice."

Frank slammed his hand down on the end table, sending still-hot coffee shooting out of his mug and spilling across the embroidered table cover. Dawn made a startled peep while Tess just continued her stoic stare in his direction. She took another sip of tea and placed the cup back down on her own end table without so much as an audible tap.

Leave it to jolly old England to have such a cockamamy approach to dying. It reminded Frank of that old *Holy Grail* movie he'd watched in high school. In a fit of inspiration, he sang out, "Bring out your dead! Bring out your dead!" He flailed his hands around, imitating the bold hand gestures he always pictured Alex Meter making in his studio when he went on one of his glorious rants. "But I'm not dead yet. Blam! Quiet now, yes you are." Frank grinned ruefully. "I thought it was just a Monty Python skit, but it's the real deal!"

"She's not in any pain," Tess said. Her voice betrayed strains of irritation but remained firm. "The morphine drip manages that completely."

"She doesn't need a morphine drip!" Frank shouted, though the pounding at the sides of his head made him suspect *he* would need some painkillers soon. Or a whiskey. "People in a coma don't feel pain!"

"We don't know that," Tess said.

"Yes, we do! All the morphine does is stop her from coming out of the coma!" He raised his hands to massage his temples.

"Listen," Tess said, her voice rising for the first time. "Who on earth gave you your medical license? That dreadful right-wing radio knob your father made Mum listen to? She wasn't coming out of the coma. All the medical team agreed that she was within forty-eight hours of dying."

"And exactly when was that?" he asked.

"Last Thursday."

"So," Frank said triumphantly, "almost six days later, she's still alive. How inconvenient! You know, the courts put Dr. Kevorkian in jail, but at least he gave his patients a choice! I'll bet no one asked Mom how she felt about being starved to death! I sure as hell know that no one asked me!" Frank bit his lip and tried to will the growing headache away. He turned to Dawn, who was still curled up and looking out the window. He turned his best Alex Meter fake smile her way. "How about you, Dawn? Did they ask *you*?"

Dawn looked in his direction after an internal struggle. "Yes." Her voice was as soft as ever, reminding Frank of a particularly inspired ass-chewing his father had given her not long before he died. *Darn that girl! If my daughter had to be a queer, she could at least be the "man" there! Isn't that how it works? But she's lettin' that Black she's with have all the balls!*

"It seemed like a good idea," Dawn said.

Frank waited for her to continue, but that was all she had to say. "Oh, that's just great," he said mockingly. "It seemed like a good idea!" Frank looked at Tess. "Maybe I don't want to stay on your couch after all! You and Dawn might decide I snore too much and smother me with a pillow for my own good!"

Dawn began to sob like she was still a little girl throwing one of her childhood tantrums. She heaved herself out of the chair and fled upstairs.

Tess fixed him with a stern look. "That was needlessly cruel, Frank," she said. "Even for you. It's an unfortunate fact of life that people die, and when they come to the end of their lives, what they want most of all is to die free from pain. The last thing they need is endless observations, blood tests, and injections. They need a clear decision that the time is right to focus on their comfort and dignity."

Frank threw up his hands. "The last thing anyone needs when they are dying is to be murdered!"

"When's the last time you've been out to see Mum, Frank?" Tess asked. "Oh, right. Never. Not a single time in the six years she's been living with me. And six months ago, when her health started failing, I don't remember you volunteering to take care of her."

"I would have if she asked me to," Frank said. A sour taste rose into his throat, and he swallowed it back down.

"That is such a bullshit excuse," Tess said. "You and your two sisters sit back in the States, enjoying your lives, while I'm over here working as a full-time nurse for our mother and also running the pub. Even if you couldn't take her in, at least you could have come out and visited occasionally."

Frank grimaced. Even though they weren't related, Tess had a few qualities in common with his father. Her jaw jutted at the same aggressive angle Frank Sr.'s did whenever Frank Jr. was misbehaving.

"I called her," he said.

"On Mother's Day," Tess said. "And holidays."

"More than that."

"Not much more."

"She knew that I loved her."

"She assumed that you loved her."

"Look." Frank took an angry sip of his coffee. "She was the one who decided to move back to England. She could have stayed in Clayton." He reached into his pocket for his packet of Tums, before remembering he had eaten all of them on the plane.

"No, she couldn't, Frank." Tess's matter-of-fact British sternness was infuriating. Who was she, Winston Churchill? "Don't you remember? After your father died? You didn't have room for her. Dawn wasn't sure if she was going to stay in Berkeley or go on the road singing. Elizabeth had the apartment in New York but was so busy with work. Everyone talked and talked, but I was the only one who asked her to come live with me. That's why she's been in England. So tell me, Frank, why is it that her life is so valuable to you now that she's dying, but it wasn't worth more than an occasional phone call for the past six years?"

Frank burped. "Do you have any Tums?"

Tess raised her eyebrows in surprise. "Yes," she said. "Just in the kitchen. One moment."

She left Frank to stew by himself on the couch. His only company was his ever-growing headache, the occasional tremors in his hands, and the cloud of dread that had been chasing him for the past month and was currently threatening to swamp him.

13

Jim spent the better part of a minute staring into the fridge in his trailer's tiny half kitchen at the few remaining beer cans scattered across the otherwise empty shelves. As if actual food would appear, if only he looked hard enough.

But it didn't work, just like looking hard enough didn't manifest his Afghan girl when he wanted to see her. He had been checking in on her for a full week but given that she slept through more than half of his shift and was in school for most of the rest of it, he usually only got glimpses of her on her commute. He knew a week had passed, though, because one day she and her dad hadn't left the house like usual. He'd been alarmed, but that night he'd done some digging and learned that Afghan schools have Fridays off. Ever since, he'd been counting her school days to track his week.

It didn't usually matter to Jim what day it was. He worked twelve-hour shifts seven days a week, and mostly played Call of Duty in his off hours when he wasn't sleeping. If it wasn't for the few Christmas decorations some asshole on the base had starting putting up, he'd have had no idea it was almost Christmas. The weather in the Nevada desert didn't exactly scream "Santa's coming!"

He shut the fridge door and opened the freezer. Score. Among the deep layers of accumulated ice were the half-eaten remains of a single 7-Eleven burrito, stored away God knows how long ago and now more or less frozen solid. Jim dusted some of the frost from

it, popped it in the microwave, and blasted it on HIGH for ninety seconds.

He had the radio on in the background, and Alex Meter's voice
cut through to blend in with the hum of the microwave.

"*They see a gunman go into a school and he happens to be white and
male . . . and 'Aha! See? You're all violent and you're oppressing us!' It's a
load of hogwash, people. Pure crap. They see a lonely nutjob who badly
needs to get laid slaughter a bunch of kids, and their mouths water. They
love these mass shootings. It's like Christmas to them. It's their excuse to
openly scream about wanting to dismantle our constitution.*"

The microwave dinged and Jim pulled the soggy burrito out,
then stumbled back into what the Air Force dubbed a living room:
an eight-by-eight space with a well-worn couch and the forty-eight-
inch flatscreen he'd bought after his second paycheck. He had Call
of Duty on pause, watching the game's chaos play out on the screen
courtesy of other players around the world.

"You got my little message there, faggot?" The voice that screeched
into his headset—lying on the dusty couch next to him, but still audible—sounded like one of the thirteen-year-old shitheads he usually encountered during gaming sessions. Jim flipped the headset the
finger with his left hand while opening his can of beer with the other.
The beer was mostly foam, bursting out of the tab and spilling down
onto the dusty cushions of the couch, joining the other stains of past
beers, microwave meals, and who knows what else. He was not this
couch's first owner, and he preferred not to think about the shit it
had seen before him.

"I sent one to your mother last night, you mother's whore." This
voice had a thick East Asian accent, and the speaker stumbled on
his words.

"Ha!" the thirteen-year-old shot back. "If I'm a 'mother's whore,'
that means you got my sloppy seconds!"

"Why would I eat your sloppy seconds, you butthole?"

And on and on.

Jim took a swig of foam and a bite of freezer-burned burrito before picking up his controller. He gazed down the sights of an HK33 rifle, pointed in the general direction of human forms running in and out of a warehouse-looking complex in a desert location that vaguely resembled the Afghanistan he saw on his screens every day. Jim pressed his thumb against the trigger button on his controller with the same dexterity he used to operate his drone. His rifle unleashed an improbable number of bullets in rapid-fire, tearing through the CGI combatants in front of him. Their bodies convulsed in the most dramatic death throes the game developers could imagine, complete with intricate red clouds of blood erupting from the bullet wounds. Jim was always amused that the developers put such a huge amount of effort into getting the actual weaponry, armor, and locational details correct, but went Hollywood when animating the violence.

That's not how people die when they're shot.

After wasting a group of five CGI terrorists, a few pulses of return fire forced him to duck his avatar behind a pile of crates that would not be enough to stop AK-47 fire in the real world. But whatever.

"Who just did that?" some indignant teenage voice raged through his speakers.

"Hey, suck my dick!" another offered.

"Eat my excrement," said a third, heavily-accented voice.

The players traded insults over each other and the sounds of gunfire and explosions until they all blurred into generic background noise.

After about fifteen minutes, Jim had accumulated a kill count of thirty, give or take. It was easy pickings, and he was getting bored, and tired. He dropped his controller in his lap and settled back on the couch, watching as a wave of CGI civilians fled the battle with their hands stretched into the air. One of the edgier players thought it would be funny to riddle the entire group with an onslaught of bullets, and vast spatter-clouds of blood exploded around the animated men and women who began flailing in violent spasms to a soundtrack of stock scream sound effects.

Jim's mouth twisted when he caught sight of a young girl, meant to be part of a local tribe but dressed in remarkably striking clothing for a non-player character. As she ran, a bullet caught her between the shoulder blades and sent her sprawling.

Jim switched the game off, and the TV screen went dark. A sense of discomfort began to rise in his chest. His mind stuck on the image of the girl. Her 3D-rendered robes and black hair. His in-game rifle trained on her bleeding-out form. He suddenly felt nauseous.

He shook his head. It's just a game, asshole.

He went over to his computer and woke it up with a swipe on the mousepad. He'd left his browser open to Google's main page, with a few tabs of porn still up from last night. He clicked in the search box and stared at the blinking cursor for a bit. Then he drew his fingers to the keyboard and typed "Khewa, Afghanistan." After another few seconds, he added "girls living in" and hit ENTER.

The results were news articles about women's rights issues in rural Afghanistan, plus a few hits on international relief and aid organizations and some links to girls' schools. He noted that one of the links referenced the school he had seen during his drone observations of the area. He clicked on the "images" tab, and his screen became filled with pictures of Afghan girls and young women, most wearing traditional robes and headscarves, some wearing school uniforms or more traditional Western dress. Some were smiling at the camera and flashing goofy faces with their friends, while some looked somber or contemplative, maybe even unaware that they were being photographed.

None, however, had green eyes.

And none held a leather-bound diary.

Jim clicked out of the page and looked out the window. It was as black and featureless as ever. Somewhere above him, a plane's engine roared. Somewhere above Afghanistan, a drone's engine roared.

14

When Tess put her fifth kettle of the day on the hob, she was dismayed to realize it wasn't even suppertime yet. She stood alone in the kitchen, relishing the momentary quiet and watching the first whispers of steam rise in smooth, intricate patterns. An inversion of the path of the snow falling on the other side of the kitchen window. From elsewhere in the house, Frank's too-loud footsteps thundered across the old wood. A vein in her temple thumped in syncopation, and a familiar ache began to gnaw at her eyes. Before the kettle's shrieking could make things worse, she pulled open the drawer closest to her and grabbed the bottle of paracetamol. She swallowed three in one gulp.

As she put the bottle back, she noticed the much larger container of antacids was empty. It had been half full just a day ago, before Frank arrived in a storm of jet lag and rage, his proudly protruding belly branding him American while his comb-over confirmed him as someone who either never looked in a mirror or looked but never really saw. It was no wonder she had a headache. She should see if Dawn needed some paracetamol too.

Despite Frank's boorish behavior—quite predictable but aggravating nonetheless—Tess felt a maternal impulse to caution him against ignoring the medication instructions on the package of antacids. Ironic given she'd never had any desire to have kids herself. And yet here she was, having spent the past six years mothering her own mother and now hosting two half-siblings who were acting like children, though in opposite ways. Frank throwing tantrums, while Dawn retreated into herself.

Dawn walked in, bussing her empty cup of tea to the sink.

"Ah, let me get that for you, love," Tess said, more out of reflex than anything else. Mum had been prone to try and wash her dishes herself even as her condition deteriorated over the last year or two of her life. Tess had learned to take over to keep her tableware intact.

"Oh, no, I've got it," Dawn said. Her eyes were still puffed and red from crying, though her voice had steadied to its soft and melodic mezzo-soprano. Tess thought back to her surprise, and Dawn's surprise as well, when they happened upon a performance at a local coffee shop the day after Dawn arrived, and the singer recognized Dawn from her YouTube videos. It had been a real treat hearing Dawn sing a few songs on the café's small stage that evening.

"I do apologize for Frank," Tess said. "I supposed it was a given that he would react like that, though one cannot say we didn't try to get on his good side."

"Oh, don't worry about Frank," Dawn said. "He still knows just how to set me off. But it's nothing I didn't get used to when I was growing up."

"The relatively few interactions with him I've had over the years were . . . an experience, to say the least," Tess said. "When Dale died, you may remember that I sent all of you memorial cards with the particulars of the funeral and so on. I didn't expect any of you to attend, but it didn't seem right to send out cards and not include the American side of the family. Frank wrote back the most nasty note, accusing me of asking for money or flowers or something. I can't imagine growing up with him." She glanced through the door to make sure Frank wasn't eavesdropping and saw that he was asleep on the couch.

"On a 'cheerier' note, I guess," Tess said, "I did get through to Mum's care team at hospital just now."

"Oh? What did they say?"

Tess bit her lip. "Well, they're willing to take Mum off the NICE protocol for the time being and restore her life support. But . . ."

"But?"

"You must understand," Tess said. "It's not something that can really be done indefinitely."

"No, no, I understand," Dawn said. "Are you sure this is a good idea, though? Don't you have power of attorney over Mom, or whatever it's called here?"

"Yes," Tess said. Her thoughts drifted momentarily. "Just, with Frank's . . . reaction, I thought it best to wait until we have full family consensus on what to do with Mum. At least until Elizabeth gets here. She texted me about an hour ago that her flight got in, so she should be arriving shortly. Once she decompresses, we can have an official discussion on Mum's end-of-life-care."

"That makes sense," Dawn said. "I'm glad the hospital can resume Mom's feeding tube for the time being. But do you think Frank—"

Tess was saved by the door buzzer. From the couch in the living room, Frank let out a porcine snort. Tess buzzed the door open and switched the kettle off, then turned to see Elizabeth striding through the entryway. The sight of her other half-sister briefly sent a small shock wave of bemusement and envy through Tess's mind. The tall, broad-shouldered Elizabeth showed no symptoms of jet lag or prolonged confinement in an airplane. Her shiny brown hair was pulled into a professional bun and her makeup was immaculate, hitting a perfect balance of grace and subtlety. She wore a grey pin-striped pantsuit, and a small but noticeable crystal necklace sparkled on her neck. She was the epitome of a businesswoman, in looks and demeanor.

"Oh, Tess, darling, how are you holding up?" Elizabeth hugged Tess with a bit too much of a grip on her shoulders, a move Tess imagined Elizabeth perfecting as a feminine variation of the "strong handshake" business cliché.

"Well," Tess said, "I thought I was doing pretty well, but recently things have taken a turn for the worse."

"I thought we already expected the worst?" Elizabeth said.

Tess looked to the living room at Frank, whose head tilted across his shoulder at what looked to be a painful angle, brief shudders erupting across his hands and his torso as he slept. "I mean here," she said. "But never mind that. I'm so glad you made it! Where are your bags?"

"I dropped them at the Hyatt on the way from the airport," Elizabeth said. "That was a bit more convenient, I thought, than coming here first."

"Oh," Tess said. "You could have stayed here. It would be tight, I admit, but you could have bunked with Dawn in Mum's room. I hate to see you at a hotel."

Elizabeth waved her hand in a dismissive fashion and popped a lozenge into her mouth. "The Hyatt Churchill is in such a convenient location," she said. "Plus, I knew you'd be crowded—I didn't want to impose upon you more than you've already been imposed upon." Elizabeth pulled out her phone and scrolled through something on the screen. "And don't tell anyone, but I'm sort of combining business and pleasure with this trip, so it's all on my expense account."

"Ah, yes . . . I see," Tess said. Elizabeth's visits to Mum always occurred during business trips. Apparently she'd been able to finagle one to coincide with her dying too.

"Just a meeting with a London client," Elizabeth went on, looking up from her phone. "Shouldn't take too long. Oh, Dawn, forgive me for being rude!" Elizabeth embraced her younger sister in the same efficient motion she had Tess. "How are you holding up?"

"I'm doing okay, more or less," Dawn said.

"And not just this unfortunate business with Mom, but the tragedy in Haiti on top of that!"

Dawn's mouth twisted in something of a grimace. "Yes, that's been a bit stressful as well, on top of everything."

"Wasn't it only a day or two after you flew back to California that the earthquake hit? And Angela . . . that's correct, yes? Angela?"

"Yes," Dawn said. "Well, I mean, Angelique, really. Or just Angie." She swallowed. "She just goes by Angie most of the time."

Tess felt a strange sense of relief that it wasn't just her who had neglected getting to know Angie.

Elizabeth nodded while glancing back down at her phone. "And did she manage to get out okay?"

"No, not yet," Dawn said. "But she's okay, if a little rattled. I was able to speak with her the other day, although the phone reception was bad, as you can imagine. Her parents survived, too, and their house and shop were only minimally damaged. Angie's got US residency, but her parents don't, and she doesn't want to leave without them, so we're going to investigate legal options with the State Department."

"Well," Elizabeth replied, still looking at her phone, "if you need legal help, I can recommend some excellent lawyers from a few top firms in New York. We have relationships with—"

"Which part is the business, and which is the pleasure?" Frank suddenly boomed from the kitchen door, and all three women turned in surprise. Tess hadn't heard him get up from the couch, but he'd clearly been listening for a couple minutes at least. Shit. He plopped his empty coffee cup on the counter, waiting for a refill. Tess set her jaw, but Elizabeth and Dawn, on the receiving end of such things for years, just ignored it.

"It's just a phrase, Frank," Elizabeth said. "The client meeting won't take more than an hour or two, and since Mom's in a coma . . . She's still in a coma, right?"

"Oh, yes," Frank said. "Fortunately for your meeting plans, she's still in a coma."

Tess could hardly believe her ears. What an utter ass.

"I'm just saying that since she's in a coma she won't be bothered if I pop in on a client for a couple of hours." Elizabeth pocketed her phone and gave Frank her full attention, as though to make clear she could focus on family. "I'll still have plenty of time to spend with her."

"How tender." Frank smirked, which accentuated his double chin. Tess realized then that Dawn was no longer in the room. She must have snuck away to avoid Frank's toxicity. Tess would have liked to sneak away, too, but someone had to stay and be the grownup.

"And by the way," Elizabeth said, "it's good you see you as well. All my love to you and the fam." She turned away from Frank, who went stumbling around the kitchen to find more coffee on his own. "So, Tess, have the doctors given us a prognosis yet?"

"Yeah," Frank said, the sarcasm evident even in that one word. "They said she's in a coma."

Tess inwardly rolled her eyes. "Her condition hasn't changed since I talked to you on the phone," she clarified.

"You know," Frank said. He had found the coffee pot, taken the last of the coffee, and put the empty pot back on the warming plate. "Now that I think of it, you Brits should do this with complete efficiency. Instead of starving Mom to death, why don't you just schedule a specific time to strangle her? That way Elizabeth could put it into her calendar and—"

"Frank," Elizabeth cut in, her face reflecting impatience. "What are you talking about?"

"I'm talking about Mom being murdered!" Frank shouted. "Oh, sure, they've got universal health care over here in England, but they should call it universal death care. Once someone gets old, once they're a liability instead of an asset to society, they stop giving them food and drink and starve them to death. It's a preview of the system that Comrade Nobama wants to put in place for us."

Tess cringed. She hated that she immediately recognized what the phrase "Comrade Nobama" was supposed to mean.

"But what does—" Elizabeth began, but Frank interrupted.

"I mean, I can see families saying to themselves, 'Gosh, I'm so sick of cleaning up Aunt Jane's poop. She's ready for a carbon exchange.' And President God will be there with his new stimulus package, Cash for Codgers, where you can turn in old family members for forty-five-hundred dollars and help reduce the Social Security and Medicare deficit in the process."

"I don't understand what—" Elizabeth tried again, but this time Tess cut her off. She'd had enough of Frank and his radio-inspired diatribes.

"Since when did this become about your US health care problems?" she demanded. "And as long as you bring it up, your dysfunctional system knocks off far more people every year than an army of death panels flying from hospital to hospital in black helicopters could do!"

"Bill O'Reilly had this guy on—"

Tess wasn't standing for it. "A system that ranks first in cost of health care and thirty-seventh in quality of care," she interjected, getting them back on point.

"We rank number one on the same survey for timeliness of care, science, technology, new drugs, and the other factors that matter if you're sick," Frank said, sticking up an index finger.

"Well done, Frank," Tess said, shaking her head. "You've just made the stupidest argument in the history of arguments. Maybe your system works for you, and other people with insurance, but what about the fifty million people without any insurance or access to health care?"

"Half those people are illegal aliens who shouldn't be there anyway, so screw 'em!" Frank hollered. "Oh, sure, you can find your poster child case where a family can't get insurance and loses everything, but that's no reason to socialize medicine."

"But isn't Mom covered here?" Elizabeth asked. "Even though she's not a citizen?"

"And that's the real root of the problem!" Frank railed on, and Tess had no idea if he was responding to what Elizabeth said or continuing his own train of thought. "No one has a right to health care beyond what they're willing to pay for! Let people make their own decisions. Sure, lots of people will make bad decisions, but then let them suffer the consequences! Want to smoke? Buy smoking insurance. Like being a fat pig? Then buy obesity insurance. Think you don't need insurance? Then give 'em your credit card when you check in and when you hit your limit, you're out of there. That's exactly how it works in the hospitals in Mexico!"

"There's something to strive for," Tess said. "If you want Mexico's health care system and Fox News's politics, go enjoy yourself and leave us Brits in peace."

"Maybe we should have left your country in peace back in 1940 instead of getting our asses shot at to bail you out!" Frank yelled.

"Wait a minute!" Elizabeth raised her hands to the sides of her head and shook them. "What does all of this have to do with Mom!?"

"The hospital," Frank explained, all diplomatic and official-sounding now, "with the blessing of her daughters Tess and Dawn, has been starving Mom to death for the past week. That's how national health care works in the UK. Very cost-effective. What I want to know is why the UK didn't use this lovely little program on that Libyan terrorist who bombed the plane. Too cruel for a terrorist, but just fine for Mom, eh?"

"Hang on, I'm confused," Elizabeth said. "I thought Mom was in a coma. How do you starve someone in a coma?"

"You stop giving them food and water!" Frank said. "Then you just sit back and watch them wither away!"

"It's not the way Frank is describing at all," Tess said, shaking her head and turning to Elizabeth. Her half-sister regarded her with a look that said both "I'm listening" and "Don't bullshit me" that she'd clearly honed in corporate boardrooms. "It's a completely humane ending to a person's life, a form of hospice care. And this happens in the United States every day. You just don't talk about it."

"Oh, we talk about it all right!" Frank paused for a sip of coffee, not that his fire needed any more fuel. "When those ICU physicians in New Orleans were trapped by Hurricane Katrina and euthanized their patients, they were brought up on murder charges!"

Elizabeth turned her boardroom expression on her brother. "Frank, the value proposition of keeping a person alive a short period at the end of their life just isn't there. The cost can be astronomical, approaching a million dollars."

Tess was elated to finally have an ally in the conversation. "It's one thing to treat a patient, to help them recover," she said, nodding. "But another thing entirely to try to maintain life in a patient whose systems are failing."

"Even if you could keep them alive for a while, for what?" Elizabeth said. "What exactly would this do except prevent the family from getting on with the inevitable grieving process?"

Frank blinked several times. "I mean . . . You're both telling me that you wouldn't mind being starved to death by the people who are supposed to love you, if you end up like Mom is?"

Tess thought of Dad's heart attack and that painful month during which he was too sick to live and too alive to die. "When it's my time, I'd rather pass quietly than have a team of specialists competing to figure out how to squeeze the last dime out of me." She inhaled to steady her nerves. "But it's good that we're all talking about this. At Frank's . . . request, I have had Mum's feeding tube and life support restored." Frank's bullying, more like it. "For the time being, at least. I figured it would be best if the four of us came to a consensus on the best path forward before making any ultimate decisions on Mum's care plan."

"Care plan!" Frank laughed, a big guffaw that shook his gut.

Tess sighed. There was no winning with Frank.

Frank eyed his coffee, then slapped both hands on the counter. "I think we all need a drink," he said. "Can I assume you have something to drink here?"

"I don't think so," Tess said. This was a lie, of course, but she didn't want to add alcohol to his already fired-up thoughts.

"I thought you ran a pub," Frank scoffed, and Tess detected a hint of quiet desperation creep into his tone. "You're telling me that you don't have anything to drink?"

Tess sent a wayward glance toward her kitchen cabinet. "There's a half a bottle of wine by the stove I use for cooking," she said. She wasn't about to tell him where she kept the good stuff, and she knew he'd never find it.

Tess instantly recognized the subtle expression of longing that took over Frank's face. It was the look of one truly desperate for yet another drink—so much so that they are willing to consider drinking anything with an alcoholic kick, even past-its-prime cooking wine. Or something far worse. "I suppose I can look through the cabinet, to see if I have any beer left over. But do understand, Frank, Mum preferred not to drink, and I don't go raiding the pub willy-nilly; it's a business, not my own personal liquor store." Not that she couldn't—her assistant manager, Jack, was running things while she took time off to tend to family affairs, and he wouldn't stop her—but she didn't want to, not for an overbearing, overwhelming half-sibling.

Still, her answer appeased Frank, who licked his lips and loosened the tension that had been building in his jaw and shoulders, just a bit. "I mean, don't kill yourself," he said. "If you find anything, I'll take it. But I'm sure there's a bar open somewhere. You guys love to booze it up over here, right?"

That was drunkard talk, alright. She supposed it wasn't a surprise Frank was a lush. She would be, too, if she was inundated with right-wing garbage day in and day out. "I live above a pub, Frank," she said with a sigh. "It's a weekday evening. The Hangman is open just downstairs. But I'll check my cupboards first."

"Actually," Elizabeth said from her side, "if you happen to find a nice bottle of wine, or sherry, I can't say I would mind a glass of something like that." Tess looked over at her half-sister, exasperated. Elizabeth coughed awkwardly. "But, of course, only if you happen to find anything like that. Otherwise, it's no worry."

"Well," Tess said. She clapped her hands against her front thighs in the manner their mother had done during her limited childhood with her. Tess hoped her half-siblings had also witnessed it during their formative years, at least enough to recognize its desired note of finality. "I am going to go find Dawn and see how she's doing. Don't forget that she has reasons to be stressed in addition to all of this. How would you be feeling, Frank, if Nancy were trapped in a country just ravaged by an earthquake? Or you, Elizabeth, if Liam were? Now, if you'll excuse me."

She hustled off before either could respond and sought refuge in her bedroom. It had once been her dad's, but she'd decided it was easier to live on one level after he died, so she'd moved her stuff from the upstairs room to this one off the parlor and moved his bed and dresser upstairs to become a guest room. And then Mum's room. And now Dawn's, for a short while anyway. Tess hoped Dawn had found a way to block out the arguing from below but knew sound traveled all too easily in this flat. All the sound-proofing money had been spent ensuring the pub noise didn't infiltrate the living space above.

Tess fell backward onto her mattress, catching her pillow with the back of her tension-riddled neck and letting her hair flop freely across her face. She breathed deeply, one, two, three times, and felt her body begin to relax. Frank and Elizabeth's voices reverberated from the kitchen, ruining any shot she had at a nap. She might need to invest in a white-noise machine . . .

Tess let out a full-body sigh, then sat up and opened the bedside desk underneath her reading lamp. There, half-buried in shadow, was her bottle of ten-year Laphroaig, about two-thirds empty and unblemished by the layer of dust that had settled upon everything else in the drawer.

She pulled the cap off the bottle and took a long, deep swig, letting the smoky peat seep through her mouth and down her throat, eventually landing with sulfurous urgency in her stomach and—she hoped—rising to her brain to burn the stresses of her life into a dizzied but peaceful dream.

15

"Matant Angie?" The girl's voice was barely a whisper. Angie waved her hand at a cluster of flies swarming around her face and rubbed yet another stream of sweat from her nose and lips. She swallowed as best she could, but her mouth and throat had turned into sandpaper. She had to assume the kids were equally parched. But what could she do? They had no water. And, she quietly admitted to herself, they were lost. Lost in the city where she was born and raised, whose streets she had explored endlessly during her own childhood.

Guilt choked her as much as the dehydrated flesh of her throat. She clutched Lovelie's hand a little tighter as she pulled the train of children through the shattered pavement of Port-au-Prince. Every few feet she had to step around a crushed pile of concrete or the shell of an abandoned van half-hidden under a rubble grave.

"Where are we goooooing?" one of the children called from somewhere behind her, whiny and piercing. "I'm tiiiiiiiiiiiired!"

Angie clenched her jaw against the urge to snap at the voice.

Which one was that? Evans? Antoine? Wait, was that even a boy? Or was it Celeste? Camille? They all sounded the same, except for Lovelie, whose glorious silence gave her away.

"Listen." Angie squeezed Lovelie's hand with too much force and the girl let out a soft whimper. Angie's rage began to dissipate, giving way to yet another current of guilt. She swallowed against the dryness in her mouth and continued. "We're going to find your parents, remember? Or even better, we're going to find some people who can help you find them."

"But Matant Angie," another voice—or the same one?—erupted a grating whine. "*You're* helping us find them!"

Angie's lips clenched so tightly she imagined them turning bleached white. "Yes," she said, biting her swollen tongue. "I'm helping you as best I can. But when bad things like this happen . . ." She glanced around at the destroyed buildings, crushed cars, and decaying bodies, hoping for something to appear that would help prove whatever point she was trying to make. Nothing did. "When bad things like this happen," she soldiered on, "good people show up to help. The Haitian government has people who are trained to deal with emergencies like this. And rescue organizations have come from all over the world just to help us. They have rescue gear, medicine, and food and can give you everything you need. And they can help you find your parents better than I can!" This was all a lie, of course, but maybe if she believed her own words they'd come true? She was running out of options.

The children were silent for a few seconds and Angie closed her eyes, hoping they had been reassured by her words. But a dread reverberating through her chest told her they were taking their own look around the ruins of their city—and seeing nothing in the way of help.

The hot wind picked up, dry, sunburned, and failing to provide any relief from the sweat drenching her face. Angie forced her eyes back open, and they landed on a row of blankets lying in a malformed row along the sidewalk. A wave of nausea began to rise when she noticed several pairs of bloated and fly-addled feet sticking out of them. A flock of seagulls was walking around the bodies, darting in to peck at the maggots, or the corpses. Whoever had tried to gather the dead and preserve their dignity with haphazard funeral shrouds was nowhere to be seen.

"You lying!" a girl's voice erupted from the cluster of kids behind her. "No one who comes to Haiti wants to help us! They only want to steal and take our things! My mama told me what they do! They're going to rob us of the clothes off our backs!"

"Yeah!" a boy's voice cut in. "My dad told me those whities come here to steal Haitian kids and take them to rich white families across the ocean!"

"Matant Angie!" another kid cried. "Don't let them steal us!"

And with that, several of the children burst into tears. Angie didn't allow herself to think, only tilted her head to the bare sky. Circling clusters of seagulls glided and swooped above them. Once upon a time that might have been a soothing sight, a reminder of the peaceful nature of her island nation. Now all it reminded her of was vultures.

"Why don't we go over here!" Without letting the kids respond further she gave a harsh pull on Lovelie's hand and dragged the train of children to the next block. As they rounded the corner, they encountered a long line of people stretched the entire length of the block. A flutter of relief batted away the lingering nausea. "Here!" she shouted at the kids. "Here's some of those helpers! We can get in line here and they'll help you find your parents!"

But as she dragged the kids closer to the line of people, her hope dried up as quickly as it had arisen. The line stretched much farther than she had thought initially, in a dismal, hopeless display. Some people were hobbling on bloodied, broken legs. Others lay in a heap, trying to forge cooling shadows with their hands against the onslaught of the sun. The line did not appear to be moving at all.

Angie slowed her group's pace as she reached what she thought was the end of the line. They took up position behind an older woman who stood on uneasy legs, looking like she was fighting a losing battle to remain conscious, while she dabbed her dirty and blood-caked forehead with a rag.

"Uh, excuse me," Angie began. The woman didn't seem to notice her. "Excuse me," Angie tried again. "Do you know what this line is for? Is this a relief organization?"

The woman slowly turned a blank gaze on Angie, looking her up and down. "Relief?" she finally said, shaking her head. "You see any relief here? You stupid or something?"

Angie gulped another mouthful of dry air. "Well, can I ask what you're standing in line for?"

"What the hell else I'm going to do?" the woman snapped.

Next to her, an old man with a half-crazed sneer leaned in. "This here's the United Nations, what I heard," he said with a strange cackle that didn't inspire much hope in Angie. "They gonna take real good care of us!"

"Ain't no United Nations here, you fool!" another old man broke in. "Them UN assholes don't care about us for two hundred years; you think an earthquake gonna make them give a shit!"

"Hey, dipshit!" the first man fired back. "You in line too!"

His rival laughed through raspy lungs. "Look at this fool. We already lambs heading to the slaughter! Might as well line up now!"

Angie tried to force her throat clear again. "You see, it's just that I have these children with me, and I wanted to see if I could find people who could help—"

"Children!" another voice erupted from farther up the line. A younger man emerged, shirtless and waving a crowbar in Angie's direction. "There ain't no room for no kids here! You wanna take all the food for yourself, you selfish bitch! I been in line all day; you and your brats ain't gonna steal what I been waiting for!"

Angie recoiled, pushing her backside into Lovelie and forcing the cluster of kids back several feet. "No, no!" she attempted. "I just wanted to see—"

"Hey, asshole!" another man's voice shot in. "Put that thing away! You a big man? Threatening a bunch of kids and a lady?"

The speaker emerged from the crowd, wielding a hatchet.

The man with the crowbar made to spit at him, though nothing came out of his dry mouth. "Asshole!" he shouted. "Pretending to be some kind of knight! You just trying to get all the food for yourself!"

Each man hoisted his weapon in the air and they stepped toward one another, but before Angie could see what happened next, the crowd descended into chaos, wrapping around the men in a crazed spectacle and losing any semblance of organization.

Angie pulled Lovelie's hand once more and fled.

"Matant Angie?" Lovelie's voice whispered a moment later. They had cleared the crowd and were making their way through a much emptier street. Angie looked down to find Lovelie gazing at her with quivering eyes.

Angie swallowed the clod of thick, sticky mucous that formed at the sight of the tears and spoke in a reedy rasp. "Yes?" she said.

Lovelie's mouth folded in embarrassment, and she looked back down at the ground. "I have to go potty."

Potty. Right. Angie slowed the group to a stop, pondering what to do. She tried to imagine Dawn's singsongy voice offering words of reassurance and comfort to the little girl. She tried to hear exactly what the words were, so she could mimic them for Lovelie. But while her girlfriend's tone and richness came through loud and clear, the actual words were a garbled mess. Angie was alone in this. Dawn was back in the safety of the States, or England, anyway, both a world away from the devastation in Port-au-Prince. For a split second, Angie allowed herself to indulge in envy that Dawn only had to deal with a dying mother and not any of this shit. Then she got back to business.

"Okay," Angie said, giving Lovelie her most encouraging smile. "Do you think you can hold it for a bit longer? We're almost there." Where "there" was supposed to be Angie had no idea, but she hoped the girl's battle with a full bladder would distract her from asking questions.

Lovelie, however, merely grimaced and shook her head. "I have to go real bad."

So much for holding it. Angie glanced behind her. The rest of the kids were wandering around, some pushing or play fighting each other—including Evans and Emmanual, who still had the toy plane—and more than one picking their nose. Nearby, Angie spotted a thick cluster of bushes and palm trees that looked like it would provide some degree of privacy.

"How about back in those bushes?" she asked, gesturing to the cluster.

Lovelie looked down at the ground for a few more painful seconds, and then, with a protruding lip, said, "Will you come?"

"Oh. Uh." Angie hadn't expected her to need an escort. "Do you need help going to the bathroom or do you just want someone to go with you?"

Lovelie didn't say anything but continued looking at the ground sadly.

"Or is it a bit of both?" Angie asked with a sudden intuition.

Lovelie paused for a second and then nodded.

"Okay, then." It was okay, Angie could do this. "Hey, kids?" She turned to the rest of the group. Their chatter and playing diminished as they looked up at her expectantly.

"So, uh, we're going to take a quick bathroom break. Does anyone else need to go?" The heads all shook side to side in unison. That was good, at least.

"Okay, great. So, you're good here for just a minute?" Now the heads nodded. "Okay, then you all stay right here, okay? Don't go anywhere. Matant Angie will be right back. Right back."

She backed away, Lovelie in tow, keeping eye contact with the children, who thankfully made no attempt to follow. She finally turned and led Lovelie to the thick grove of bushes. Twigs snagged on their dresses as they forced their way into the thicket, and once they were well enough hidden from prying eyes, Angie stood guard while Lovelie squatted down. When she returned to Angie's side, her wide smile conveyed her relief. Angie took Lovelie's proffered hand

and led the charge out of the bushes, taking the brunt of thorns and sharp twigs that cut into her skin and further tore her already-torn clothing.

Emerging from the thicket, Angie found the block surprisingly quiet. Where were the other children? She scanned left and right, but the block was empty. Her throat, already dry, began to constrict even further as she whipped her head back and forth for any signs of the children. Lovelie eventually gave a small peep of pain, and Angie realized she had been squeezing the girl's hand harder and harder in her increasing panic.

She looked down to find Lovelie gazing up at her with a dim and blank expectancy, surrendering to the faith that Angie, now the sole adult in her life, would take care of any problem. Angie forced a cheerful smile. She was getting good at forcing smiles.

"Say, would you by any chance see any of your friends around? Down there you might have better eyes than I do." Lovelie looked blankly at Angie for a few seconds, and then meekly pointed in the direction of a row of half-leveled slum houses in the next block.

There were no children visible, but a cluster of men stood in a tight circle, several wearing matching uniforms and many armed with rifles or handguns. They were police, or military. Thank god.

Angie sprung forward with Lovelie in tow, but as they got closer, she noticed more details about the men, details that tempered her desperate hope and slowed her approach. The men held guns, yes. But not with the authority of trained police officers or soldiers. Rather, they held their guns with a kind of haphazard abandon, pointing them skyward or across their bodies with no apparent regard for safety. In addition to the guns, some were armed with other more primitive, improvised weapons, such as machetes, knives, and clubs. Not, Angie realized, standard issue for most police departments or militaries.

While some were indeed wearing matching pale-blue uniforms, others were shirtless, their backs and arms covered in dark tattoos. To

her horror, Angie realized the uniforms were not police or military—
they were the pale, bleached blue of prison inmates.

And then, she remembered the sign they had passed earlier that
day: Pénitencier National de Port-au-Prince. Her mind swam with
images of the bloodied, bloated faces of the murdered guards strewn
across the grounds of the destroyed prison. She swallowed anxiously.
They had to get out of here. She would just leave, take Lovelie back
home to Mama and Papa. If they asked where the rest of the children
were, Angie could honestly say she didn't know.

Except she couldn't. Not when Lovelie was still pointing directly at the group of escaped prisoners across the street from them.
Escaped prisoners who had formed a tight ring around *something*,
and Angie was afraid she knew exactly what that something was.
She didn't allow herself time to think. She hardened her expression
into what she could only hope would come across as resolute and
intimidating, then marched herself and Lovelie toward the group
of men. As they neared, Angie could make out the crude tattoos, all
featuring images of skulls, daggers, and teardrops. The implication
of violence was clear.

It was one of the larger, most muscular men who noticed her
first. He gave a brief shout in a slang-ridden form of Creole that
Angie didn't understand, and the rest of his prison comrades turned
to look at her and Lovelie. As they did so, a gap was created in
their circle and Angie was sickened to have her suspicion confirmed.
The children had bunched themselves into as tight of a ball as they
could, the littlest ones protected in the center, the rest forming a ring
of their own around them, facing out and clasping hands in some
vague imitation of a defensive position.

"Ha! Lady, what you looking for?" boomed a cold and raspy
voice, reeking of years of cigarettes, drugs, and improvised prison
alcohol but at the same time holding a grating, high-pitched sneer.
"You lookin' for protection? Your man Junior's got all the protection
a pretty lady like you's gonna need, ha!"

A man emerged from the far side of the circle and came to stand next to the guy with the slang Creole. His faded blue uniform was worn with an air of authority, his shoulders thrown back, the front of the garment straightened with military precision. It took Angie a few seconds to notice how short he was, the top of his head just grazing the big guy's shoulder. Junior, as he was apparently called, stood with a sadistic kind of passive expectation, twirling a sharpened and bloodied machete like a baton.

Angie cleared her dry throat and attempted the most authoritative voice she could. "Can I assume you are Junior, then?"

A confident sneer split the man's face, and he burst into laughter, his crew following suit as if their boss had just told a hilarious joke.

"Let me tell a pretty lady something." Junior stepped forward, his machete draped casually over his shoulder.

Angie took a reflexive step back but refused to break eye contact. Something about the situation had dredged up Dawn's advice on what to do if you encounter a bear or mountain lion. "Make yourself look big and threatening," Dawn had told her the first time she'd dragged her on a day-long hike in the California wilderness. "Don't break eye contact. Back away slowly."

Angie took another small step backward as Junior continued. "I'm Junior to all my good friends here but make no mistake. For a pretty lady like yourself, there ain't nothing 'Junior' about your boy here!" He laughed again, clutching his crotch with the hand not holding the machete.

The children had seen her by now, and while they still looked too frightened to break out of their frozen circle, they seemed to recognize that her return meant some hope of rescue.

An adult would save them from these armed criminals. And that adult was her.

"Look, Mr. Junior," she said in her most formal Creole. "We don't want any trouble here. I was watching those kids. I just ducked into those bushes for a bathroom break. I appreciate your . . . concern, but I can easily take them now and leave you and your friends in peace."

Junior's ever-present sneer widened. "My my my!" His cigarette-strained voice boomed with much greater command and gravitas than Angie's meek, thirst-addled one. "Listen to that posh accent my lady here has! Where you been livin' these past few years, lady? America? England? France? You sure pick a great time to come back to ol' Haiti, don't you! Ha!"

Junior sauntered forward, extending his machete in a slow, callous manner. Angie's heart thudded alarmingly as she struggled to keep her expression stoic while backing up even farther, Lovelie tight at her side. When her shoe hit an unexpected curb behind her, she swiveled her head to find their route of escape blocked by several tattoo-covered men. Oh, god, they were trapped. She pulled Lovelie close in front of her with both hands and met Junior's gaze directly, her chin held high. He circled his machete a few inches from her face as if he were some kind of insect feeling her with his bloody metal antenna.

"My lady sounds thirsty too," he said. "A dry throat's not good for a lady's posh accent! But don't you worry your pretty little head, I'm gonna take care of you! I've got the finest water you can find! Make the stuff those charities are handing out taste like shit water from a toilet!"

Junior swung his machete toward a wagon being guarded by another group of escapees. Inside were a stack of five-gallon jugs of clean, clear water, all labeled with the logos of various luxury brands, all still sealed as if right off the truck.

Angie's dry tongue scraped her equally dry lips at the sight. She could almost feel the moisture rejuvenating her mouth, her throat, her whole body. The jugs had to be from the hotels, or the high-end stores. She stopped herself from thinking too hard about how Junior and his gang got their hands on the water. Or what happened to the people they stole it from.

Angie turned back to face Junior, whose machete was again draped over his shoulder, a passive threat. He smiled with the sadistic glee of a man without conscience but with unquestionable control of his surroundings.

"But, uh-oh! For such a pretty lady, you don't got much money, do you?" He snorted and spat a greasy wad of phlegm onto the sun-scorched ground. "That's okay, not too many people in poor ol' Haiti has much money, even before the Earth decided to take a shit on us. But, lucky for you, I'm a fair man, and I'm willing to make a nice deal with you, even if you weren't as sexy as you are."

Angie had little doubt what this "deal" would be. It had been a long, long time since she'd been intimate with a man, and those few excursions had borne no joy or memorable gratification in her path of self-discovery. But water was a need, not a want, and Angie's years of gender studies and gay activism began to dry up like dead autumn leaves. For water, enough for her and the kids, she could take Junior, even there, on the street, if he just dropped his pants . . .

Junior, seeming to read her thoughts, began cackling again. "Ha! I see this pretty lady undressing me with her eyes! But you're merely flattering yourself!" He whipped his machete from around his shoulder in one sharp motion and gestured to a group of people that had appeared from thin air behind his water wagon. Where had these women and girls come from? Many of them looked little older than their mid-teens and all bore obvious signs of having originated in the worst slums of Port-au-Prince. Most of them had bruises visible across their necks and shoulders, and they shuddered and winced as Junior pointed his machete in their direction. They had not, Angie was sure, received those bruises from the earthquake.

"Man, I've already got more coco than I know what to do with!" Junior cackled. "Besides, I got no interest in posh American Haitian lady like you! You forgot how to handle prime Haitian meat like mine! You wouldn't know what to do with it!"

Angie needed that water, and she needed those kids. She had to turn the tide somehow. "Look," she started. Her voice was growing weaker in the face of her growing dehydration and the worsening afternoon heat. She drew her fingers through Lovelie's hair, hoping to both give and receive emotional support. Lovelie just continued clutching Angie's leg and staring at her friends, who remained cowed in a tight cluster. "We don't want any trouble," Angie continued. "I have a bunch of kids I'm watching. We don't know where their parents are. We . . . they need water. I'm not looking for charity here. What would you be willing to trade? My parents have a store—" Instantly she realized the stupidity of mentioning her parents' lootable shop to criminals like these.

But Junior wasn't listening to her, and instead, speaking in a Creole dialect so fast-paced and slang-ridden that Angie couldn't understand a word, shouted something to one of his underlings while waving his machete in her general direction. The man, a foot taller but with dull eyes that gave off an infantile passivity, pulled from the wagon a whole jug of water in one of his massive arms. He opened the lid and poured some into a small tin cup, which he handed to Junior. Junior traded his machete for the cup, then approached Angie with the offering extended in his hand, like she was a stray dog he was trying to lure in with a hunk of raw meat. In many ways she was, lost on the beleaguered streets of Port-au-Prince, racked with thirst.

"Here, pretty lady," he said as he brought the cup to her lips. His own curled upward, revealing a mouth of dirty, half-missing teeth. "I'm gonna offer you a free sample."

Desperate as she was, Angie didn't move. Junior tipped the cup across her stony lips, and the water blended with her sweat as it dribbled down her chin. When a single drop breached her closed mouth and found its way to her tongue, her animalistic survival instinct took over. Forgetting the peril of the situation, she gaped her mouth open and tilted her head back just enough for the water from the cup to pour into her mouth, across her tongue, and down her seared throat.

"There, that's nice, isn't it?" Junior said, his voice a mockery of paternal comfort, and Angie's immense relief almost allowed her to believe it was the real thing.

Almost.

"But let me tell you the good news," Junior said, withdrawing the cup from Angie's mouth, leaving her puckering her lips out in front of her like an amorous fish. "You already brought me all the payment I need." He took a gulp of water himself and made a gesture with his index finger back toward the wagon. Angie followed where he was pointing, drawing her gaze past the water jugs, past the gang's bruised and bloodied harem of women, to the cluster of children, formerly under her ward, now surrounded by criminals.

Without thinking, Angie swung at Junior. With reflexes he undoubtedly developed in his years in prison, Junior dodged, just missing Angie's attempt at an uppercut. Instead, her fist connected with the tin cup still raised to his lips, and as it flew from his hands, the last of its contents splashed across his face and into his eyes. Angie grabbed Lovelie and pulled her back, gesturing frantically to the other children. "Kids!"

The sudden chaos worked to her advantage. Junior's gang seemed torn between moving against Angie and attempting to help their boss, and in that instant of confusion, several of the children broke from their fear-induced spell and rushed toward Angie. Dodging an attempted grapple from a nearby gang member, Angie pulled Lovelie close to her and reached her free arm to clutch as many of the kids as she could.

From all around, the gang members spurted curses and profanities in Creole. Junior, however, just wiped the water from his eyes and regarded Angie with blunted amusement, as if this whole escapade were merely a matinee movie of mediocre entertainment.

By the time she could settle her mind and take note of the situation, Angie was standing outside the circle of gang members with a clump of children clutching every piece of free space on her legs and torso. The gang members, called back by a shrill whistle from Junior, had retreated toward the water wagon. Angie, keeping her eyes on Junior, ran her hands over each child's head, trying to arrive at a haphazard headcount. Seven? No, nine. Or eight? Did she count that one twice? She touched each head again, and then again, arriving at varying numbers in her still-panicked autopilot. But regardless of where she landed, the basic assessment was still the same. She had fewer children around her than when she left her house that morning.

A stifled cry from a few feet away drew her eyes back to Junior. There, huddled in a fearful bunch behind him, were the remaining children. Five, she counted, noting that Evans and Emmanuel were among them. Their little plastic plane was crushed under Junior's shoe. Three members of Junior's crew were clutching their shoulders with nothing resembling gentleness.

Angie stared down Junior, who brandished his machete and took a few steps forward. She herded the children closer, ready to shield them with her body if need be. But Junior just picked his tin cup up off the ground and offered a brief snort of a laugh.

"Ha! Lady knows how to fight, at least for a girl. She didn't forget her roots in Haiti after all!" Junior used one foot to roll the jug of water toward Angie. "There's five gallons in there. Five gallons for five kids. That's fair, no?"

Despite his rising tone, she knew this wasn't a question. The jug of water came to a stop at her feet. She made no move to pick it up.

"Kids make me a lot of money. Lots of white folks want a Haiti kid to make them feel good about themselves. You help me out a lot. And who knows, maybe you'll see one of them on your nice block back in the USA!"

Junior tossed his machete over in his signature stance and gave a caustic laugh. His gang, taking this as a signal, started steering away the kids, their captive harem, and the water jug wagon.

Junior didn't follow. He turned back to Angie, showing her a vile smirk like a cat torturing a mouse. "Of course, you did take a swing at Junior. Nothing I can't handle. But to get where I am, I don't let no man who takes a swing at me live to tell about it." He winked at her. Angie's throat somehow became drier. "You ain't no man, though. So we'll compromise."

Without warning he pulled a pistol out of his pants and fired in Angie's direction. She yelped and held her breath, waiting for a bullet to pierce her flesh after each loud crack of gunfire. *Crack! Crack! Crack! Crack! Crack! Crack!*

It went silent, and Angie's body was so sore she couldn't tell if she had been hit. She looked down. No fresh blood leaking from a new wound. None of the kids' grips on her legs had loosened either.

What the hell was he shooting at?

Junior gave another crude laugh, nodding and returning the gun to his waistband. "You and your kids best start drinking before that all becomes mud!" He gestured to the water jug, which now sported six holes in its plastic sides, each leaking water in a steady stream.

Angie could only gape in anguish as she watched the lifeline bleed into the dirty ground.

16

Frank stared awkwardly at his older sister. While he couldn't remember the last time he and Elizabeth had been alone together, he'd been hoping a moment like this would crop up while they were in London. As he tried to game-plan how to proceed, his right hand erupted in spasms. He clutched it with his other hand and pursed his lips, trying to will the tremors away. If Elizabeth noticed anything, she didn't show it. She never was much for noticing when it came to family.

"So," Frank began. He decided on a Hail Mary of small talk to try and ease into the discussion. "How's life in New York been treating you?"

"Pretty good." Elizabeth's voice was impossibly calm, given the blowout with Tess they'd just endured. "About the same, really."

An unpleasant emotion bubbled up in Frank's chest. Envy? No, of course not. Frank did not feel "envy" for *any* of his sisters.

"Oh, well, I just completed the Goobers Chocolate acquisition," Elizabeth continued, "so my schedule isn't quite as booked as usual. I have some breathing room, at least for now."

"Goobers Chocolate?" Frank said. "Isn't that the stuff we used to eat in the theater during those Saturday matinees Mom would take us to?"

"Yep, that's it. I think I gained ten pounds putting that deal together." Elizabeth frowned and gazed down toward her waistline, which was as trim as ever.

Frank's hand twitched. But he wasn't craving chocolate. "I used to love those Saturday double features," he said. The Tarzan movies were especially great. And the Elvis Presley movies were good, except for the kissing parts. He could still remember all those years when they were kids. Even then, Elizabeth had perfected a calm and professional expression no matter what shit was going down at home. But for Frank, going to a different world, a world inside the movies, was the escape that he needed.

"Nowadays no one would dare just drop their kids off at a movie theater all alone for the afternoon," Elizabeth said. "But fortunately for us, kids will also find new and clever ways to get their hands on sugary snacks, so I don't think Goobers Chocolate has much to worry about." She poured herself a cup of tea from the pot Tess had left on the counter. "So, how are things going with you? Still driving that big rig cross country?"

As she gazed at him with that self-assured confidence, Frank was suddenly consumed by the idea she had x-ray vision and was looking right through him. Like he was nothing more than a spineless, boneless blob on a truck windshield.

"Things are good," he said a bit too quickly. Tess's cooking wine was beginning to sound better and better. "Everything's real good. Nancy's fine. The kids are fine. Sue's applied to Northeast Iowa Community College, and we think she has a real good chance of getting in. She's trying to become a beautician."

Elizabeth set her tea down and took out a small pocket mirror, which she used to check her eyeliner. Not that she didn't already look immaculate, despite just getting off a trans-Atlantic flight. "When was the last time I saw Sue?" she mused. "Gosh, it was some kind of cheerleading thing. And how's—

"The county championships," Frank interrupted, not wanting to let her steer the conversation in a direction he wasn't willing to go. He shot her a proud-dad smile. "Second place."

"Yeah, that was it," Elizabeth said. "Eighth grade, right?"

Frank nodded. "She was on the high school squad, too, made varsity as a junior."

Elizabeth tilted her head and narrowed her eyes, as if appraising him, like a business deal. "So, everything's going great with you. I'm real glad, Frank."

"Well," Frank began, ready as he was going to be. "There is one thing that's been bothering me. Been on my mind quite a bit recently, in fact."

Elizabeth flashed Frank something resembling a human emotion. But Frank couldn't tell if this was surprised annoyance or the smugness of having her suspicions confirmed. "What's that?" she asked.

Frank remembered the countless times she had gotten concessions from their parents with her calm and collected bargaining, while Frank's own impulsiveness and ill temper only got him a whuppin' and a grounding. He could still remember her patiently convincing their father to let her stay out past her curfew—until midnight, if you can believe that—and then getting him to give her a twenty-dollar bill for spending money to boot. She'd called it "mad money" and explained that she needed it to get home in case the boy got fresh with her. Of course, Frank was a guy, so he didn't have a curfew. His equivalent was, "If you get her pregnant, you're going to marry her."

Frank tried to think of the best way to ease into the subject. "Do you remember that time I made over a thousand betting on the Cougars?"

Elizabeth brushed a rebel strand of her otherwise perfectly sculpted hair away from her eyes. "Not really," she said. "You sure you told me about it?"

"Oh, yeah, I'm sure. But that's not important. All you need to

know is it was sweet. Real sweet. Like one of those 'sure things' you
see on TV or the movies but never think would happen to you."

"You know I don't follow sports, let alone bet on them." Elizabeth's
tone remained neutral, which made it sound even more condescend-
ing and self-righteous than if she were outwardly judging him. "But
I can imagine this was a sure thing, as you called it."

Frank couldn't let her get to him. He had to keep going. "It
was great. I bought Nancy a new TV, and we spent the weekend in
Prairie Du Chien—took the kids to Prairie Fun Land. It was great.
Really great."

"Actually," Elizabeth said, nodding slowly, "I think I do remember you talking about that. Or, rather, I remember you mentioning
a trip to Prairie Du Chien, some time ago. You had just come into
some money, if I recall correctly, though I had assumed you'd finally
followed some of my investment advice."

Leave it to Elizabeth to make everything about her. "Oh, well, I
was never much for the world of finance—as I'm sure you know. But
you have your investments, and I have mine. And on my end, I've
done pretty good over the years. Maybe not that good, but I won
more than I lost, made a little drinking money."

"And by 'investments' you mean gambling, yes?"

Elizabeth's tone still didn't sound judgmental. Her mouth was
relaxed in a soft semi-smile and her eyes were unblinking. But Frank
knew how she worked.

"No, not gambling," he said. "Just putting a little money down
on the games. Just enough to keep things interesting. Nothing serious. Nothing I couldn't afford to lose."

"Okay." Elizabeth folded her hands on the counter like she
must have done during so many high-stakes business negotiations.
Bargaining over more money in one lunch than Frank would earn in
his entire life. And yet, somehow, Frank's stakes felt so much higher.
"So why are you telling me this?"

He had to pitch this just right. "Recently I've had an unbeliev-ably bad run of luck. I mean, something that from a statistical per-spective is completely impossible. I mean, I knew I was in further than I should be. And I'd lost this string of bets that was, like, amaz-ing, impossible. So, I was thinking, it's like a coin. You flip a coin five times, then ten times, then fifteen times, and every time it comes up tails. Tails, tails, tails, tails. What are the odds of that? I was helping Sue with her homework, this math assignment, and it was talking about this very thing. Flipping coins. And do you know what the odds are that a coin will turn up tails fifteen times in a row?"

"I have no idea," Elizabeth said, but Frank got the distinct im-pression that she did, in fact, have an idea.

"Guess," he said, trying to lure her into his story. "Just guess."

"One in a thousand?"

Ha! Not so smart after all. "One in thirty-two thousand, seven hundred and sixty-eight."

"So I'm guessing that you lost a string of bets. How much did you lose?" Curiosity tinged her voice, but it was the same curiosity she might express in asking what was for dinner. If he had a poker face like hers, they wouldn't be having this conversation.

Despite his best efforts, his mind flashed back to all the previous times he had "borrowed" money from his big sister. Five hundred bucks, when he'd gotten skunked at the Trojan High School basket-ball game on his first-ever bet. He hadn't known what he was doing back then, of course. The other times were just bad luck. He'd bor-rowed a thousand, then seven-fifty. Fifteen hundred. She didn't seem to be keeping a tab, even though he had yet to pay any of it back. But this time . . . this was different.

"Not too bad," Frank said. "Fifteen thousand." He waited for her to react, to raise an eyebrow at the unusually large sum. But her face remained a blank slate. He pushed on. "But I got to thinking . . . what about sixteen?"

Elizabeth blinked, her first show of not being totally in control. "Sixteen what? Thousand?"

"No, sixteen tails in a row." Frank couldn't stop his voice from rising. "The odds. It's one in sixty-five thousand, five hundred thirty-six." Another loss was basically impossible. It had been the surest sure thing he'd ever done.

"Frank," Elizabeth said, sounding genuinely concerned. "What did you do?"

He would let the math explain. "I mean, how could I lose? If you took every single person living in Dubuque, you still wouldn't have sixty-five thousand. I'm talking one out of more people than everyone in Dubuque. That was the odds of me getting one more tails."

"It doesn't work that way, Frank." Elizabeth shook her head sadly, gazing around the kitchen as if she, too, needed something stronger than tea.

"I knew this was a golden opportunity," Frank continued. "I mean, when else in my life would I have a chance to place an even money bet where my odds of winning were sixty-five thousand to one? Never!"

Elizabeth let out a dismayed sigh. "How much do you owe?"

Frank looked at the floor. "Forty thousand dollars."

Elizabeth nodded sagely, taking this in. "Forty thousand dollars?" she echoed.

"Plus interest. One percent."

Elizabeth raised her eyebrows in an unspoken question.

"Per week. One percent per week."

She set her teacup down on the counter with a thud. "And what did Nancy say when you told her?"

"She doesn't know." She couldn't know, not ever. She'd never forgive him.

Elizabeth stared at Frank until he met her intense gaze. "You've got to tell her," she said. "I mean, even if you take on extra runs, that's going to take years to pay off. She might need to go back to work."

"Winning that money was real important to me, Liz," he said. "I mean, real important. More important than you could know."

"You didn't need it, Frank. You had no right to take chances like that. You've got a good, steady job. Sure, you're on the road a lot, but you make good money for someone living in Clayton."

"Oh, shit," he said, letting his anxiety pour out. "I really screwed up, Liz. Not just with the gambling. I really, really screwed up."

"What, Frank?" she asked. "What else?"

"I lost my job." He pounded his fist on the counter. "After twenty years working for the same company, I lost my job."

"Okay, Frank, that's bad, but it's not terrible," Elizabeth said, ever the voice of logic and reason. "There's lots of work out there for experienced truck drivers willing to drive cross country. Hell, maybe I can get you a job driving Goobers around to the theaters. Listen, you're taking this much too seriously. You'll have another job in a week or two. Sure, it's going to be hard to pay that money back, but you've learned your lesson."

"I lost my license." He hadn't said those words aloud to anyone. It filled him with a nervous energy and he began to pace.

"Lost your license?" Elizabeth squeezed closer to the counter as he barreled past her.

"I lost my license." Frank pulled open the cupboard door near the range, looking for the cooking wine. "Indefinitely. No more truck driving."

"Why did you lose your license?"

"They said I was drinking," Frank said, moving on to the cupboards near the sink. "When I was driving. It was a lie! They pulled me over and did these tests. Tightrope walking, balloons, and shit like that. It was a regular freakin' circus. So then they tell me that I'm drunk, but I swear to you, Liz, there's no way I was drunk. I was perfectly fine to drive."

"Then why did they pull you over?"

"I drifted over the line. Just not paying attention and the truck drifted a bit." He tried one of the lower cupboards. No dice. The wine had to be here somewhere.

"Had you been drinking?" Elizabeth asked, like she was talking to a child trying to suss out a lie.

"I'm telling you, I was perfectly fine."

"Had you been drinking?"

What was this, the Inquisition? "Nothing significant," he mumbled.

"Significant?"

She just wouldn't let up.

"A few beers. I had a few beers when I stopped for dinner. I mean, there's nothing wrong with having a beer with a meal at dinnertime, right?"

"Oh, Frank," Elizabeth said with a sigh. She shook her head.

"I know," he whispered. "I know I screwed up."

"Have you looked for help?"

"From who?" Frank snapped, but then checked himself and continued more calmly. "I mean, Nancy would never understand. She'd just pack up and leave me. Reverend Jones would stand me in front of the congregation, drive the devil out of me, and then tell me to go in peace. But nothing would really be any different."

"You could have called me," Elizabeth said.

"No . . ." How many times had he thought about it but failed to dial?

"I've lent you money before."

"I know. This whole thing is so hosed. I'm your brother. I know you're older than me, technically, but I'm the only son! I'm supposed to provide for everyone! And here we are. I mean, even when we were kids, you were up here, and I was down there"—he held one hand up above his head and the other as low as it would reach—"and sometimes . . . sometimes it feels like . . ." He let that trail off. "But yeah. Since you brought it up. Maybe you can loan me the money I need to pay these guys back and get back on my feet. Nancy wouldn't even need to know about it."

Elizabeth regarded him with that impenetrable poker face. "I don't know, Frank," she said slowly. "This is a lot of money. New York's an expensive place to live, and we've got a mortgage that you wouldn't believe. I'd have to dip into my 401(k) and there's a penalty for that, plus taxes. By the time you add it all up, we'd be getting something like thirty cents for every dollar we pulled out, and . . ."

"No—" Frank tried to interrupt, but Elizabeth talked right over him.

". . . to be honest, Frank, thirty cents on the dollar is stretching the limits of sibling love pretty far."

"No! I mean, listen." She had to finish hearing him out. "I was talking to a friend of mine about this. You can take the money out for up to sixty days, then put it back with no penalty or interest. It's like an interest-free loan for sixty days."

"What good would that do?" Elizabeth asked, looking truly baffled.

He'd saved the best part for last, though. And he couldn't hold back his excitement. "Do you know what the odds are of seventeen tails in a row?"

"Frank!" Elizabeth exclaimed.

"One in one hundred thirty-one thousand!" he shouted.

"Oh, Frank." It wasn't sympathy so much as pity in her voice now. "You might be a lost cause, you know that?" She left the kitchen and Frank heard the bathroom door in the alcove clank shut.

He'd failed. In his mind's eye, his father's twisted face screamed at his screwup of a son, calling him a pansy and a faggot and calling on God to answer for why his only son should be like this. Then, Alex Meter glared down in disgust, wondering out loud why such a disgrace to his God and his country should ever have thought he deserved a place as a proud citizen of Meter Nation.

"Screw it," he muttered to no one. "If Tess doesn't stock her own house with anything, I'll find a liquor store and stock it for her."

As he forced his trembling body into his coat, struggling to get his twitching right hand into its sleeve, a sound came drifting down from upstairs. It was a woman's voice, singing softly. Elizabeth? Gah, what was he thinking? No, idiot. Dawn, obviously. He paused, letting her voice calm the twitching. After a few seconds, he realized he recognized the song.

He'd never given a shit about the hippie folk stuff she usually sang, but this was a song she had often sung from the room she shared with Elizabeth when they were kids. The room that was right next to Frank's, where he could hear her voice drifting through the house's old and dusty ventilation grates. He never learned the title but had taken to calling it "Oh, Death" after the one line that always stood out.

Oh, death, what is this that I can see,
With icy hands taking hold of me?
I am icy death, and none can tell.
I open the door to heaven and hell.
Oh, death, oh, death, please spare me over till another year.

The song ended and he closed his eyes, stretching his arms over his head. He pictured giant but soft hands coming down from the adult world to scoop him up, soothe him, sing him a lullaby, and tell him that everything would be okay. For a moment he could almost believe that.

But then his reality swarmed back into his mind and body, his tremor picking right up where it had left off. He bowed his head, zipped up his coat, and fled down the stairs and out into the chilling winter air of a foreign land. Alone.

17

Jim's shift always started with a lick of anticipation. Would the green-eyed girl sit out on her balcony, bare leg exposed, reading or writing in her diary? Most nights, sadly, the answer was no. Apparently that first night, after the escaped Jihad-Johnny came knocking at her door, was an exception. But thankfully he still got a chance to watch her most days, on her way to school. Some days her dad drove her all the way there; others he dropped her off in town where she still had many blocks to walk. Those were Jim's favorite days, when he could get lost in the sway of her hips as she moved, her face always buried in a book.

This was one of those days. Her dad's beige car stopped at an intersection near the Khewa market, and the girl stepped out, a stack of books clutched to her chest, like some kind of secret treasure that might be taken from her if she let her guard down. As her dad drove off, she transferred the stack into one hand and used the other to prop open the book on top of the pile. She walked slowly down the block, face hidden in the pages, and Jim was amazed she made it more than a few steps without crashing into something. How could she see with that thing right in front of her face? And moreover, how could Jim see her?

He let his imagination take hold, painting in the details of her wavy, dark hair, the gentle curve of her ears, the striking emerald green of her eyes. Her lips moved occasionally as she came across a particularly striking word, her eyes lighting up.

Beautiful.

"What's that?" Brian asked from across the trailer, startling Jim from his fantasy. Had he said that out loud? Shit.

"Wasn't talking to you, asshole," Jim said, then to himself whispered, "Beautiful." And she was, even with her face buried in a book.

She needed a name.

Jim pulled out his phone and opened Google Translate. He found the Pashtun tab and typed "beauty" into the English line and waited impatiently for the translation.

"Uzuri," he whispered after it popped up. "Uz—ur—ee."

"What?" Brian barked again.

"Shut the hell up," Jim said without looking up.

He maneuvered his joystick to readjust the camera angle, getting the girl back in the center of his screen, and zoomed in. Her face grew to the size of a quarter, then even bigger. Big enough that Jim could make out the contours of her lips, her cheeks. Her green eyes were studying her book with what looked like hunger.

Uzuri. That was as good a name as any.

Jim focused on her lips when they moved and tried to mimic the motions. Maybe he could figure out what she was saying and cram it into Google Translate.

Just then, as she was about to walk out of view, she lifted her eyes from the book and turned her head, right at Jim. He gulped nervously, his chest tightening. But the look was short-lived, a stopover on the way to fully turning around. As her body spun, he thought he saw her eyes perk up. He thought he saw a smile creep across her face. A second later she waved a friendly greeting at another person, just off-screen.

A classmate, walking the same route to the girls' school? A fellow book-lover, a kindred spirit she could share her love of learning with?

But no. It was a boy, around Uzuri's age based on his height and build. He wore the standard school uniform, though his was less tidy than Uzuri's. Jim's eyes narrowed as he focused the drone's camera on this new character. Uzuri and the boy began to chat in a lighthearted manner, sharing occasional laughs and smiles as they walked toward the schools. Every so often, Jim noticed their hands beginning to creep together, coming closer and closer to touching, but pulling back at the last moment in a sudden, awkward retreat.

Crap, Jim thought, then checked himself. Wait. Was he jealous of that Afghan asshole?

The last time he remembered feeling anything like that was years ago when he was still in high school. He'd had a crush on Brianna McKay, gorgeous with silky brown hair that cascaded down her back in waves except when it was tied up in a perfect ponytail for cheerleading. But she had gone for the point guard on the basketball team, and Jim was left with clenched fists and burning resentment that he couldn't resolve.

Was he feeling the same thing now? It was ridiculous, of course. What was he going to do, ask her to the prom via drone? Did they even have proms in Khewa? She didn't speak English, so how would he . . .

What was he doing? He shook his head, trying to rattle some reality back into his brain. She was just some girl on his screen in Afghanistan. He had no right to be jealous, to want to protect her. And from what, from some teenage boy who wanted to . . .

Without thinking, Jim leaned closer and closer to the screen. He could see the boy's muscular shoulders, tall frame, the beginnings of the beard starting to form on his chin. He stared as Uzuri and this strange boy talked, still trying to decipher words that he wouldn't know the meanings of even if he could read their lips. He watched their eyes share glances, glances that seemed more than friendly, hinting at something . . .

"Wilson!"

Jim jumped back in his seat and, in a frantic motion, zoomed the drone camera away from the scene. Major Udall was standing directly behind him, holding a cup of the shitty base coffee with limited interest.

"Yes . . . uh, sir!" Jim managed, trying to will his heart to stop hammering so hard. Was it as loud to Udall as it was in Jim's own ears?

The CO took a loud and sloppy sip of coffee. "How're those subjects looking?"

Shit. Udall was onto him. "Uh, what's that, sir?" he choked out.

Udall looked annoyed. "Lieutenant, are you retarded? The subjects you were monitoring. The girl and her dad. Any new info?"

"Oh." Jim couldn't shake the feeling he'd been caught in the act of something shameful, even though Udall's question was vague enough to confirm he hadn't been. "No, nothing right now, Major. The . . . girl is walking to school. Her father dropped her off and is driving to his job at the university."

Udall looked bored as he took another loud sip of coffee. "No more potential targets show up?"

"No, sir." Jim tried to keep his voice steady despite the anxiety still pounding in his chest.

"Well," Udall said, "keep your eyes open. I'll let you know if you get authorized for another strike or even more direct reconnaissance."

And with that, Major Udall engaged in the one superpower that all superior officers had, and immediately ceased giving any and all shits about Jim, turning his attention to bitching at Brian at the other end of the trailer. Jim sank into his seat.

As his heart rate returned to normal, he grabbed his controls and found Uzuri and the boy again. They had just reached an intersection, and he watched as they separated, waving to each other, and walked off in opposite directions. Uzuri turned back for one last glance at the boy, and Jim thought he saw a flash of desire cross her face.

"Sir?" he suddenly called out before he was even aware of what he was doing.

Udall jerked his head around. "What?"

"Sir, uh, it's me again," Jim said.

Udall shot him a scowl but wandered over. "What do you want this time?"

"There's something else, sir," Jim said.

"What? What do you mean?"

Jim swallowed. "There's a boy."

Udall paused. "A boy?"

"This your lover?" Cooper called from across the trailer.

"Shut the hell up," Major Udall barked back. Then, to Jim, "What 'boy' is this?"

"With the girl, Uzur—I mean, the girl I've been monitoring. She's been talking to a boy, and I, uh, figured that would be something to report to you and to the chain of command."

"Hell's bells," Udall muttered. "Who gives a shit if she's talking to a boy! She's a teenager! Probably wants to get finger-blasted or whatever the Afghan equivalent of that is. I dunno, having him touch her bare ankles? Why do we give a shit?"

"We" don't, but Jim did, even if he wasn't willing to articulate why. The boy was still just visible on his screen, a few humanoid pixels nearing the edge of the picture. The look of desire that Uzuri had given him flashed back into Jim's mind, and he again spoke without fully thinking. "He was acting suspiciously, sir."

Major Udall perked up. "Acting suspiciously" was a magical phrase for the intelligence service. Like catnip. "How so?" Udall asked.

"Well, you know . . ." Jim turned his stupid thoughts over and over, trying to find some kind of justification. "He matched a description. Of a person of interest. Might be associated with the Taliban, based on his looks."

Udall scratched his cheek with partial interest. "You said he was talking to the girl whose house was previously visited by the high-profile target? From the strike?"

"Yes, sir."

Major Udall considered this. "Well, then, I'll let my superiors know. It's probably just some horny teenagers screwin' around, but you never know. Keep an eye on it in the meantime."

Jim gave a brief smile and nodded. "Yes, sir, I will."

"And continue keeping an eye on that girl and her dad. Their house, specifically. See if the original target shows up again."

Jim nodded from his seat. "Affirmative, sir."

Major Udall went back to not giving a shit about Jim or his assignment, and Jim returned to his screen, the slight smile still on his face, though he wasn't quite sure why.

18

Once upon a time, a lifetime ago, or maybe just a few months, Angie walked through Golden Gate Park with her hand wrapped around Dawn's. The central California sun was shining above them, the breeze coming off the nearby ocean cool and comforting as it blew across their skin and hair. A husband and wife passed them with three young kids in tow, and Dawn squeezed Angie's hand.

"We should have kids," Dawn said, turning her eyes to peer at Angie as they walked.

"What's that, now?" This was the first she'd heard about Dawn wanting to be a mother.

"There are so many poor kids sitting in foster care. We could adopt one. Provide them a safe, happy home."

Angie shook her head, a low chuckle escaping. "Honey, we can't even get married."

"We can't get married, *yet*," Dawn corrected, and the hairs on the back of Angie's neck perked up. "'But the times, they are a-changin,' as Dylan sang."

Angie smiled in her partner's direction but couldn't suppress the bitterness staining her thoughts. Why couldn't it just remain the two of them? Wasn't their love enough? They were barely getting by financially now, and there's no way they could take on the added cost of raising a child. Plus, Angie was pretty sure she'd be a terrible parent, and it's not like she could take the kid back to Target, show them her receipt, and return it. And even if she could return it, doing that would prove beyond a doubt that she wasn't a fit mother. No, better to not even go down that treacherous path.

But Angie merely squeezed Dawn's hand in reply, her inner voice not able to speak up and make her point.

Lost in that memory, Angie could almost forget the crushing heat of the Haitian sun bearing down on top of her. And the guilt and fear screaming in her chest. Five children, lost to a monster. No longer entertaining fantasies about finding competent government officials or relief agencies to hand the kids off to, Angie could only stagger herself and the remaining kids in the direction of her parents' home, which thankfully she'd finally found her bearings toward.

"Matant Angie?" Lovelie's voice cut through Angie's daydream.

"Hmmm?"

"Matant Angie," Lovelie said in a sad, chapped voice. "I'm thirsty again."

Angie bit her lip. "I know, love," she said, and quickly checked herself in surprise. Where did that come from? Was "love" even what you were supposed to call little girls? Maybe just thinking about Dawn had allowed Angie to siphon off some of her maternal instincts. "We're all thirsty. You can have another drink in just a few minutes. We'll get some more when we get back to the store. There's still so much water on the shelves."

I hope, Angie's thoughts helpfully added in her head.

She suddenly heard Dawn's soft voice cut through her pain and tired haze: "*I have faith in you.*"

Angie swiveled her gaze, looking for the source, but of course it was only in her head. *That's great, honey*, she replied in her thoughts. *Now if only I could have faith in myself.* But even if she didn't yet have faith, Dawn's words buoyed her spirit.

She smiled down at Lovelie. "Thatagirl," she said.

As they kept walking, Angie wondered how Dawn was doing,

what was happening with her mother. They hadn't been close—Angie had never met Margaret Wilson and knew Dawn hadn't seen her since she moved to London six years ago—but that didn't make losing a parent easy. Angie may be trapped in a living hell, but at least both her parents had survived alongside her. Now she just needed to get back to them, to make sure Junior or some other band of criminals hadn't found his way to the store . . .

"I'm thirsty," a girl's voice complained, only this time it was Celeste, halfway down the line.

Angie was trying to again channel her inner Dawn when a new voice stepped in. "Excuse me, do you need water?" It was an adult voice. But not Dawn's.

Angie turned and saw where the question was coming from. A middle-aged, heavyset woman with a bandana around her head that was already soaked in sweat was coming up behind them on the road. She wore a tank top and several metal crosses around her neck, and she was carrying a box filled with supplies and food rations. How she had avoided being mugged was beyond Angie, with Junior and his band of cretins on the loose out there.

"Sorry to bother you," the woman said, offering a sincere smile. "I overheard you talking to your little ones about your water supply, and I was wondering if you needed assistance."

"Oh, yes, sorry." Despite the welcoming tone, Angie felt a wave of caution pull her shoulders back and place her body between the woman and the children.

"These can't all be your children, can they?" the woman asked.

A rough laugh escaped Angie's lips. "No, not mine. I am watching them now, though." She twisted her mouth. "I've been trying to find their parents. Or at least some aid group that would be more qualified to take care of them than me."

The woman nodded with a knowing expression. "I see," she said. "Thank God you found them. So many children have been left orphaned, and so few adults have stepped up to help them. I've always said that tragedy makes one person's child everyone's child. I had thought that all of Haiti agreed with me there, but I suppose not." A sad look came across the woman's face. Angie suddenly realized this may not be the first time the woman had come across someone in Angie's situation over the past week.

"But," the woman continued, "you were looking to get help for the children? I'm currently working at an orphan—" She stopped abruptly before saying the word in its entirety, and Angie saw her send a quick glance at the children. "I mean, I work at a place that takes care of children like this, while we work to reunite them with their parents."

Angie's heart fluttered, despite the atmosphere of mistrust that had settled across her thoughts since the incident with Junior's gang. "You do?"

"We are . . . quite filled up, at the moment," the woman said. "As you can imagine, I'm sure. But we are not going to refuse any children who may need our help. We have rations of water back at the facility, as well as food and clothing that we got from charity organizations. Lord knows it's hardly anywhere near what we need, but it's something."

Angie tried to conceal her desperate joy at finding someone who seemed vaguely qualified coming to finally take the children off her hands. "I certainly don't wish to overburden you, but I'm not sure I'm the best person to be taking care of these children, and if you have knowledge and supplies . . ."

"We have *some* supplies," the woman said with a sigh. "As I said, it's never going to be enough to help everyone who needs it. And these international aid organizations are not as much help as they could be. They're more intent on getting good photo ops or converting us to their branch of Christianity than they are on getting us clothing and toys. But what else is new?"

"Yeah, I imagine you're right about that," Angie said with a laugh. "So, where is this orphan—I mean, the facility."

"Down the road a bit," the woman said, pointing in a direction Angie and the kids hadn't been yet. "I came out this way to try and gather some more supplies, but it wasn't exactly safe to go too far away. I heard that a group of criminals who escaped from the penitentiary are running around, causing who knows what kind of trouble."

Another stab of guilt ripped through Angie's heart. "Yes, I heard that as well. Hopefully, they don't cause much trouble." The children, bless them, did not expose her lie of omission.

"So, kids," Angie said, kneeling to address the group that had congregated behind her. "Do you want to go with this nice lady here, whose name I now realize I never got?"

The woman gave a maternal chuckle. "It's Roseline," she said. "Though the kids I've been watching have taken to calling me Matant Wozie."

"So, kids," Angie tried again. "Do you all want to go with Matant Wozie here, to a nice place with other kids where they can help you find your parents?"

None of the kids moved, except Lovelie, who wrapped her arms around Angie's thigh. They all continued looking up at her with sad eyes.

Wonderful, Angie thought bitterly.

"They seem attached to you," Roseline said. "It makes sense, you're the one who helped them when no one else would. Maybe they're better off staying with you.

"No, no, no," Angie said, much too fast. She frowned and tried to save face. "What I mean to say is, I'm not really qualified to take care of these kids. Hell, even one kid. In normal circumstances, let alone a time like this." She gestured at the carnage surrounding them, her point left hanging in the air.

But Roseline merely offered a soft laugh in response. "Not qualified?" she said. "It looks to me like you've kept them alive and in one piece! That's about ninety percent of taking care of kids 'in normal circumstances.' Plus, it looks like the kids have faith in you."

There was that faith thing again. Did everyone have faith in her but her?

"But if you're sure you aren't able to continue caring from them," the woman offered with a rueful smile, "you could accompany me to the . . . facility to bring the children there yourself. I'm sure they will be happy enough to stay once they see it in person."

Relief flooded through Angie, and she looked back at the kids, who all stared at her with puckered mouths and deferring eyes. She was so very ready for a break from this crushing responsibility. "Yes, of course," she said.

So she followed Roseline through a maze of twisted and broken buildings, the children cued up behind her like ducklings, aside from Lovelie, who never left her side or loosened her tight grip on Angie's right hand.

"I don't mean to be too intrusive," Roseline said after a few blocks. "But I was curious about something."

"Sure, what's that?" Angie asked.

"I noticed your accent," Roseline said. "I caught some traces of American there. Are you from the States, by any chance?"

Angie blinked, embarrassed. In the shock and stress of the post-earthquake world, she had forgotten to try and hide whatever American affectations she had picked up in California.

"Well, in a sense," Angie acknowledged. "I'm from here originally. Port-au-Prince, born and raised. But I've been living in the States for the past several years. I went over there for the degree but stayed because of the acceptance. Acceptance of me, I mean. Plus, my partner's from there, so there's that. I guess it's rubbed off on my Creole."

"Where in the States, if you don't mind me asking?"

"Sunny California."

"Ah, yes, California!" Roseline's eyes lit up in what looked like childhood reverence. "I'd love to go there sometime. I've only seen pictures and heard stories. Surfers and waves, Hollywood, the Beach Boys, all that. It must be incredible!"

That's how Angie had felt when she'd first arrived. Starstruck at being in the Golden State. Then she'd learned firsthand that though California was far more tolerant, and she didn't have to hide the fact she was a lesbian, it had plenty of poverty and crime, just like Haiti. The shine had quickly sloughed off, replaced by the reality of jobs and bills. "Yes, well," she said. "It's nice enough, for what it is. Pop culture may have painted a different picture than what's there in reality. And the cost of living is something you wouldn't believe. I'm pretty sure I could buy a nice house here for how much I pay for one month's rent in California. And that's before the earthquake!"

"Yes, of course," Roseline laughed. "Isn't that always how it goes? The reason I asked is that we are in contact with several American agencies."

"Oh?" Knowing what Angie knew about Americans, this could either be for good or ill.

"Yes." Roseline looked back at the children, then leaned closer to Angie's ear, lowering her voice. "For some of the children whose parents did not survive, or who seem to have been completely abandoned, we're trying to place them with families in the United States. Even before the earthquake, we were working on adoptions. Now, the tragedy has become news in the States, and many people there are suddenly interested in getting Haitian kids for themselves. Trying to help however they can." Roseline punctuated the point with a sardonic laugh.

Angie rolled her eyes. "I know the type. Are they mostly evangelical groups?"

"Yes, for the most part." Roseline nodded. "There's one group in particular, Shepherd's Flock Relief Fund. Very religious. But nice enough. Not that I don't have any notes I could give them, but they mean well. Seem to genuinely want to follow God's word, as best they understand it, at least. But though we have some connections established who may want to bring some of our children to the States, the issue is, of course, cost."

"Really?" Angie had a flashback to all of those TV commercials she had seen in America, featuring sad yet sanctimonious missionary types walking through some third world village to a theme of somber music, informing the viewer they can literally save the life of a poor, brown child for just the cost of a cup of coffee per day. "How much does it cost to get a kid from Haiti to the United States?"

"You have to understand," Roseline said, "it's not just the trans-portation cost, though even that is more difficult than just plopping them on a plane and having someone meet them at the airport state-side. There are all sorts of legal fees, for both Haiti and the United States. There are medical issues, checkups, vaccines, and all that. Social workers, background checks, educational requirements, and so on. All in all, it adds up, totaling into the thousands. Sometimes tens of thousands."

"Tens of thousands?" Angie said with a gasp.

"Yes." Roseline shook her head sadly. "Tens of thousands, and in your American dollars, mind you. I honestly have no idea how much it is in gourde. The currency conversion rate got away from me some time ago. But suffice to say, it's quite a bit."

A bit more than a few gallons of water. It wasn't guilt that gnawed at Angie now, but anger.

"Anyway," Roseline continued, with the tone of someone testing the waters of a potential situation. "The reason I bring that up is I assume you have strong English language skills?"

"Yes, more or less," Angie said. "My accent threw a lot of Americans the first year or two I was there. I had trouble with 'Th,' which became a 'D' sound. I remember someone asked how old I was, and I was trying to tell them 'thirty,' but I kept saying 'dirty.' We went round and round but finally figured it out. Anyway, it eventually improved, and now, from what I gather from you, my American accent has overtaken my Haitian one."

"It would seem so," Roseline said with a smile. But then her grin faltered, and she continued, "Communication is the other big issue we're dealing with, alongside overall costs and lack of supplies. Our organization on the Haitian side of things has some people who can speak English, but Lord knows, not enough. The American missionary groups have some people who can speak Creole, but even less than we have English speakers. We've wasted far too much time on communication challenges, running around trying to find our English speakers, or them trying to find their Creole speakers, sometimes running right past each other. The children are the ones who suffer the most. I guess what I'm trying to say is, we could use help from more English speakers."

This was the first time being Americanized seemed to be an advantage in Haiti. Angie was flattered, if a little flummoxed at the strangeness, and part of her could see herself working for a spell at the orphanage, making up for losing five children to Junior's gang by helping the remaining seven find safe, secure homes in America. But the other part knew she needed to keep her focus on getting back to Dawn in Berkeley—and bringing her parents with her. "I would love to do that, in better circumstances," she began, "but things are a bit hectic on my end as well. You see, I have elderly parents. They survived, thank God, but my father is disabled, and the shop they ran is . . . it's obviously not in great shape now. I'm trying to get them passage to the US as well, once I get means for myself to get back to California." She paused, searching for some kind of final apology. "Not that I wouldn't love to help."

But Roseline waved her hands. "Ah, say no more," she said. "Of course, I understand completely. Everyone is doing the absolute most they can just to keep their heads afloat, and Lord knows the government is about as much help as it always is. Which is, of course, no help at all."

This woman was so kind and doing such important work. Angie really did want to help. "Maybe just today," she said tentatively. "I do have to get back to my parents, but since we're going to your facility anyway, maybe this afternoon I can help with some supplies and communication issues."

Roseline's face split into a huge grin. "Wonderful! I am sure we can find something for you to do. We have, sadly, far too many children. But you have a gift for working with young ones."

"Really?" Was Roseline blind? "I never considered myself particularly good with children."

"Ha!" Roseline snorted a laugh. "Neither did I, before I had my first one. But getting thrown into the gauntlet can make you find your hidden gifts quickly. Or motivate you to make them up on the fly. Besides, I would say you have all the evidence you need." She gestured to the line of children behind Angie, and for the first time Angie looked at them with a hint of fondness rather than exasperation. Was she good at this? The kids *did* look a lot like that children's book, *Make Way for Ducklings*.

Lovelie, still at her side, was sucking the thumb of her free hand, looking up at Angie expectantly. As if her attachment to Angie was not a reflex born out of desperation but some kind of wise, conscious choice.

No, that was ridiculous. Angie pursed her lips as they neared another intersection.

"It's just around this corner," Roseline said.

A lone building stood solid at the end of the block, but it seemed less like a dedicated childcare facility and more like a random office that had survived the earthquake and subsequent looting enough to work as an orphanage on an ad hoc basis. It was two stories, constructed of blue painted concrete blocks, with minimal windows or other openings in the façade. Overall, the impression was of a military bunker, which explained why it was still standing. The scene outside was no less chaotic than most street corners across Port-au-Prince since the earthquake. The only difference was that the frenzied people clustered around the door were young children. A woefully small number of adults rushed around trying to watch them—or, in one case Angie noticed, gave up completely and sat down on the cracked sidewalk to enjoy a cigarette and cast occasional, half-assed glances toward the kids.

"My gosh!" Angie exclaimed. "How many are there?"

She heard Roseline draw in a pained breath next to her. "I've lost count. Someone was keeping records of the names of the children—or at least how many came in and when. But to be honest, even before this mess we weren't that good with the paperwork. And now . . ." She trailed off and shook her head. "I know we passed a hundred children yesterday, and with your seven added to the group, well, it's hard to see what the maxing out point is. Our policy is that we do not and will not turn away any child who may need our help. But we never imagined something like this . . ."

She didn't finish her sentence, but Angie understood well enough.

"Are the kids on recess right now?" she asked.

Roseline's expression darkened. "In a sense." Her voice had grown quieter, almost guilty, as if she was trying to avoid directly confronting an unpleasant truth that, despite her best efforts, would not go away. "We must rotate the children inside and outside in groups. This building used to be a church of sorts. It was originally run by an evangelical group, I forget which denomination, but one of the more . . . enthusiastic ones. I was working with the childcare organization here even before the earthquake. When it hit, we were in the process of trying to lease the space from them. They were less interested in paying money for church facilities and more interested in getting butts in pews. They wanted us to try to 'convert' the children. I got the sense they thought all the kids down here were

Vodou cultists or something. But once the earthquake hit, they fled, and we took over. Because it was a newer building, it stood up pretty well against the earthquake. It still seems structurally sound, thank goodness. But the amount of space inside is . . . limited. So the kids must take turns being inside. We're doing the best we can to get everyone inside if there's bad weather or other . . . issues, outside. But even a few days ago, it was getting overcrowded. The children were crammed shoulder to shoulder. And many more kids have come in since then."

Angie's head was spinning. "Wait, what about sleeping? Do you have places for them all to sleep?"

Roseline turned her head away. "Sleeping has been a challenge," she said in a sad tone. "Initially we had enough blankets and sleeping bags, but as you can see . . ." She waved her hand in the general direction of the mass of children clustered around the building. "We try to have the children sleep in shifts, so everyone can get a blanket and pillow at least. But that's as close to impossible on a scale this large as you would imagine. Some children, of course, don't sleep well, given what they've seen."

That was understandable. But if they were only able to be indoors in shifts, and sleeping in shifts, what else could they only do in shifts? "What about bathrooms?" Angie asked.

Roseline's mouth twisted. "There are two in the back, but the water got shut off, as you know, when the earthquake hit. The toilets filled up quickly. We have some buckets, some diapers from our charities and some we managed to pick up from whatever stores were still around. But there are never enough to go around."

"So how do the children go to the bathroom?" Angie pushed.

Roseline didn't respond, but as they approached the front door, the foul stench provided all the answers Angie needed. Instinctually, she threw her hands over her nose. Roseline merely sighed sadly, leading Angie and the children inside.

It took a moment for her eyes to adjust to the relative darkness. The space looked exactly as Roseline's description suggested it would, like an unfinished church sanctuary now crowded with children. The floor was cold gray concrete, with stains here and there that might have been blood. One single electric fan in the corner provided the only source of moving air, though Angie wouldn't describe it as cool. The floor was littered with soiled pants and diapers.

Angie didn't see any adults, aside from herself and Roseline.

"And what about food?" she asked, fearing for the answer.

Roseline looked around the room. "That's always going to be the real sticking point, isn't it? We have some, though of course it's nowhere near where we need it to be, especially since we have no idea how many more children are coming in and when we'll be able to reconnect these children with family members or find them new homes. Donations have been steady, but the quality hasn't always been great. People don't seem to know about—or care about—the general rule of only donating nonperishable items. We've gotten meats that are spoiled, moldy bread, milk that's curdled, and what have you. We want to throw it away, but given how scarce food is here, well . . ." Roseline gestured around, as if the obvious state of the room would provide the ending to that sentence for her.

Angie nodded. "And how many adult volunteers do you have?"

"Honestly," Roseline said, "like with the number of kids, I've lost track."

The space was noisy, no doubt, but for a room full of young kids, the sound seemed muted, dulled by trauma and fatigue. Instead of bright, happy eyes, most of the children wore blank expressions, the same post-traumatic zombified look she had noticed in so many adults wandering around the ruins of what was once their city.

Lovelie began to squeeze Angie's hand harder, which meant it was time. Angie had to just do this. She knelt to Lovelie's eyeline. "So, sweetie." She had never been able to create a "soothing voice" even before she was thrust into a life-or-death situation. "Would you like to stay here for a bit? The people here can take care of you and your friends until you all find your parents, and you can finally go back home!"

Lovelie said nothing, just continued staring into Angie's eyes with an expression that was somehow evocative of both childhood innocence and deep, age-old wisdom. Angie bit her lip, feeling tears suddenly threaten to well up. "I know it's scary, love," she said, swallowing them back. "But it's not safe out there for little kids right now. These people can take care of you. I promise."

Lovelie dropped her head to the floor and gave a small, sad nod.

"But," Angie said quickly, squeezing Lovelie's hand, and the young girl looked up again. "I promised Matant Wozie here that I would stay around a bit, just to help. So, I'll be here for you for the rest of today."

"Just today?" A wobble tinged Lovelie's voice with sadness. Or fear. Angie realized that through it all, having Lovelie at her side had given her a source of strength, of purpose. Might she still draw comfort and guidance from her, after leaving her at this place? The young girl had already gone on a full odyssey through hell and back— almost buried alive alongside her classmates and teacher.

"More than today," Angie said without thinking about what she was saying. "I'll be here tomorrow too."

"And after that?" Lovelie asked.

"Well, we'll see." Angie had some figuring out to do before she could commit to anything further. "But I'll be around for a while. We'll get you back to your family soon, and I'll be here to watch over you."

Lovelie's expression didn't change, but Angie saw something flicker in her eyes. "Promise?"

Angie gave a smile that, for once, wasn't forced. "Promise," she said. She squeezed Lovelie's hand and held it for a few seconds until the smile seemed to transfer between them and come out on the little girl's face as well.

19

Tess had just hung up with the NHS line when Frank's heavy footsteps thudded up the stairs and into the flat. She was thankful to still be hidden away in her bedroom, so she didn't have to endure his arrival, at least not yet. He was well into his drink, she could tell from the uneven, pounding way he walked, his feet no longer fully under his control. The clink of glass bottles—liquor, by the sound—accompanied his loud voice.

"Did you two just stay here the whole time I was gone?" Frank said from the parlor. Tess had heard Dawn come downstairs not long after Frank left, and she and Elizabeth had been chatting quietly for the past hour.

Tess rolled back on her bed and clutched her knees to her chest. She might as well eavesdrop on the conversation for a few minutes before going out to join it.

"We were just talking," Elizabeth said in a voice that was softer and much more collected than Frank's, though still clear enough through the closed door.

"About what?" Frank asked. His slightly slurred tone showed he was trying—and failing—to conceal his inebriation.

"Nothing important," Elizabeth said. "I was just talking to my hand."

Tess tilted her head, unsure if she'd heard right.

"You were doing what now?" Frank asked, and his confusion, rightly, wasn't just from the alcohol.

"I was talking to my hand," Elizabeth said. "This mole in particular. Dawn has a very interesting theory about life after death. She thinks . . . well, Dawn, why don't you explain it?"

Tess had to strain to pick up Dawn's meek voice as it seeped like a thin vapor under the door. "I believe that when we die, we don't need to go to heaven because we're already part of heaven. It's like our life is a splash in the ocean, and for a second, we stand out as a wave that rises above and out of it, at least a little way, but eventually we fall back into the ocean and become part of it again."

"Yeah, yeah, yeah," Frank slurred. "You've told me all that hippie shit before. But what's that got to do with her hand?"

There was a pause, and Tess could picture Dawn wilting under Frank's imperiousness, which was even more threatening when he was drunk.

"I mean," Dawn continued, even quieter. "I was just using our cells as an example. Like, your body has between ten and a hundred trillion cells, and thousands of those die every day. But *you* don't die. You still exist. So sure, individuals might die, but there are higher levels of consciousness that continue, that don't die. These consciousnesses don't try to talk to us, in the same way that we don't talk directly to the cells in our body."

"And I proceeded to try and talk to the cells in my hand," Elizabeth chimed in, "to try and get the pigments on my age spots to shape up and look young again."

Tess gazed down at the numerous age spots on her own hands. They were accompanied by wrinkles and visible veins that twisted just under the surface of her loose, discolored flesh. She didn't really mind, though. Aging certainly beat the alternative.

Frank's drunken laugh boomed through the wall. "Well, you can talk to my hand then," he mocked. "Talk to the hand, sis. Tell it who's gonna be the next to go."

"My age spot," Elizabeth said matter-of-factly.

"Your what?"

"My age spot. It's had a long, productive life and now it's moving on into the ocean of life."

Tess was stunned by what she heard next: singing. Not Dawn's lovely mezzo soprano, but Frank's deep, off-key attempt at playing off the opening theme of *The Lion King*. A friend had dragged her to the Lyceum Theatre when the play premiered in London, figuring it was the closest to Africa either of them would ever get. Tess had been enchanted by the costumes and surprised that a children's story could have such a dark antagonist.

"It's the ocean of life, and it moves us all . . . uh . . . choom ba boom ba, choom ba boom ba . . . In the ocean, the ocean of life."

"That's not how it goes, you drunken buffoon," Tess said to the wall. She pulled her weight out of bed, sighed, and pushed open her door.

"Oh, hey, Tess," Frank said, spinning her way with his whole body. He was still standing, for some reason. Tess would have expected him to have plopped into an armchair by then. "I thought I heard you. These walls are thin. Did you say something?"

"I said, that's not how the opening theme to *The Lion King* goes," Tess said.

"What the hell do you know about how it goes?" he demanded. "It's an American movie, written by one of the greatest Americans who ever lived: Walt Disney. Oh, sure, you guys had Shakespeare. Shakespeare, Shmakespeare, if you ask me. I saw part of one of his plays once, and it was the most boring thing I've ever had to almost sit through. But it takes America to create the really great art, the art that matters to the Everyday Joes of the world."

"That's fine, Frank," Tess said. She had stopped listening to his diatribe when he said "movie." Of course, Frank hadn't seen the stage production. She turned instead to her half-sisters, who had likewise drawn their eyes from their drunken brother. "I've talked to the hospital and explained the fact that we were not unanimous in our consensus that the Liverpool Care Pathway was the best option for Mum."

"I'm certainly not consensual," Frank slurred.

"And," Tess continued, ignoring him, "they told me we have the option of maintaining her on an intensive care regime."

"As in feeding her?" Frank asked.

Tess steeled herself. She could get through this conversation, just as she'd gotten through the one earlier. "As in full intensive care."

"Great. Let's do it," Frank said.

"Except," Tess continued, eager to see Frank's reaction to this one, "if we go that route, it is not covered by the NHS."

But it was Elizabeth who spoke up. "What does that mean, exactly?" she asked.

"It would be private care," Tess said. "Which would mean that none of the subsequent costs would be covered by the NHS—which means it wouldn't be covered by the British government. Mom would be responsible for the costs initially. But we'd need to co-sign for financial responsibility so after her estate was gone, we'd be responsible."

It had taken Frank even longer to process this in his drunken state than she'd expected. "Wait," he said, brows furrowing. "What do you mean we'd be responsible?"

"I think I was pretty clear, Frank."

"What exactly are we talking about here, in terms of likely costs?" Elizabeth asked, her boardroom tone taking over.

"Initially, twenty-five hundred to five thousand pounds per day," Tess said, cringing inwardly at the huge sums. "If she stabilizes, it should drop to about one thousand a day."

A heavy pause fell across her three half-siblings.

"Are you serious?" Dawn's voice was barely a whisper.

"It wouldn't be on us, at least initially," Tess continued. "Mom's got about a hundred and sixty thousand pounds in the bank. But after that's used up, we'd need to split the remaining costs."

"Wait a minute!" Frank cut in. "Where'd she get a hundred and sixty thousand dollars? I thought she was broke."

Before Tess could answer, Elizabeth corrected him. "One hundred sixty thousand pounds is closer to *two* hundred and sixty thousand dollars, Frank. That would be split to sixty-five thousand dollars for each of us when she dies—if we don't spend it on health care." She gave Frank a pointed look that Tess didn't follow, and it made her wonder what they'd talked about after she'd left the room earlier.

After a moment's pondering, she remembered Frank had asked a question. "She saved it over forty years of working," she explained. "She's been trying to live off the interest so that she could pass it on to us when she died. That's why she always seemed broke. That was her big plan." She took a deep breath. "Still, even with all that money saved up, with the daily cost being so exorbitant, it will only buy her, what, five or six months?"

"Wait, back up," Frank blurted, his eyes suddenly bright and alive in a way she hadn't seen them yet on this trip. "You said that she was going to leave that money to us?"

"Yes, as Elizabeth just said, each of us will stand to get around sixty-five thousand of your US dollars. As of now. But if we refuse the NICE protocol and continue Mum's care privately, that will get eaten up by the ongoing care costs quickly."

"No, no!" Frank moaned, as if the idea hurt him physically. "You can't just take away my money like that."

"Oh, for heaven's sake!" Tess threw up her hands. Frank was too much, he was just too, too much. "Not even an hour ago you were straight-up calling me and your sisters here murderers for wanting to provide Mum with the NHS's end-of-life care! And now that your inheritance—which you only learned about a minute ago—is being threatened, you're whining like a spoiled child! You are truly an impossible wanker, aren't you, Frank!"

Frank scowled. "Listen here, you . . . Wait, what's a 'wanker'?"

"I'll be damned if I'm going to have some half-relative call me a murderer over money! So what do you say, Frank, do you want the sixty-five thousand dollars, or do you want to use your share to keep Mum alive for two months?"

His face had turned an unhealthy shade of red, but there was no way he was angrier than she was. "Wait . . . I mean . . ." he spluttered. "You can't just . . . !"

What would Frank's god-awful American radio ponce say if he could see the arsehole like this, she wondered.

"Frank." Elizabeth rose from the sofa and took a few steps toward him with her hands raised, clearly aiming to disarm the situation. Dawn slunk even deeper into her chair, face turned toward the window, like she thought he would cease to exist if she stopped looking at him.

"You know what?" Frank shouted. "To hell with this! All of it! I'm done!"

He turned and stumbled out of the room, back down the stairs, and out into the cold night.

20

The blue Skype page lit up as Jim's call went through, and Marcus's face came into frame after a few seconds. He was clearly fresh off shift, still dressed in his combat fatigues with about half of his body armor on. His face was obscured with a layer of haphazard stubble, dust, dirt, and sweat that hadn't been washed yet.

"Hey, man," Marcus said. He sounded tired, even in Jim's shitty headphones. "How're things going on your end? What time is it even over there?"

"Oh, shit, I don't know." Jim hadn't looked at a clock since leaving the command trailer and heading to his quarters. It had to be late. "Past midnight or something. You lose track of time in these shitty trailers."

"Yeah, I can imagine," Marcus said. "Still, right about now I'd trade staying cooped up in a shitty little trailer for going on patrol through these mountains. The heat is insane." He scrubbed a hand over his face, wiping away some of the sweat and managing to smear a streak of dirt across his cheek. "How're you doin' stateside? You build on your kill count since we last spoke? You still beating that asshole, Bradley?"

"Oh, yeah." Jim had all but forgotten about the rivalry with Bradley. But if he'd lost his lead, the guys would have let him know, and how. "Yeah, still beating him. Numbers could be worse. Could be better too. We, uh, got a new target. Potential target. We're keeping our eyes on him, watching to see if they're planning anything at your end. Might be a strike in a day or two."

Marcus nodded appreciatively. "You see those assholes planning anything, you make sure to blow them to hell before we have to deal with them, okay? So, you free for Call of Duty later—"

"Do you have any chocolates?" Jim blurted. Huh. Not how he'd expected to break into that conversation.

"What?" Marcus blinked a few times, a look of pure confusion clouding his features.

Jim rubbed his eyes and tried to gather his racing thoughts. "Sorry, sorry, uh, Call of Duty, yeah, I might be free later, I'll let you know, we can look at our schedules. But . . . okay, so, I need your help with something. Do you have access to any chocolates? Like in your rations or something."

Marcus narrowed his eyes. "What the hell are you talking about, man? Chocolates?"

"Yeah, chocolates. I was wondering if you could do a favor for me." He paused. "But only if it's convenient."

Marcus scowled. "A favor?"

"Only if it's convenient," Jim repeated.

"Yeah, yeah," Marcus said, still confused. "I can do you a favor, no problem. But what's this about chocolate?"

He suddenly had a flashback to high school. He'd asked Marcus to bring him a box of chocolates from his part-time job at Walgreens, so he'd have something to give Brianna on Valentine's Day. This was before she started dating the point guard. Marcus gave him a Whitman chocolate sampler box, but he wouldn't take any money. ("Stole them," he said. "No big deal.") But then Jim never drummed up the courage to give them to her. The little heart-shaped box ended up in the trash, smashed with the heel of his Doc Martens.

"Well." Jim thought over how best to phrase his question. "At your base, do you guys get access to chocolates or any other kind of candy? Something sweet? Those boxes of different chocolates you can get on Valentine's Day or something?"

As Marcus tipped his head as though trying to figure out Jim's ultimate plan, Jim hoped he wasn't also flashing back to the Brianna McKay debacle. "Valentine's Day chocolates?" Marcus asked. "Like a romantic gesture?" No mention of high school, so Jim was in the clear, at least on that front. "I, uh, well, maybe? I don't know. We get care packages and stuff from stateside. Some guys here got girl-friends back home who send them shit like that sometimes. I can ask around, I guess."

Jim nodded, trying to hold back his excitement. "Yes, yes, that would be great, thanks."

"So," Marcus said, raising an eyebrow. "Is this some kind of Christmas present?"

Jim was flummoxed. What did Christmas . . . oh, that's right, it was late December. What day even was it?

"You know they don't celebrate Christmas here, right?" Marcus continued. "They're Muslim. Can I ask who this is for?"

Jim twisted his mouth. That was a question he needed to avoid answering. "No, it's not a Christmas gift. You know Khewa, right?"

"Khewa?" Marcus shrugged. "Yeah, of course I know it."

Jim nodded again. "You going on patrol there at any point?"

"We're on patrol there all the time," Marcus said. "Hell, we'll be going through tomorrow, I think."

"Great, great," Jim said. "If I send you coordinates, for a house in Khewa, and if you can get your hands on a box of chocolates—like I said, don't worry about any of this if it becomes too much of a pain in the ass—but if I send you these coordinates, and you're in that particular area of the city, could you, maybe, like, drop the choco-lates or whatever on the doorstep of the house?"

Marcus stared into his webcam with a dumbfounded face.

"Yeah," he said slowly, drawing out the vowels. "I guess I could do that. Wouldn't really be an issue."

Jim smiled. "Great! Great, thanks!"

"So are you going to explain what this is about?" Marcus asked. "You got, like, a girlfriend here I should know about?"

"No, no!" Jim said, a bit too quickly. "It's not like that. It's complicated. I just thought it would be a nice thing to do for someone."

Marcus waved his hands at the screen. "Man, sounds like you got a crush on someone over here."

"A crush?" Jim said. "No, how could I?" But that was a question he wasn't really interested in trying to answer for himself, let alone Marcus.

"Look, whatever, man," Marcus said in his familiar "no-bullshit" tone that told Jim he didn't really care enough to bother learning more. Good ol' Marcus. "I take it this is something personal, so fine. I can get some chocolates and drop them off at this house, for whoever this person is. Your business, not mine. Now, you got a name or something you want me to write on it? Like 'from Jim,' or like, address it to whoever this person is?"

"What?" Jim's mood suddenly dropped. He hadn't considered this part. Did he want to sign it or address it? What, "To Uzuri"? That wasn't even her name. And she would have no idea who "Jim" was if he signed his own. "Oh, no, no. No names or anything like that. Just drop it off on the doorstep; that will be good enough."

"I don't speak whatever language these people speak anyway," Marcus said. "We got a translator, but he'd be pissed if I wasted his time with this, so it's probably just as well."

"Yeah, yeah, it would take too long to explain anyway," Jim said. "But I really appreciate this, man. If you ever need anything . . ."

"Look," Marcus said, his tone mirroring the sudden seriousness of his expression. "You just keep blowing up those terrorist assholes over here before they screw with us, and I'll drop off chocolates for whoever you want."

Jim flashed a thumbs up to his camera. "Thanks, man!" he said. "I'll send you the coordinates."

Jim signed off Skype and emailed the numbers to Marcus immediately. As he awaited the reply, doubts flooded in. *You're not thinking this through enough*, a voice sounded in the back of his mind. He frowned, trying to brush it off.

"No," he said out loud, to no one. "It's not like that."

This wasn't like Brianna McKay all over again.

And Afghanistan didn't even have any point guards to steal her from him.

Marcus wrote back promptly. His team would be going through the city tomorrow—right by Uzuri's house, in fact. The timing would be perfect for her to find the chocolates when she stepped outside to go to school. Jim told himself that had to be a sign from God that he was doing the right thing.

Jim imagined Uzuri's face as she found the box on her doorstep. A dazzling smile would erupt; her green eyes would sparkle even more than usual. In Afghanistan, any kind of sweets—let alone chocolates—were worth their weight in gold. Hell, Uzuri might not have ever had chocolate before. Jim pictured her sitting on her windowsill later by moonlight, her book propped in one hand while the other delicately placed the candies one by one on her tongue; she'd lick her fingers after each one to devour every taste of chocolate.

Jim eventually fell asleep, dreaming of picking up Uzuri for the prom, flowers and chocolates in hand.

"Wilson!" Major Udall barked, storming into the command trailer halfway through Jim's shift. Jim's drone was trained on Uzuri's front door, and he was eagerly awaiting her coming outside to find his present. He'd already seen a truck pull up outside and a green blob that bore a close resemblance to Marcus sneak up to the door and leave a small package.

"Yes, sir," Jim coughed out. "What is it, sir?"

"Lieutenant, we got a situation. I just got off the line with command, they want you at the controls for this one."

"Sir?"

Udall placed both hands on the back of Jim's chair and leaned close, so his next words were practically shouted in Jim's ear. "Those Marines got themselves screwed again." Udall was always quick to belittle the other branches of the armed forces, and even quicker to defend his illustrious Air Force if a barb was thrown. "They were escorting a convoy of supply trucks, contractors and all that, down the Jalalabad Highway. But they just got themselves ambushed out by the Bazarak District, and now they're pinned down. They're requesting air support, so us Airdales are going to need to come to their rescue again and rain hell on those insurgents."

Not Marcus's unit, then. That was a relief. "Yes, sir," Jim said, and sprang into action. Within minutes, he had his drone camera focused on a group of Taliban insurgents who had positioned themselves in the high ground over the mountain pass. They were armed with AK-47s and old Soviet-era rocket launchers. Old, yes, but more than enough to get the job done, especially against the US Marines and contractor vehicles under fire on the highway below. By the time Jim's drone was within range, the Marines had taken defensive positions and were shooting bursts of machine gun fire in the general direction of the insurgents.

"Target acquired," Jim said into his microphone. The rest of his unit had gathered around his station, as usual, watching the drama unfold as one would watch a football game.

"Shit," Cooper said. "How many are there? I count at least a half dozen."

"More than that," Jason said. "Gotta be like nine. At least."

"Shit," Cooper said. "If old Jimbo here wasn't already at the top of the kill count, this'd rocket him up there for sure. Lucky bastard."

Holy shit, had they always been this annoying? Or was he just noticing it now?

"Target acquired," Jim repeated into his mic. "Awaiting confirmation."

"Confirmed," the voice at the other end of his line said. "Strike authorized.

"Pilot copies." Jim gripped his joystick as he had on countless other occasions. But here, now, his focus was off. He found himself repeatedly flipping his eyes down to the clock on his console. Uzuri would be leaving for school any minute now. He needed to get this strike over and done with ASAP.

"Pilot copies," he repeated through his mic. "Pilot confirms targets."

"Fire when ready," the command voice said in its robotic monotone.

"Pilot confirms," Jim said again, speaking out of reflex. "Firing rifle in three, two, one . . ."

He engaged the joystick and fired the missile. As he had dozens of times before, he watched the sudden disturbance in the air from the rocket launch and the surge of white smoke that appeared snake-like in the air, marking the path of the missile as it screamed toward its target. He tried to focus on the estimated impact data on his screen, but his eyes kept drifting back toward the clock. The image of Uzuri opening the package and finding her chocolates superimposed on his screen's image of the incoming missile strike.

"Lieutenant," Major Udall called out right next to his ear, snapping him back to attention. "Lieutenant! The time to impact, please?"

"Uh, yes, sir. Sorry, sir. Impact in three, two, one . . ." He sputtered the count, hitting "one" a half-second after the insurgents on the mountainside were transformed into a crater of smoke, debris, and atomized human remains.

The room around him burst into applause.

"Hell yes, lieutenant!" Major Udall cried. "Nice work. Never let those Marines tell you they do all the heavy lifting."

"Shit, man," Jason said. "That must have been double-digit targets. How many did you count for your tally?"

"Huh?" Jim was already fiddling with his coordinates to circle the drone back to Uzuri's house.

"The kill count," Jason said, staring at him with wide eyes. "I mean, Bradley's already buying you a case at the end of the year, but with all this, he's probably going to have to throw in a few shots as well."

"Nah, man," Cooper said. "He'll probably just offer to suck your dick."

"Shut the hell up!" Bradley snorted, then stormed back to his station while the other two laughed.

But Jim was hardly paying attention to them. "The tally?" he managed to say. "Oh, uh, didn't catch it."

"Didn't catch it?" Jason said. "What the hell's that supposed to mean?"

"I must have missed it. Just put me down for whatever. I trust you."

"Shit, man," Jason said. "What the hell happened to you? You goin' soft on us?"

"Hey," Cooper cut in. "Ol' Jimbo here's looking at a promotion, with all the towelheads he's been nuking for Uncle Sam. Soon he'll be leaving us dipshits behind for bigger and better things, so what the hell does he care for our stupid little kill list?"

Jim tuned out the rest of their conversation. He zipped his drone away from the isolated mountain highway back to Khewa, right to the entrance to Uzuri's house. He squinted his eyes and felt a sudden wave of excitement when he found the small package still sitting by the front door. "Hell yeah!" he muttered under his breath. He waited impatiently, his adrenaline surging, and a few minutes later, Uzuri popped out her door. Alone, thankfully. He hadn't even noticed that the car wasn't in the driveway anymore. Her dad must have left early for work, and Uzuri was walking the whole way to school.

Jim was awash with giddy anticipation, but Uzuri closed the door and started down the short walkway without ever looking down.

Jim held his breath. No, no, no, she couldn't miss it. The chocolates would melt if they were left outside all day. Miraculously, as if she heard his pleading—which was of course impossible—Uzuri stopped and came back to the house. She was reaching for the doorknob when she paused and glanced down. With her back turned to Jim's drone, he couldn't read her reaction. But she rose slightly and looked toward the street, then back at the package, before picking it up gingerly.

She weighed it in her hand for a few seconds, then turned the package over a few times and shook it next to her ear, before giving a brief shrug and disappearing back into her house. She returned a moment later clutching a book and headed back down the walkway.

Jim exhaled. True, he had been hoping Uzuri would open the package right there on her doorstep—in plain view of Jim's drone—and even start eating them as he watched. But that was too much to ask. She had gotten his gift, and that night she would enjoy a delicacy that was impossible to acquire in her own country. Jim wanted to smile and extend his hands in the air in a wave of triumph.

Only he didn't. He stopped, suspended on his seat, stuck between competing emotions that he couldn't really process. He'd watched Uzuri receive his gift. Her day would be brighter. But he'd also watched the flash of the explosion from his drone missile. The shock wave and black cloud of dust and debris. The bodies flying everywhere. The shell-shocked and bloodied survivors. The telling signs of a war zone. And how close all that was to Uzuri's house. Where later, he hoped, she would indulge in the gift an American Marine had dropped on her doorstep.

Jim tried to force these two images to coexist, to create one clear picture of both that made sense. He remembered all those times he had pumped his fist with excitement when his screen lit up with smoke and debris. He remembered laughing at the appearance of the white-hot shock wave rippling across the ground, and the tiny human figures fleeing, running in a way that seemed so funny from his screen in the safety of a trailer on the other side of the world.

Then he thought of Uzuri enjoying the chocolates. Simple and happy.

The two pictures were so close they almost touched. But then the shock wave appeared at the edges of the picture. The blast moved toward Uzuri's hand as she reached for a chocolate. The motion of the shock wave and the motion of her hand inched closer and closer together. The entire scene in Jim's mind began to tear at the seams in a strange kind of nightmare logic that he didn't understand. He suddenly felt nauseous.

21

Frank slowly pulled his head off the couch. It flared in waves of familiar pain while the room spun. He was somewhere between "still drunk" and "hungover." His mouth was dry, with a bitter, sick taste. He reached for the nearest bottle and took a swig of what tasted like Irish whiskey.

"So you're awake," a voice said. Frank was too tired and too worn out to jump. "And you're already drinking again. Very nice, Frank."

Frank painfully turned his head and found Tess standing in the doorway of the living room, a cup of hot tea in her hand sending a few strands of steam toward the ceiling. Behind her in the kitchen, Elizabeth stood at the counter, looking at something on her phone with her usual stern indifference. Even though both women were behaving exactly the same as always, for some reason he wasn't perturbed by them. Maybe it was the whiskey, but the sight of them filled his chest with warm fondness. He felt his cheeks softening into a smile.

"You should put down that bottle and go visit Mum today," Tess said. "You're going to need to face her before it's too late."

She wasn't wrong, and Frank was hit with a massive twinge of familial love that his big sister was looking out for him. "Tess, if something were to happen to me, say I was hit by a bus or something, I'd just want you to know that I think you're okay. I think you're a great sister."

Tess's eyebrows crinkled in surprise. "Thanks, Frank. I appreciate that."

"It's strange," he continued, after pushing himself into a sitting
position on the couch and wincing as the throb in his head stabilized.
"You're my sister, but I really don't feel like I know you at all."

Tess regarded him warily. "Half-sister," she corrected.

"Yeah." Frank started to nod, but his skull hammered in sync
with the motion so he quickly stopped. "Half-sister. But still, that's
significant. That's blood."

"Are you now in the state of drunkenness that begets sentimen-
tality?" Tess asked, a wry smile teasing up her lips as she crossed the
room and sank into an armchair.

Frank closed his eyes. "How do you know about that?"

"I run a pub, remember?"

"I never understood this whole 'blood is thicker than water'
thing," Elizabeth said, striding into the room and joining Frank on
the couch. "Are we meant to suffer through any number of insults
and behaviors if they come from people we're biologically related to? I mean, I can see where it might have made sense for those
1950s sitcoms—"

"You mean like *Ozzie and Harriet, Donna Reed, Leave it to Beaver*?"
Dawn appeared in the doorway from upstairs, sipping her own cup
of tea, and Frank once again found himself in the presence of all
three of his sisters. Instead of feeling aggravated, as he had almost
nonstop the past couple days, the warm sensation in his chest spread
into his limbs. Why couldn't it always be this way, the four of them
bantering casually, comfortably.

"Exactly," Elizabeth said. "I mean, old as we are, those were only
reruns, but in all those fifties shows you have a mother, a father, and
some kids growing up together in a nuclear family, going through
shared experiences, supporting each other. You've got a common experience bond, an underlying love. When there's a fight, it's a lover's

spat. But even there I don't think the common bond, the thick blood in the metaphor, came because of some genetic commonality. I mean just because Ward was boning June Cleaver—"

"But only fully clothed," Dawn interrupted, plopping into the other armchair, "sitting on opposite sides of the bed, each with one foot on the floor at all times."

"Sort of the 1950s version of yoga," Tess added.

"I somehow always thought that Twister was some 1950s group sex orgy in disguise," Frank said, almost giddy to share his wisdom with his sisters.

"I think Twister came out in the sixties," Dawn said.

Rather than feeling slighted by the correction, Frank just chuckled. "As a free love version of the 1950s bed-sex yoga."

"Okay, fine," Elizabeth said, and Frank preened at having made her grin. "But anyway, even accepting Wally and Beaver as evidence that Ward somehow managed to get it inserted, I don't think that's the source of their common bond, their love and support. I think it was the time spent growing up together, spending time with each other. Interacting with each other at meals."

"So," Dawn said, "without that time together, without those interactions?"

"There's nothing," Tess answered. "No bond, no support. If your parents split up, like Mum and my dad, that damages one major part of the equation. If the kids don't have the opportunity to interact with each other, like in our case where there was an ocean between us, that damages another major part of the equation. If lives have become so busy that we're seldom around, we don't eat together, that's one more piece missing."

"And," Elizabeth added, "if our limited time together is spent in front of a television, even during meals, that finishes the story. So in the end, even if blood was thicker than water back in 1955, it isn't today."

"But we *did* have time together," Frank said. "I mean, not you, Tess, but the three of us. We had a life like that. Like *Leave It to Beaver*, I mean."

"Yeah, right," Elizabeth burst out. "Dad's idea of a seven-course meal was a bucket of KFC and a six-pack."

Dawn made a sound that was somewhere between a snort and a chuckle. "But Elizabeth," she said with a bitter note of sarcasm, "he was a lite beer drinker. He started drinking beer when it got light."

Elizabeth and Dawn shared a smug laugh. A little of Frank's warmth dripped away as an urge for another swig of whiskey overwhelmed him.

"My word," Tess said with her strange British reserve. "What fun I missed out on not growing up with you three."

"Okay," Frank said, feeling like somebody had to come to Frank Sr.'s defense. "Maybe he didn't have a Harvard education like you, Liz, and he certainly didn't write poetry like you, Dawn, but he was a good man. We always had food on the table, and you two wouldn't have been able to do what you did without him."

Dawn looked down at the floor.

"Oh, bullshit, Frank," Elizabeth said. "He didn't pay for my college; I had to get a scholarship and take out loans. He wanted me to drop out of high school and take that job at the diner. Mom was the only one who supported me going away to school."

"And what about me, Frank?" Dawn said in a rare fit of defensiveness. "Ostracized and not allowed in the house from when I was twenty. Did you know he sent me a Christmas card the year before he died?" Frank had no idea what she was talking about. "You didn't? Well, he might not have remembered sending it, it looked like he was drunk when he wrote it. But I still recognized his handwriting on the envelope." Dawn scowled. "The outside of the card was this beautiful snow scene. Bethlehem, light streaming out from the stable, angels overhead. I mean, I'm ninety-nine percent sure it doesn't really snow over there but it was pretty, anyway. So I figure, maybe he's ready to accept me for who I am. I do a little internal debate. Can I forgive him? Can I be big enough to accept his apologies and forgive him for everything? I open the card, and inside there's this scrawl that says, 'You're going to hell.' That's it." She shook her head slowly side to side. "And I blame Mom for putting up with it."

Frank considered this for a moment, familial love suddenly replaced by loathing. But he followed Meter's approach and kept his tone neutral. "And what about me?"

"You?"

"Yeah, do you blame me too?"

Dawn drew her face into something like contemplation. "Why would I blame you? You were my older brother, of course. You took part in it. But most of the bullying was standard older brother shit, not really reaching the level of hate crimes. Part of me always saw you as a scared little boy, so terrified of Dad that you'd just go along with whatever terrible path he decided to take. So, no, I don't blame you."

Frank's temples thundered. "A scared little boy?!" he shouted. "I was the man of the house, after Dad! And you can be darn sure I'm a man now! I'm your older brother, not some scared little shit-pantsed kid! I'm—" He cut himself off as tears threatened to spill over from his own eyes. Damn whiskey.

None of them spoke for a few seconds. Finally, Frank, his voice under as much control as he could muster, tried a different tack. "He talked to the preacher once. You know, about 'it.'"

"About 'it'?" Dawn wrinkled her brow in confusion.

Frank shrugged. "You know, the whole lesbian thing."

"Shit," Dawn muttered. "About me, you mean? I'm not an 'it.'"

"Give him a break," Tess said, her mouth perched just above her teacup, almost mid-sip. "You know the kind of nonsense he listens to on those right-wing radio stations he's so fond of."

Frank wasn't sure if she'd backed up him or insulted him.

"All too well," Dawn said. "Keep in mind, he got that from our dad. And everything else. And Dad wasn't what you would call 'hesitant' about making his children listen to it. Especially after one of his daughters came out as gay."

"Yeah," Frank said, attempting to get the conversation back on track. "What I meant was, Dad talked to the preacher about you. About the whole lesbian thing. He asked the preacher if a queer, sorry, I mean lesbian, could go to heaven."

"Ha!" Bitterness choked Dawn's laugh. "Wrong question. He should have asked him if there really is a heaven."

"He should have asked the preacher about the cells in our hands," Elizabeth said, holding hers up and regarding the backs with a small frown.

"The preacher said no," Frank continued. "I mean, not exactly no. He first said that if someone was born homosexual—like, really born homosexual, instead of just choosing to be homosexual out of lust or a desire to hurt God or something like that. If they were born homosexual, then they couldn't help that, and God wouldn't punish them."

"Oh, he said that?" Where was meek Dawn finding this confidence and sarcasm? "Well, hallelujah." She turned to Elizabeth. "And to think I had problems with the church."

"But that's not all," Frank went on, eager to finish his point. "The preacher told Dad they needed to live a pure life. They could be born homosexual, but they couldn't act on it. Because that was something in their control. They needed to overcome their handicap, get married, raise a family, and with time God would grant them the grace to feel normal about it all."

"Oh, hell, Frank," Dawn said. Was that pity on her face? She was the one who needed pity, not him. "Do you really believe that crap?"

Frank did, he was pretty sure. But it was one thing to think it and rail about it in the abstract, and another to admit it directly to his queer sister's face. "Sort of," he managed. "I mean, Dad did. We did. Do. Kind of."

"Uh-huh," Dawn said, her voice flat. "Like I said, a scared little boy, believing all of this bullshit because he's scared of his mean, drunken, asshole father."

Frank was too stunned to respond. He'd never heard Dawn talk like this before, with such a strong voice, strong opinions.

"So," Elizabeth said. "Do you guys remember watching Shock Theater on TV?"

Dawn ignored her. "It's bullshit, Frank. I am not an 'it' and I am not a sin."

"I never said you were," Frank mumbled. "I was just telling you what the preacher said."

"It was that cheesy horror series on local public access TV," Elizabeth tried again.

Frank had vague recollections of what she was talking about and wanted to lean into her change of subject, but Dawn was looking directly at him.

"Who gives a shit what the preacher said?" she barked. Frank could only ever recall her using such a hostile tone when she was playing with her dolls in the back corner of her room, pretending her stuffed wolf was a big bad monster coming to threaten the rest of her toys.

"I just wanted you to try and understand where Dad was coming from a bit more," Frank said, more to the floor than to his sister. "So you wouldn't be too mad at him."

"You're still his son through and through, aren't you?" Dawn said, and as Frank again found himself craving a drink, he knew it was true.

"Yes, this is all fine," Elizabeth said, her voice louder now. "I wasn't asking you all any questions about our childhood or anything. Just go back to ignoring me."

Tess, who was quietly watching the sibling drama unfold between Frank and Dawn, brought her teacup to her lips again and then gave a warm but deliberate smile to Elizabeth. "I'm afraid I don't have any frame of reference for this, er, Shock Theater," she said. "Not having grown up in Iowa, of course. But I'm sure we had things like it here on the BBC."

"Shock Theater?" Dawn asked, evidently ready to move on to the new topic. Frank was ready too.

"Yes," Elizabeth said, nodding. "It was a kind of horror variety theater thing on the Des Moines affiliate of PBS"—she turned to Tess then—"that's our Public Broadcasting System, like the BBC, but with much less funding. They used to show all kinds of cheesy old horror movies. I mean, we didn't have a lot of channels back then. But we loved to watch it when we were kids."

"Oh, yes, I remember that." Dawn's tone had fallen into a soft and dreamy whisper. She looked out the nearby window. "I was always a little scared of the movies. But I didn't want you all to think I was a chicken, so I'd end up watching them with you anyway. I kept my eyes closed for most of them."

"I loved the way we'd get our blankets all set up," Elizabeth said. "And then lay out our candy in a row, then sit there in our pajamas and wait for the skull."

Frank had forgotten about the skull, but a wash of memories flooded in with the reminder. "And that host, what was his name?" he asked.

"The Mad Man of Des Moines." Elizabeth gave a mock evil laugh.

"The Mad Man of Des Moines," Frank echoed. "He always creeped me out, but in a fun way."

"I remember watching that *Dracula* movie," Dawn said. "And afterward asking you guys if there really were vampires."

Frank laughed. "And we told you, 'Yes, of course.'"

"I mean, everybody knows they really exist, Dawny," Elizabeth said.

"And for the next six months, the only way I could sleep was to wrap my baby blanket around my throat to protect me from bites." Dawn grimaced, but Frank couldn't see why.

"I still believe in vampires." He offered Dawn a meek smile. "And ghosts."

"Yeah, right," Elizabeth said, at the same time Dawn asked, "Why?"

"Because the world is a more interesting place if they exist," Frank said.

Elizabeth rose from the couch and went to the kitchen to pour herself another cup of tea. "But what you want to believe has nothing to do with whether or not they exist in reality," she said as she came back.

"It has everything to do with whether or not they exist in reality," Frank insisted. "It *is* reality. It's the only reality that matters. If you believe that vampires exist, then they do exist for you. I mean, you of all people were just talking to the spots on your hand for some reason."

"Oh, so you agree with me now," Dawn teased, but Elizabeth shook her head at Frank and continued.

"But if you carry reality around with you, then reality disappears when you die. What's the use of that?"

Frank nodded, pleased she was finally tracking his logic. "That's exactly right. All those problems you worry about, those webs of stupidity that you've surrounded yourself with, they disappear when you disappear."

"Given all that's going on with Mom," Dawn said, "and all of us being together at last, I've been remembering a bunch of things, from years ago." She planted her gaze first on Frank, then on Elizabeth. "Do you guys remember the time Frank saved our lives?"

Frank felt his brow tilt upward, his face apparently as surprised by these words as he was. "Saved your life? When was this?"

"Well, you weren't there, of course, Tess," Dawn continued, and their half-sister tipped her head in agreement. "But it was back when we were kids in Iowa. After Mom married Frank Senior, she moved to Clayton and had us. God only knows why. I guess she was on the rebound, shifting from things foreign and exciting to things American and stable. She was punishing herself, I can see that now."

At this, Tess's eyebrows rose, but it looked like disagreement more than surprise. Dawn's own eyes widened and she quickly exclaimed, "Oh, I don't mean I can see why she'd want to punish herself. I didn't mean anything like that." She rolled her shoulders a couple times, working out a kink on the right side. "This may seem weird to you Tess, living in a big city like London, but for us, Clayton was always something of a prison."

Elizabeth looked at the floor, nodding. "A prison without bars or walls," she added.

Frank rubbed his head and glared at his sisters. He couldn't have them talking shit about his hometown. "It's a great place! Not fancy, like San Francisco or New York or London, but for good, hard-working Americans—"

"Yes, Frank, we get it," Dawn interrupted, but the excitement in her voice showed she wasn't mad. "Can I finish the story? It's about you being our savior after all, I'm sure you'll want to hear it. Now, if I recall correctly, it was your idea to go see the reservoir. You were the one who was bored."

Frank remembered it a little differently. "It was Liz's idea too!"

Elizabeth rolled her eyes and turned to Dawn. "I vaguely remember what you're talking about."

"Well, this reservoir was the only 'interesting' thing in Clayton when we were growing up," Dawn said. "One day, I think this was in the fall—"

"It was," Frank said, picturing the fiery colors of the forest in autumn.

"Yes, well, one day Frank and Liz and I took a hike to the reservoir. We were technically forbidden from going up there, but, like I said, there wasn't much to do in Clayton. I was still a little kid, eight or nine. Frank and Liz wanted to go by themselves, but I insisted they take me, too, and I guess I was annoying enough that they eventually let me come along."

Frank chuckled. "Good lord, you were so annoying whenever you wanted something. And it must have helped to know that Mom and Dad would never punish you for anything, since you were their 'baby.'"

A scowl darkened Dawn's features. "Yeah, let me tell you about coming out to them, and we can reassess that. But, to get back to my story, the three of us were hiking up this path to the reservoir, the trees all glorious in their fall colors, the leaves crunching under our feet. Like the way I picture the forest when I read that poem, 'The Road Not Taken.' Anyway, we get to the top and the reservoir's just this little concrete wall waist-high and about ten feet across. And water on the inside. Frank said it was hundreds of miles deep and this was just the entrance to a huge underground cavern that was filled with water, like some kind of giant womb. But I was disappointed, it looked so small."

A sudden burst of laughter shook Frank. "I do remember that," he said. "I remember I was going to piss in it, because I wanted everyone in Clayton to have to drink my piss. But Liz wouldn't let me because she didn't want to drink my piss when she got home."

Elizabeth scoffed. "And you can all thank me for that."

"I don't actually remember that part, thankfully," Dawn continued, "but the reservoir's not really the important part of the story anyway. The real excitement happened on the way back. See, we decided to just cut down the other side of the mountain, skip the path altogether. The trees were tall and dense in the canopy, and there wasn't much underbrush at all. We started down and we got the idea to just sit back on our heels and slide right down that mountain. The leaves made everything real slippery like, and let me tell you, we were flying. Using our hands to steer, swerving between trees, whooping and hollering. It was pure joy. And there was Frank, out in the front, leading the way, when suddenly he grabs this little sapling and spins around and around. And he's yelling 'grab a tree, grab a tree!', but Liz and I don't really know what's going on, only Frank sounds scared, real scared. So Liz grabs a tree, but I can't find one. They're all too big for me to get my arms around. I'm still sliding down that mountain like a tire rolling down a hill. But as I go past Frank, he grabs me by the shirt and pulls me up short. I still don't know how he did it. See, the mountain on that side didn't go down to the valley. On that side, the mountain ended at the bluffs over-looking the Mississippi River. Another ten feet and we'd have gone sailing five hundred feet straight down to the water. The distance between the biggest thrill of my life and violent death was ten feet. The three of us just stood there, panting, on the edge of that huge cliff, looking at the suddenness of death, the beauty of death."

Oh, death. Frank heard Dawn's song in his mind, though a heavy silence had descended on the room.

"Well, then," Tess eventually said. "This reminiscence is all fun and good, of course. Certainly, much more pleasant than the ear-lier difficulties we were having. But we cannot pretend that there are no pressing matters that affect us. For example"—she turned to Frank—"why haven't you been to hospital yet? You flew all the way to London, and you haven't even seen Mum."

Here was the Tess Frank knew and didn't love. Playing the mar-tyr yet again. "Well," Frank said, "she's just lying there, right? She's not even aware. So what difference does it make?"

"It does make a difference," Tess said. "You should go see her."

"I don't want to see her," Frank said, hoping his matter-of-fact tone would quash the conversation.

"Why, Frank?" Tess pushed. "Why don't you want to see her?"

Any fondness Frank had felt for her earlier flew right out the window. "Because I don't know what to tell her, that's why!" he shouted, surprised at his own honesty. "Because I can't face her right now!"

Tess recoiled at his outburst, gave him a reproving frown, and then got up and crossed the room, kneeling by Dawn's armchair. Frank realized Dawn had drawn her legs to her chest, her arms wrapped firmly around them as she stared out the window at the snow.

"Are you okay, Dawn?" Tess asked.

A low huff escaped Dawn's lips. "Sure, I'm just fabulous." She was back to her little girl ways, her brief stint in adulthood apparently over. It figured it wouldn't last.

"I know this is hard for you," Tess said, reaching out to touch Dawn's forearm. "It's hard for all of us."

"You're right, you know," Dawn said, so softly Frank almost couldn't hear.

"About what?" Tess asked.

"I wasn't there for her. I was so wrapped up in me, and my life, that when she needed me, I wasn't there for her."

Tess sighed, rubbing her hand back and forth above Dawn's wrist. "We all do the best we can."

Dawn let out another huff. "You know, when you first enter this life, you're a helpless little baby. You're completely dependent on others for your survival. We were all like that, completely dependent on Mom for our very survival. And then, at the end of your life, you're like that again. Completely dependent on others. But your mom's not around this time. No one is."

"Mum didn't see it that way," Tess said. "She followed your career. She celebrated every time one of Frank's kids won some award. She didn't really understand what Elizabeth does for a living, but she knew it was important and she was proud of her too."

"I just want her to wake up long enough for me to thank her," Dawn said. "Long enough for me to say I'm sorry she was all alone. I mean, I know she had you, but I'm sorry I wasn't there too."

"Let's go see her," Tess said, standing up.

"But she's still in a coma." Dawn unfurled a little in the chair. "She won't hear my apology."

"The doctors say people in a coma can still hear what's going on around them," Tess said. "You could still talk to her, say goodbye, and she'd hear you."

"Do you think so?" Dawn asked.

"I'm sure of it," Tess said, offering her a hand. "Let's go right now."

Dawn smiled and rose from the chair, and Elizabeth followed suit. She turned to Frank. "Are you coming?"

Frank tried to picture himself getting up and following his sisters into the cold streets of London to the hospital where his mother lay dying. "You guys go," he said, unable to move. The fingers of his right hand started to twitch, and he shoved them under his thigh. "I'll call a cab or something and meet you there later."

"Are you sure?" Elizabeth asked, and a small part of Frank wanted her to insist he get up this instant, wanted her to drag him to his mom's bedside.

"I'm sure," he said. "I just need a little time. I need to sort through some things."

A frown crept across Elizabeth's face. She turned to Dawn and Tess. "You guys go ahead. I'll be right behind you."

Tess paused in putting on her coat, as if she sensed something bigger going on, but Dawn eagerly cried out, "Let's vamoose!" and swept Tess into the kitchen and out the door. The clunk of it shutting behind them felt like a door slamming in Frank's heart too.

Elizabeth stared at Frank, and he waited for her to say something, anything. Finally, she did. "I'm going to look for someplace I can get some food to go. Do you want to come? Or can I bring you back something?"

The thought of a meal caused Frank's abdomen to seize. "I'm not hungry." He was pretty sure he could devour a whole bottle of Tums but not any actual food. "My stomach's been bothering me. But you go. I'll see you at the hospital."

Elizabeth hesitated, then nodded once, grabbed her coat, and left. Frank leaned his head against the back of the couch, took a large breath, and let it out slowly.

Oh, death.

22

The buzz and commotion of the children in the makeshift orphanage had become a vague and pleasant background noise in Angie's ears. A few feet away, Lovelie sat in a shaded corner of the room, playing with an old set of letter blocks that was missing several pieces. The other six children Angie had brought were scattered throughout the space. Some ran around playing games with more energy than rules while others sat browsing through picture books or making do with whatever second- or third-hand toys they were able to find. Angie tried to keep an eye on them—to keep an eye on the entire room—but her gaze always returned to Lovelie.

"I can't thank you enough for all you've done to help us," Roseline said, coming up behind Angie with an infant in her arms, while trying to wrangle several younger children with her legs.

Angie smiled. "It hardly seems like I'm doing anything at all. I told you I was never great with kids."

"Oh, I don't know," Roseline said. "You have much more of a knack for this than you give yourself credit for. Even just having another set of adult eyes here is more than enough of a help."

Angie nodded, and her gaze drifted back to Lovelie. "I would really love to stay and help more. Really. But my parents . . ."

Roseline waved her one free hand. "Of course, don't worry about it. Like I said, given the circumstances, you've been far more helpful than we could ever hope for."

Lovelie was still playing with her half-missing letter blocks, as safe and comforted as could be. The thought of leaving her there sent a strange wave of something through Angie's stomach. Was that sadness? Grief? Pain?

"I mean . . ." Angie muttered. "I mean . . ." She shook her head. What was she doing? Dawn was the one who wanted kids, not her. Besides, these kids were much better off here than wandering around the ruined city with criminals and gangs and . . .

"Really, it's fine," Roseline said. "We have enough hands here for the time being. Go back to help your parents. Honestly, the best thing you could do to help us out is spread the word when you get back to America. Let those rich California types know about all the kids in need here if they feel like opening up their pocketbooks."

Angie forced a smile. "Thank you, again, for everything," she said. "I will try to be back, in a day or two, if I can make it. I'll try to send some money your way if I can find any to spare."

Angie and Roseline shared an awkward hug with the infant in Roseline's arms stuck between them. Roseline's attention turned to two older kids who had gotten into a fight, and Angie turned back to Lovelie.

On the floor, Lovelie looked like she had tried to spell out the Creole words for dog and cat. Angie briefly thought she may have also tried to spell out mom and dad, but her already-overburdened heart didn't let her consider this too long. She got down on one knee and brought her face as close as she could to Lovelie's eye level, offering her most kind and reassuring smile.

"Hey there," she said. Her voice, though still dry and raspy, had taken on what she hoped was a soft and maternal tone. "How you doing over here, love?"

Lovelie looked up. Her eyes full and innocent, the trauma of the past few days visible but not in control. "Okay," she squeaked.

Angie widened her smile as best she could. "Do you like it here?"

Lovelie looked down at her blocks and the dirty floorboards around her feet. "It's okay," she said.

"Do you like your new friends?" Angie attempted.

Lovelie paused for a second, then nodded slowly. "I like them."

"Good," Angie said. "That's good. Listen, I need to talk to you about something." She raised her hand and brought it gently to Lovelie's shoulder. "You remember Mama Celeste and my dad, right?"

Lovelie smiled. "Uh-huh. They're nice. Mame Celeste gave me some candy."

"Yes," Angie said. She wasn't quite sure how to proceed. "Well, they're old, as you remember. And they sometimes have a hard time taking care of themselves. Especially after the . . . after things got bad." Angie's heart began to seize in her chest as Lovelie's innocent eyes showed no sign of dawning realization. "I'm going to have to go back to their house, just to check up on them."

Lovelie's face was overtaken by a broad smile. "Okay!" she exclaimed. "Is Mama Celeste going to have more candy?"

Angie bit her lip and tried to stem a disruptive sob from threatening her voice. "Well, here's the thing, sweetie," she began. "I think it would be best if I went by myself."

Lovelie's smile deteriorated into confusion, and then into the early stages of blunt but not unexpected sadness. "I can't come with you?"

Angie shook her head. "I'm afraid it would be for the best if you stayed here, with all your new friends, and with Matant Wozie and all her helpers. It's not safe out there, just yet."

"I can protect you!" Lovelie said, the smile returning to her face.

"I'm sure you can, love," Angie said, forcing herself to meet Lovelie's eyes. "But, like I said, right now it's best for you to stay here. I just need to check up on my mom and dad myself, and I'm sure you have so much fun planned with your new friends here, I don't want you to have to worry about taking care of me as well!"

Lovelie pursed her lips together, but her eyes and breath remained steady. "Okay," she said. Her voice had skipped grief and gone straight to sad resignation. Angie wasn't sure if this was better or not. "Will you come back to visit me?"

Angie tapped her on the nose with her index finger, and Lovelie offered up a single giggle in response. "Absolutely," she said. "I'll be back sooner than you'll know."

"Promise?" Lovelie said.

"Promise," Angie said. "In fact, you'll probably be having so much fun here, you may not even recognize me when I get back!"

Lovelie giggled. "I'm not dumb!"

Angie leaned forward and drew Lovelie into her arms. The little girl leaned onto her shoulder, and Angie felt tears beginning to form at the periphery of her vision. "Like I said, love," she managed while stifling the emotion in her voice, "I'll be back soon."

Lovelie said nothing but gave Angie's shoulder an extra squeeze.

A moment later, Angie had made her way through the impossibly thick cluster of children to the entrance of the orphanage. She froze in the doorway. Despite her internal protests, she found herself turning her gaze back into the room. She looked at the children crammed inside, now numbering in the hundreds, all orphaned, few with any clear prospects for a safe or secure future beyond tomorrow. And there, still sitting in the corner, still bearing her sad stoicism, was Lovelie, looking down at her blocks and radiating all the innocence of the world when her own world seemed to have forgotten it.

This was for the best, Angie told herself. Lovelie was where she needed to be.

Angie managed to find just enough of the spark she needed to break from her frozen state and turn and walk outside. But no matter how many times she repeated that final line to herself, like a mantra—Lovelie was where she needed to be—Angie could not shake the deep, troubling uncertainty that burned deep in her thoughts. At the center of that uncertainty was the haunting image of Lovelie sitting by herself in the back corner of that overcrowded orphanage, alone and on her own.

Just like Angie was alone and on her own as she made her way through the destroyed streets of Port-au-Prince and the orphanage fell out of sight behind her.

23

Uzuri left her house in a tense rush, her back and shoulders tight. Her face wasn't buried in a book, and the slow, dreamy gait she usually walked with was nowhere to be seen. This was a girl on a mission. And not at all what Jim was expecting, given she must have opened the chocolates the night before. He'd been anticipating a contented, happy look on her face.

Jim zoomed the camera in closer, making small adjustments to the angle and focus so he could get a clear look at Uzuri's face. It was contorted in grief and fear. Her lips quivered and her brow was caught in a tortured furrow. Her quick pace meant Jim needed to constantly readjust his camera focus, and he only got a second or two of a clear image before he needed to adjust it again.

He followed her like this down a couple streets—he couldn't keep track—and at some point, he realized she was now speaking to someone off-screen. No, pleading, was more like it, calling out in what Jim imagined to be a sad voice after someone walking away from her. Her green eyes were stained with tears that he thought he could make out spilling down her cheeks in single strands.

Jim frowned and rubbed his own eyes, tired from the strain of trying to read Uzuri's face from his distance.

Why the hell was she upset? And who the hell was she yelling at?

Jim pulled the drone camera back to try and get a fuller picture of whatever drama was unfolding. Uzuri was walking down a sparsely populated city street, calling after a male figure, dressed in a standard Afghan boys' school uniform, a backpack perched over one shoulder.

"It's him!" Jim said with a sudden gasp.

"What's that?" Major Udall asked from across the trailer. But Jim ignored him.

Instead, he focused his attention on the boy who was storming away from Uzuri, the same boy she had been chatting with so happily only days ago. Now the boy was clearly pissed off, his back to Uzuri and his shoulders held stiff and high as if to build a wall between them. Jim zoomed in on his face and saw his mouth twisted into a scowl, an expression that grew even more bitter each time Uzuri called out to him.

As they neared an intersection, Uzuri broke into a run, coming up behind the boy and grabbing his sleeve. He finally turned to face her directly, yelling something Jim couldn't hear or hope to understand. But the disgust, anger, and betrayal were clear enough on the boy's face. He flung his finger in a violent, accusatory manner at Uzuri, while she continued to plead her case through her tears. Eventually, the boy made one final angry hand gesture toward the sky and stormed off in the direction of the boys' school.

Uzuri fell to her knees and buried her face in her hands, her shoulders shaking.

Jim suddenly felt like he was intruding. Without thinking, he pulled the camera away from Uzuri and settled it on an empty and boring section of the city. He leaned back, resting his head on the back of the chair, lifting his eyes to the ceiling, and letting the sense of dismay and foreboding cluster around his lungs with every breath he took.

What the hell was that all about? Jim twisted his mouth in thought. He had of course been a teenager himself, not all that long ago. His thoughts turned back to Brianna McKay and the point guard, and his lonely, angry nights of browsing her Facebook profile.

Had he just witnessed some kind of lover's spat? A stupid mis-understanding that the boy's young mind blew up into the worst possible betrayal? Jim tried to put himself in the mind of a teenage girl. He thought of Uzuri attaching way too much emotional signif-icance to something silly until she sagged into a ball and sobbed in the middle of the street.

Is that what teenage girls were like?

Is that what Uzuri was like?

He let out a deep sigh. For the first time, his complete powerless-ness in this situation became clear. Here was Uzuri, the girl whose beautiful green eyes and soft, dreamy face he had seen by moonlight, the same moon that was hanging over Nevada right at that moment. He felt the enormity of the distance between them, the thousands of miles of mountain and desert and ocean and more desert. How powerless his own hands and voice were to comfort her.

At least he'd been able to get her the chocolates . . .

His eyes shot open, and he bolted upright in his chair.

Shit! The chocolates!

Jim smacked his head for being so stupid. How could he not have foreseen it? Uzuri gets a strange package left on her doorstep, containing a box of artisanal chocolates. Even in Afghanistan, this must usually serve as a romantic gesture. And this boy, the one who must have thought that he and Uzuri were a "thing," suddenly hears about this—maybe she even called to thank him?—and becomes consumed with jealousy, left wondering who Uzuri is seeing on the side.

But who else could have gotten their hands on chocolates like that? Jim had assumed most Afghans couldn't just stroll down to the corner store and pick up a box. That's what was so special about his gift. In the whole of the country, Jim assumed that only American troops would be able to get their hands on chocolates of that quality . . .

"Shit!" Jim shouted before he could stop himself.

"Wilson?" Major Udall barked from his desk. "What's going on?"

"We, uh, may have a problem, sir." Jim fumbled with his words. The sinking realization was still falling through his chest, and his fight-or-flight panic had not untwisted his mouth yet.

"A problem?" Major Udall echoed. Around the room, all the other pilots started to look up. "What is it?"

"It's, uh, the target." Jim's heart rate had jumped to a surging pulse.

"The target?"

Jim nodded through his gulped breaths. "Yes, sir."

"Which one?"

"Pardon, sir?"

Udall stood up from his desk and began to make his way over. "Which target do we have a problem with?"

Jim tried to focus his eyes on his screen for any half-assed answer. The screen, of course, was focused on an empty section of the city.

"Uzur—I, mean, the university professor, sir." Jim's words mashed into each other. "The one whose house the potential terrorist went to after he escaped the drone strike."

Major Udall placed his hands on the back of Jim's seat and looked down at the lifeless city corner displayed on the screen. "Yeah? What's the problem exactly?"

Jim swallowed several times before responding. "They know!" he said, more forcefully than he intended. "I mean, uh, there's some concern that the targets—I mean the terrorist targets, the ones connected to the survivor—there's concern that they may know we've been monitoring the professor. And his daughter."

Udall scratched his head. "I see. And what's bringing you to that conclusion?"

Jim was so frazzled he nearly blurted out the entire story about the chocolates.

"She—I mean, the daughter of the professor . . . she has a friend, a boy . . . I mentioned him before, in my report. Anyway, I think he may be connected to the terrorists. And he was, uh, confronting her.

Earlier today. He was accusing her of something. And she, uh, she was, like, scared, you know?"

Though his tone was more informal than what a junior officer would normally use to address a superior officer, Major Udall didn't seem to notice.

"So, Wilson, what you're telling me is that you saw this girl, this daughter of the university professor, be accosted and potentially threatened by this boy who may be connected to the terrorists we're monitoring?"

Jim nodded a bit too quickly. "Yes, sir."

"And you, therefore, believe that the terrorists may know we are using the family as a source of intelligence and that they, therefore, may be planning on eliminating the family entirely?"

Jim nodded again. "Yes, sir." *We must save them!* he shouted internally. *Call whoever you need to call, get the Marines in there, and get Uzuri and her dad out before anything happens—*

But Major Udall just shrugged. "Well, let's hope that doesn't happen. At least before we get valuable intelligence on some of the higher-profile targets."

Jim choked on his own spit. "Uh, what, sir?"

Udall shot him a confused and nasty look. "The hell do you mean, 'uh, what?' We need that family to get good intelligence on the terrorists, so we can blow them up. You know, like we always do? But if they get eliminated, we can find another way in, like we always do."

"But, sir . . ." Jim couldn't finish the sentence. *But, sir, this is my fault.*

Major Udall waved his hand dismissively. "No buts, lieutenant. I know you like getting your kill hits. I know all about that stupid little death pool or whatever you guys run. But don't get emotionally attached to it. You'll have more than enough opportunities for strikes in the future, no matter what happens to our university professor here."

Jim's tongue flicked up and down the roof of his mouth, struggling to find something, anything, he could say that would shift the course of the conversation. But, of course, he found nothing.

"Yes, sir," Jim finally said, defeated. "I understand, sir."

The CO walked back to his desk. "If you see anything else suspicious, report it. But don't get an itchy trigger finger just yet. Now, the rest of you, get back to work."

And with that, he sat down and returned to whatever it was he had been doing before.

Shit. How the hell could Udall be so callous? How many innocent people had he ordered blown up? How many did he cry over, watching them get turned to ashes and dust? How many times did he cheer his crew on when they were deemed "legitimate targets" after the fact, just so he could add even more tabs to his own kill list?

Jim dropped his gaze to the floor. In his mind, he again pictured Uzuri's crumpled frame, curled up and sobbing on the sidewalk.

It wasn't until he'd been weaving the story for Udall that he realized the full impact of what he'd done. He had no idea how he hadn't seen it before. Why hadn't it occurred to him before he made the idiotic decision to get Marcus to drop the chocolates off at Uzuri's front door?

It wasn't just a jealous boyfriend he now had to contend with. Only American troops could get their hands on chocolates like those. Her family had connections to terrorists. Which meant the terrorists were watching, listening. They would know about the box of chocolates that only an American service member could get, left on her doorstep. Shit, they might have seen Marcus drop them off himself, in full uniform and all! Which would beg the obvious question: Why would US troops be giving her a gift? And there was only one answer.

24

A ngie heard the van before she saw it. The engine had a dinosaur-like diesel roar, and whatever was left of the muffler did nothing to dampen the noise.

She paused. She was only a few blocks away from her parents' house.

Was it a military vehicle? Ever since the earthquake, few cars or trucks had been driving the streets of Port-au-Prince. Angie assumed most had either been destroyed or damaged or were unable to navigate the almost-impassible streets with all the cracks and debris. The only moving vehicles Angie had seen recently were military vehicles and truck convoys from international aid organizations.

The prospect of aid brightened her hopes. But her relief was tempered by the low, guttural rumbling of the engine that was making its way toward her. Despite the chronic underfunding of the Haitian military and the haphazard fleet of vehicles picked up by the relief organizations, most of them were in good working condition. This vehicle sounded like it was running on fumes.

Sure enough, from the other side of a row of half-ruined houses, on a street adjacent to the one Angie was on, thick black smoke rose in a moving cloud, indicating an antique, souped-up engine burning its way down the road. As the vehicle approached, Angie noticed something else. The people around her were fleeing into the remains of their homes or whatever shelter they had available. Angie's mouth tightened and her pulse began to quicken.

Within a minute the offending vehicle came into view. At some point it may have been the dull, placid white of most forgettable, working-class vans that fade into the background on your average city street. But this van had been so strained by rust and dirt that it had taken on a weird brownish-yellow coloration. The side nearest to Angie was covered with graffiti, spouting Haitian obscenities and what she guessed were gang-related signs. A man leaned out menacingly, clutching interior support with one hand and gripping an assault rifle with the other. He was shirtless, and thick tattoos were etched up and down his muscular arms. He wore a bandana around his head, and his pants were faded light blue—prisoner uniform.

Angie jumped out of the street and ducked behind a tree just as the van raged near. It swerved across the median and revved its engine in a savage howl of defiance. Angie crouched behind the tree, watching the machine gun–wielding passenger as he scanned the surrounding cityscape with a violent glare.

She didn't recognize him individually, but there was no doubt he was part of Junior's gang.

As the van careened past, the back door swung on its rusty hinges and Angie saw what was inside the back compartment: a large group of young children, crammed tightly into the space with several more gun-toting gang members clustered around them as guards.

Just as the van reached the corner, one of the children turned his terrified, trauma-stricken eyes out the open door and looked directly at Angie. In that split second, she saw not only the fear, grief, and desperate tears that had built on the young boy's face, but also what she realized with immense horror was familiarity.

She knew the boy. He was one of the seven children she had just left at the orphanage.

Angie jumped up from her hiding place and raced back the way she had come, ignoring the fatigue in her legs, the dryness of her throat, and the pathetic emptiness of her hands against any kind of threat.

25

Tess stood just outside the hospital room, talking to the balding, middle-aged doctor du jour, this time joined by a fifty-ish hospital administrator with her hair in a tight bun and wearing a brown tweed suit that might have fit her twenty years ago. Both looked overworked, underappreciated, and frustrated. Inside the room, next to Mum's bed, Dawn was singing an old hymn in a soft and almost-whispered mezzo-soprano. Tess appreciated the way Dawn revised the original phrasing to personalize the song for Mum:

> To Canaan's land she's on her way,
> Where the soul never dies.
> Her darkest night will turn to day,
> Where the soul never dies.
> No sad farewells, no tear-dimmed eyes.
> Where all is peace, and the soul never dies.

"So," the doctor said in a flat monotone, unmoved by the song. He was holding a clipboard containing medical images that Tess had no means of deciphering. "When we analyze these brain scans, what we're primarily looking for is activity in a few main parts of the brain." He flipped a page on his clipboard and showed her two images. "This is the cerebral cortex. In a healthy brain, which you can see here, our fMRI machines can pick up distinct increases in blood flow. This denotes higher levels of consciousness. However, in your mother's scans, we are not seeing such activity. We sadly must maintain our initial diagnosis of permanent loss of all higher-level neurological functioning and hold to our conclusion that your mother's condition is moribund."

Dawn had stopped singing, and from the corner of her eye, Tess could see she was gently brushing their mother's hair.

"Yes, of course, I understand that—"

"Based on the confirmation of this diagnosis," the hospital administrator interrupted, and Tess tried to stop her with a "If I could just—" but the administrator droned right over her: "I'm afraid that we still must insist that resuming the NICE protocol for your mother's end-of-life care is the best course of action."

Tess grated her teeth but tried to keep her exterior expression as outwardly pleasant as possible.

"Yes, yes, of course," she said, unclenching her teeth. "I understand all of this. Really, I do. If it were up to only me, we would be resuming NICE right now. We never would have stopped. But, as I explained earlier, the situation has gotten more complicated. Mum had three other children from the States, all of whom are in town right now, and we are currently not in agreement as to how to proceed with her care."

"Yes, you've already explained this," the administrator said. "And I am sympathetic, of course. But unfortunately, we do not have inexhaustible time to dedicate to this process."

"I know, I know." Tess swallowed against the tension tightening her throat. "I do certainly appreciate the, er, patience and understanding you all have shown us. I am only asking for a little more time for the four of us to get on the same page."

The administrator sighed. "As I said, I do understand how difficult this is for all of you. But we have limited resources and cannot dedicate them to continuing your mother's care under normal NHS funding."

"I understand," Tess replied, her own patience and understanding wearing thin. "If we could just get a small extension, just a bit longer . . ."

The administrator looked down at her papers, flipping through several sheets of indecipherable data. "Well, I do believe we can extend you another day or two. If we do not have an ultimate decision from the next of kin very soon, though, I am afraid we will need to begin billing your mother's estate to cover continued care."

Tess nodded grimly. "Yes, this has already been explained to me. Thank you for your understanding, and . . ."

"Tess!" Dawn called from inside the room.

". . . and I will convey the urgency of the situation to my siblings, to ensure that—"

"Tess!" Dawn shouted more loudly.

Tess grimaced and let out a small grunt of annoyance. "What is it, Dawn?"

"Mom just opened her eyes!"

Tess looked back over at her half-sister. She was sitting on the far side of the bed, just in front of the window where the grey light of the winter's day streamed into the room. Next to her, Mum lay under a couple thin beige blankets, still and pale, emaciated, with tubes and wires streaming from her mouth and nose and off her fingers. Machines beeped and whirred, the chorus that had become omnipresent in the hospital room.

Tess walked over. "What's this now?"

"I just saw it!" Dawn exclaimed. "Mom just opened her eyes and looked around the room for a few seconds! She looked at me!"

Tess dropped her eyes again to Mum, who lay as still and unresponsive as ever. Her face was pale and expressionless, her muscles relaxed in a crude imitation of life. Her eyes had fallen back into a fallow state. Their sunken, unthinking pupils were behind drooping eyelids that Tess knew all too well only flickered out of reflex rather than life.

"Oh, Dawn," Tess said. "That happens from time to time. It doesn't mean anything, I'm afraid. It's just a neurological tic, nothing more."

"No, I saw it!" Dawn protested. "She opened her eyes and looked directly at me! She saw me!"

"Dawn, love." Tess's jaw was beginning to hurt from its constant clenching. "I've seen that, too, several times over the past week. I thought Mum was waking up the first time, as well. But I'm afraid it's just an involuntary reflex. A few random neural firings that are causing movement in the eye muscles, nothing more."

Dawn shook her head. "How can you be so cynical? I know what I saw, and I saw Mom in there!"

"Dawn, love, I'm sure the doctor here can explain this better than I can."

She glanced over at the doctor, who was tinkering with his clipboard of paperwork. "What's that?" he asked. "Oh, yes, let me show you some of these charts. As I was just explaining to your sister, I'm afraid that our brain scans do not show any higher-order neurological processing. Her stroke caused catastrophic damage to much of her brain, and she has no hope of regaining anything like consciousness."

The doctor displayed his numerous charts to Dawn, but she just shook her head. "But . . . but I saw her. I saw her open her eyes. She looked at me . . ." Dawn's lower lip quivered, and tears began to stream down the sides of her face.

The doctor froze with his mouth slightly agape, his eyes darting from his clipboard to Dawn and back again, as if embroiled in an internal debate over whether to dedicate his dwindling mental energy to expressing appropriate emotional support or maintaining his intellectual faculties for his next patient. He chose the latter. "Well, as I said, our scans do not show any such thing." He paused, then added, "I'm sorry."

A vacuum of awkward silence ensued for the next several seconds, broken only by Dawn's muffled sobs.

Tess decided to use the moment for leverage. She made her way to the other side of the bed, lightly placing her hands on Dawn's shoulders. "As you can see," she said, turning to the hospital administrator, "we are still dealing with some issues here. We don't have much of a consensus as to what to do about Mum's future care, and if we are to delve into her savings, we will need a joint agreement from all four of us."

The administrator nodded with genuine sympathy this time. "I do understand," she said. "Believe me. I can try and pull some strings and get you a few more days on NHS care. It is Christmas Eve, after all."

It was already December twenty-fourth? Tess was stunned. She'd completely lost track of time.

"But if we do not have a family consensus soon . . ." the administrator finished, and Tess forced a smile.

"Thank you," she said. "I'll convey the urgency to all my siblings."

The doctor and administrator both left, and Tess slowly removed her hands from Dawn's shoulders and brought them back to her sides. "I'm sorry this has been so stressful," she said. "For you, above all, given . . . you know."

"I know," Dawn said through sobs. "I'm sorry I made a scene. I guess it's just wishful thinking."

"Don't worry about it," Tess said. "At least you're here. Frank and Elizabeth haven't even bothered to visit Mum yet."

Dawn produced a tissue from her pocket and dried her eyes. "Why not?" she asked.

Tess shrugged. "You know them better than I do. I'm sure everyone handles stress differently."

"I don't know if they're 'handling' anything," Dawn said with sudden bitterness. "Elizabeth is burying herself in her work, as always. And Frank, well, gosh, where do I even begin with him?"

Tess had often asked herself that exact question. "They're family," she said. "We can't choose who our families are, but we can choose how we deal with them."

"Well," Dawn said. "I'd like to 'deal' with them by telling them that only those who have bothered to visit Mom in the hospital get to make decisions about what happens to her. Frank can go off and listen to his fascist radio all he wants, and Elizabeth can just claim another business expense. And at Christmas at that." She scoffed.

Tess was inclined to agree but knew that wouldn't resolve anything. "We're all doing the best we can." She patted Dawn's shoulder again and sat down on the chair next to her mother's bed. The machines continued to beep and whir, doing God knows what to keep Mum alive. A few nurses chatted outside the door as they passed down the hallway. Tess rested her head against the cold window, imagining the frost and chilly wind that still circled up and down the glass outside. She closed her eyes. A moment later, she heard Dawn resume the hymn from earlier:

To Canaan's land . . .

Lost in the soft melody of her half-sister's voice, Tess began to doze. Just as a waking dream was overtaking her, something startled her back awake. She turned her gaze to her mother, lying comatose in the grey light.

As she focused on her mother's face, there was a split second where Mum's eyes drew open. She looked directly at her eldest daughter with the same kind, gentle wisdom she had given just before the stroke. Her deep brown eyes twinkled, and she blinked once, twice. Then they closed again, and Tess was consumed with a feeling of peace. It lasted even as she realized the incessant beep of the heart-rate monitor had become a droning whine, and a nurse rushed into the room.

Mum was gone, hopefully dreaming of things far, far out of reach.

26

Jim grabbed another refill of shitty trailer coffee. It was his third so far, and he figured at least a couple more were on tap to get through his shift. He'd not slept well after the incident between Uzuri and the boy, kept awake by nerves and then restless in sleep with nightmares featuring hands covered in blood and melting chocolate. He'd wanted to rush his drone to Uzuri's house the moment his new shift started, but he'd had other coordinates to target first. He had a hard time concentrating, his thoughts circling back to Uzuri and the potential impact of what he'd done.

He'd finally had a chance to scope out her house around 3 a.m. Khewa time, and it was unsurprisingly dark. If Uzuri had told her father about the chocolates or he had learned through other means, or if either sensed that they might be in danger, Jim had no evidence from his camera.

He slumped his head onto his right hand. The clock read 03:32. He was unlikely to see any signs of life at Uzuri's house until at least 05:30. He might as well patrol the mountains for a while.

He grasped his joystick with a weary hand and pulled the drone's camera back from its focus on Uzuri's house and let the shot of the street corner fade away as both the resolution and his weary eyes drifted out of focus.

And that's when he saw it: a large, unmarked truck sliding in from the right of the screen. Jim froze, his hand gripping the joystick, unable to move. His eyes, though, already in motion, homed in on the truck. It streamed down the street, approaching Uzuri's house.

Keep going, just keep going. Please, Jesus, let it keep going.

But the truck slowed, pulling up onto the curb and parking right in front of Uzuri's front door.

Jim bit his tongue. The surge of panic that appeared in his chest seemed oddly muted, as if the horror at what he was seeing came with an additional note of inevitability. *See?* his mind told him. *This was always going to happen.*

Jim's hands, paralyzed by thousands of miles and his own uselessness, fell to the sides of his chair and dangled comically toward the floor. He watched as a group of three men jumped out of the truck. They wore ankle-length robes made of military camouflage. Their heads were wrapped in black turbans, their faces obscured by ski masks save for the beards that seeped down to their chests. Taliban. Shit. They filed out the side doors of the truck and crept up the walkway toward Uzuri's front door while the driver waited at the wheel.

One of the men pulled a crowbar from his robe and smashed the cheap wood of the front door right at the knob. He pushed his arm through the hole and undid the lock from the other side. The three men disappeared through the dark rectangle of the entrance.

The seconds ticked by. Jim, his mind paralyzed to the point of laughing at himself, drew his eyes across the trailer in search of help for Uzuri, knowing full well there was none he could give. The other pilots were looking at their own screens with various degrees of boredom. Major Udall sat at his desk, scrolling down his computer screen and making occasional notes on papers that were probably not important.

What's that? Jim heard the CO's voice say in his head. *The towelheads got our professor and his daughter? Oh, well. We'll have to find another way, I guess.*

Udall yawned a bit too loudly and scratched his crotch under his desk.

Jim shot his attention back to his screen. A full minute had passed, soon followed by another. Finally, the three men emerged from the house.

They were lugging something large, which Jim quickly realized was a person, dressed in only underwear and a white T-shirt, barefoot and looking like he had just been rudely woken up. His hands were bound behind his back, and a sack had been thrown over his head. The man struggled, but one of his abductors kicked him in his ribs while another hit his head, and he fell still.

Jim didn't need to see the man's face to know he was Uzuri's father.

Then Uzuri herself came running out of the house, just as the three men threw her father's limp body into the back of the truck. Uzuri's face was torn by panic and fear as she screamed at the men. Jim gripped the leather arms of his chair with sweating hands.

The man with the crowbar pulled it back out of his robe and went over to Uzuri.

"No!" Jim whispered.

But Uzuri, with more sense than Jim himself had, drew back, throwing her hands in front of her face. The man easily overpowered her, covering her mouth with one hand. The other men struck her father in the head once more for good measure and slammed the truck's back door, shutting him out of Jim's view. The man holding Uzuri's mouth seemed to whisper something to her, something threatening judging by the look of horror that came across her face. After a few seconds, Uzuri nodded sadly, and the man let her go, joining his comrades at the truck. Uzuri fell to her knees and cried as she watched the men drive away—her father lying in back—out of sight of both her eyes and Jim's watching camera.

Jim spent another minute stuck on Uzuri's crying form crumpled by her front door. Eventually, her sobs died down to occasional shudders in her shoulders. Only then did Jim realize he should have followed the truck.

In desperation, he zoomed out, losing focus as he did, and swung his camera randomly around the surrounding streets. But, of course, the truck was gone. And Jim was left with no option but to zoom the camera back on Uzuri.

I just wanted you to have some chocolates, he thought. *Just something nice in the middle of a war.*

The middle of a war . . .

If any of Uzuri's neighbors heard the commotion, they merely watched from their bedrooms and returned to their already-troubled sleep. No one came out to help her, to see if she was okay. She stayed like that, slumped over on her knees, crying tears that Jim could tell were silent, completely alone, with not even the bright light of the moon to help her or the useless, pathetic arms of the man who, though she didn't know it, watched her helplessly through an electric eye thousands of miles away.

You tried to do something nice and look what happened, dipshit, he chided himself. To drive this point home, he repeated "dipshit" over and over, squeezing his fingernails into his thighs so hard he had to be leaving marks. *You must be the stupidest asshole that ever lived.*

Prompted by absolutely nothing—or everything all at once— Jim began to laugh.

27

No children ran and played on the street outside the orphanage. In their place was a garrison of men wearing faded blue uniforms and armfuls of sinister, crude tattoos.

Angie had raced back as quickly as her legs could take her, ignoring the choking breathlessness in her lungs. As she tried to pull to a stop, she stumbled forward with the force of her momentum until her hands caught a rusted old car perched on the corner. She fell to her knees and gasped in the largest gulps of air she could, which still seemed oceans of oxygen less than what she needed. Her vision blurred, and dark spots of unconsciousness threatened her thoughts.

She forced her exhausted brain to conjure as clear a picture of Lovelie as it could. Focusing on that, she took a minute to catch her breath and give her burning legs and torso a much-needed, but insufficient, rest.

From her hiding spot, she took in the scene outside the orphanage. The dozen or so gang members who stood guard were armed with a variety of weapons. Some held rifles, handguns, and shotguns. Others gripped sharp machetes, some of which bore reddish-brown stains along their bleared steel. A few others held hammers, clubs, or other makeshift weapons that looked more-than-deadly enough for their purposes.

"Angie! Angie!" The whisper tapped against Angie's ears for a few seconds before she recognized it as her name. She blinked, then turned her head and noticed a hand waving at her surreptitiously through the leaves of some nearby brush. Staying low, she crawled across the broken pavement, doing her best to ignore the pain as the stones and shards of broken glass cut into her palms and kneecaps. "Angie! It's me!" The voice was female and familiar.

Angie pushed her way into the thicket, and a hand grabbed her shoulder and pulled her in. She stifled a yelp as the twigs tore into her shirt and the flesh underneath.

Roseline lay crouched among the shrubs, her face bloodied and bruised. Her clothes were torn, and part of her sleeve had been ripped off and tied in a tourniquet around her thigh.

"Wh-what's going on?" Angie sputtered.

"The orphanage," Roseline whisper-shouted. "They've taken the children!"

"The prisoners?"

"Prisoners?" Roseline asked. "Is that who they are? I assumed they were from some of the local gangs here, judging by their tattoos."

Angie's thoughts came pouring out of her dry mouth so quickly she erupted in a coughing fit before she could get any coherent words out. She tried to conjure some saliva to soothe her throat. After a couple difficult swallows she said, "They are. They escaped from the prison nearby. I came across them earlier today, and then a little while ago I saw a van—"

"Where?" Roseline's eyes flashed with urgency. "Did you see . . ." She didn't finish, but Angie could read her thoughts all the same.

"Yes. They had children with them. I don't know how many. In the back of the van. I recognized a boy I'd left with you, so I came running back."

Roseline nodded. "They stormed in, not long after you left. They had guns and machetes. I tried to fight some of them off, but . . . well, you can see how well that went."

"Oh, hell!" Angie choked. "I should have been here . . ."

Roseline shook her head. "There was nothing you could have done," she said. "It was better that you weren't here, otherwise, you'd probably be dead too."

"Dead!" Angie gasped.

But Roseline waved her silent. "We can't worry about the dead right now. We need to worry about the living. As far as I can tell, these men are planning to sell the children. To human traffickers. Corrupt adoption agencies. Some 'good-natured' American do-gooders who'd like to swoop in and 'save' poor Haitian children to satisfy their egos. Who knows?" She laughed ruefully. "The police and military are all but useless, even before the earthquake. And the international aid organizations are more concerned with their bottom lines than making things better here."

In Angie's mind, the single, sharp image returned and gave her purpose. "Lovelie," she managed to spit out.

"She's still in there," Roseline said. "As far as I know, at least. But I'll warn you. She might be particularly valuable to them. She's young, pretty, she'll look good in photos and the like. She'll fetch a high price."

"This is all my fault," Angie moaned.

Roseline gently put her hand on Angie's shoulder. "Hon, no, it's not your—"

"No!" Angie shouted, louder than she intended. "It's my fault! All of it! I never wanted to have to deal with that kid in the first place! I never wanted to be a mother! Then, I thought maybe . . . maybe . . . but . . ." She closed her eyes and dropped her head into her lap. "I should have listened to myself," she said, softly. "I tried to be something I wasn't, and I screwed everything up." She began to weep.

"Honey." Roseline rubbed comforting circles on Angie's back.

Angie gathered herself as best she could. "My girlfriend, Dawn, she was always the maternal one. She was the one who always wanted

to adopt some poor kid from another country. I never wanted that
for myself. And yet when all this shit goes down, I get stuck watching these kids." Angie began to cry again. "But Lovelie . . . I thought
I felt some kind of attachment to her. But I didn't understand her.
I thought she was like an old friend. Some wise soul I had a deeper
connection with. But she wasn't. She was just a scared, snot-nosed,
shit-pantsed kid who needed her real mom and dad, and who only
got some stupid childless lady who couldn't even keep her from getting kidnapped and sold by criminals. And now I'm supposed to
rescue her? Hell, she's probably better off with the criminals. At least
they'll keep her from getting kidnapped again."

"Angie," Roseline said gently. "Lovelie, well . . . she loves you!
When you left—before they showed up—she kept asking when you
were coming back. You clearly did something right."

"I was just going through the motions," Angie said through
her tears.

Roseline squeezed Angie's shoulder. "Hon, love *is* the motions.
Do you know how easy it is to do nothing? Do you know how easy
it is to just dump those kids on a street corner somewhere and go
about your day? How easy it would have been to just piss off and
leave the kids to their fate? But you didn't! You came back here."

"That doesn't mean anything!" Angie moaned. "What else was I
going to do?!"

Roseline offered a soft smile. "You could have treated her as
something worthless. You could have treated her as something without any value."

Angie felt herself snap. "Of course she has value! She's a kid! She's
a person! That doesn't mean anything!"

"Honey," Roseline said quietly. "In times like these, that means
everything in the world."

"No, I just . . ."

"That's why you went through the motions in the first place."

Angie wiped a glob of tears from her cheek and inhaled deeply against the surging sobs in her chest. "And that's supposed to mean I love her?"

"Honey, that's what mothers do every day. That's all love ever was."

Angie was consumed by the vast ocean of emotions surging through her, larger than even the Caribbean expanding around them in all directions, and stormier than hurricane season. She felt no overwhelming divine revelation. No flash of insight or magical thinking that threw everything into clarity. No sudden shift or evolution in her being. But she had faith. She had the single fact that, for all else, she had no option other than rescuing Lovelie and the rest of the kids.

She had nothing but motions to go through. But go through them she would. She had faith in that. Roseline was right. That's what love was.

"What do we do now?" she asked at last.

Roseline frowned and cast her gaze back across the street to the orphanage-turned-prison. "I don't know."

28

In his left hand, Frank swirled the pint bottle of whiskey that had been sitting on the floor by his side. Judging by the sound, it was almost empty. He didn't look up from the note he was writing to check. His back was propped against the couch so he could use the coffee table for a writing surface. His slumped body almost mirrored the dozens of crumpled wads of paper scattered across the floor around him with his half-formed drunken handwriting.

He didn't feel very drunk. Despite the mostly empty bottle of whiskey next to him, his mind felt clearer than usual. His hands were tremor-free. With effort, he guided his pen across the notepad and looked down at what he had written in a shaky but legible scrawl: To my wife and children,

The sentence trailed off into a few blots of ink where he had tried to scribble his dying pen back to life.

"My wife and children?" he said out loud. "Who the hell writes like that?"

He felt like he could shotgun a whole other bottle of whiskey and his mind would be as clear and focused as ever. Was this what it was like for everyone else when the moment finally comes? Unavoidable clarity, sharp focus on everything, even those small things that a less-addled mind might overlook? He glanced around the room. For some reason, his eyes caught on three stupid oval paintings of owls that Tess had hung in a diagonal pattern along the wall.

"Aren't owls supposed to be an omen for something?"

He crossed out the first line and tapped the pen a few times against the page, leaving small dots of ink in its wake.

"To Nancy, Sue, and . . . No, screw that," he said. "Shit, how the hell does anyone write these notes?"

He scribbled over these new words, watching the ink blur into a dark splotch before the trail of black gradually broke down into gray as the pen once again began to lose ink. He gave up and flung the pen across the room. It bounced off the wall and landed on the carpet with a muffled tap.

"You know what?" he said to himself. "Screw the note. I should just check myself into one of their hospitals and let them do it for me. I can explain everything to the NICE doctors, they'll hook me up to the tubes, and pretty soon . . . soon . . . soon . . ."

He pulled himself awkwardly into a standing position and walked a bit shakily over to the phone on an end table in the corner of the room. He pressed the receiver against his ear and dialed his home number, listening to the resultant fast beeps.

"Shit, still busy," he said, hanging up. He looked at the wall and its stupid owl paintings as if they would say something.

"How is the line busy every time I call? What are the odds?" Though after his conversation with Elizabeth, he had come to think he might not have the firmest grasp on odds after all. He stared at the dull white plastic of the receiver for a few seconds. Then he once again lifted it from its cradle and brought his finger toward the dial pad. He pressed zero.

"Operator," a British woman announced.

"Uh, yeah. So, I'm trying to place a call, but it's always busy and this is an emergency. Can you break in or something?" Frank said.

"I can see if the line is in service. What number are you trying to call?" the operator asked.

Frank gave the operator his phone number, first quickly, then more slowly.

"Where is that number located, sir?"

"Clayton, Iowa."

"That's in the United States, correct?" the operator asked.

"Yeah, right. Absolutely." What kind of moron didn't know Iowa?

"The number shows as in service and not busy. Are you dialing the international prefix and the country code for the United States?" the operator asked.

"Uh, prefix? Country code?"

"Yes, sir. Dial double zero, that's zero zero, to get an international line, then dial the country code for the United States, which is one. After that, dial the area code and phone number and you should be fine," the operator explained.

"Oh, thanks. Thank you, operator. I'll do that." Frank hung up.

A brief smirk. "USA number one, baby."

He hit zero zero on the dial pad, heard a different dial tone, pressed one with a flourish, then in a fit of inspiration dialed a different phone number.

If he doesn't pick up . . . Frank didn't want to consider whether he preferred an answer or not. At least it was ringing this time. He bit his lip.

Another ring.

His son's voice picked up clearer than should have been possible given the distance between them. "Hello?"

Frank coughed. "Hello, uh, hello, Jim? It's your dad."

"Oh." There was a moment of silence. "Oh, hi, Dad."

"How the heck ya doing?" Frank blurted. "I, uh, hope I caught you at a good time."

"Yeah, you're fine." Jim's voice sounded guarded but cordial. "It's around 11 a.m. here. My shift starts in about an hour. You're, uh— Mom told me you were going to England?"

Frank nodded, taking a second to realize Jim couldn't see him. "Yeah, England, I'm in London. It's okay. Cold. Cloudy all the time. It's been snowing." He had no idea what else to say. "The phones don't work right here. Well, it's working now, but they make you punch in a bunch of extra crap at the start." Stupid. Nobody cared about how the phones worked. He switched gears. "How are things on your end? Everything going okay there at the base? Where're you stationed again? Nevada?"

A loud exhale, then, "Yeah. Creech Air Force Base. I've been here a whole year."

"I gotta pay attention more," Frank said, feeling foolish for not knowing that. "Anyway, you following orders and all that? I hope they're not making you peel potatoes or scrub latrines with a tooth-brush or some shit like that. How are things going with, uh, shit, I can't even remember what you do there."

"Well, I'm a drone pilot, so I don't—"

Frank cut in too soon, trying to get ahead of the slur in his voice. "Yeah, yeah, I know, you've already explained it to me. Drones? Ha! I guess your old dad is a bit too far behind the times. My idea of war is still just putting a rifle in some grunt's hands and pointing them in the direction of the enemy." He heard himself laugh. "Yeah, well, I don't think I'll understand it, but I'm sure as hell glad that you and your comrades are out there doing what needs to be done. Tell your friends your dad thanks them for their service."

"How's Gran doing?" Jim asked.

"Yeah, your grandmother. I visited her the other day," he said, aware of his lie but unable to stop it. "She's not doing so well. They said it was a stroke. She's in a coma. Not waking up. Hooked up to tubes and stuff. Well, I'll spare you the details. We're deciding now what to do, me and your aunts are still discussing it. We'll come to a decision soon, you believe that." Frank knew he was rambling but couldn't stop himself. "Look," he went on, "don't you worry about Gran or any of this. Lord knows you have more than enough to worry about, defending our country and killing all those towelhead terrorists. I just, uh, I just wanted to call to check in, see how you were doing. Lord knows . . ." He swallowed. "Lord knows we don't talk enough, you and I."

Another pause, and this time when Jim responded there was a softness to his tone that hadn't been there before. "Yeah, yeah, that's for sure. Things are going pretty well on my end. I mean, my CO is an asshole, but what else is new?"

"You making friends?" In the silence that followed, Frank realized he had no idea why he even asked that. Jim wasn't in summer camp, dumbass.

"Um, yeah, I mean, I got some friends here at the base. And Marcus—you remember Marcus, he joined the Marines?—he's in Afghanistan, and I chat with him online from time to time."

"Uh-huh. You seeing anyone?" The question came out of nowhere and he instantly regretted it. They'd never talked about girls, even before.

"What's that?" Jim asked, clearly taken aback.

Frank doubled down. "I mean, you got a girlfriend or something?"

"Yes, but—" Jim stopped suddenly, and Frank heard a sharp intake of breath on the other end of the line. He rubbed his eyes and groped around in his pocket searching for any stray Tums that may have fallen out in there.

"What's her name?" he pushed.

"Uzuri."

Frank wasn't sure he'd heard properly. "Ooze . . . Oozerey? What kind of name is that?"

"Never mind," Jim spat abruptly. "It's not important. Forget I said that. I just, uh, I'm doing well, is all."

"Well," Frank continued. "Like I said, that's good to hear."

Neither spoke for several seconds. Frank's eyes drifted to the pile of abandoned notes crumpled up on the floor by the coffee table.

To my wife and children . . .

"But hey," he said, "I just called to see how you're doing. You take care of yourself, hear?"

"Yeah," Jim said. He sounded relieved that the conversation was ending. "I will."

"Yeah," Frank said. "I know you will. Okay, well, goodbye."

"Goodbye."

Frank rushed to put the receiver back in the cradle. He took several deep breaths, unsure how to feel about what he'd just done. Whether it changed anything.

He snatched up the whiskey and downed the rest in one big gulp. He considered searching for a new pen to resume his farewell note, but it was easier to just pick up the phone again. He dialed his home number. After three rings, his wife picked up with "Hello."

"Hi, Nancy?" The room suddenly wobbled around him, and he sank into the couch cushion for stability. He was dizzy and so tired, more tired than he had ever been in his life.

"No, Dad, it's Sue." Really? She sounded just like her mother. How had he not realized that before? "Merry Christmas. How's Gran? Are you coming home soon?"

Too many questions. She'd always been inquisitive that way. "Oh, hi, Sue. Sad to say, Gran's not doing great. Not sure how much longer I'll have to stay here. Is your mother around?"

Muffled voices in the background, and then his wife's voice: "Frank, I miss you!"

"Nancy, hi. Yeah, I miss you too. I'm sorry about calling so late at night, what with the time zones and everything."

"What do you mean, dear? It's afternoon."

Afternoon? Frank was thoroughly confused. "I must have got it backward."

"That's okay, dear. Merry Christmas!"

Was it already Christmas? The days were blurring together. "Oh, yeah. Merry Christmas to you too! I'm sorry I'm not there."

"You're right where you need to be. How's London? How's your mom?"

"London's good. I haven't really seen much of it. Mom's still in a coma. It doesn't look good."

"You're praying for her, aren't you, Frank? I've been praying for you all. How are your sisters? How's Tess?"

"Sure, we're praying too," Frank lied. Like he could get Dawn anywhere near a Bible. "Tess is fine. Dawn and Liz are fine, too, holding up okay. Not much else to report." He didn't want to talk about his mom or siblings. "So, how's Boo?"

Nancy chuckled. "He's been moping on the couch ever since you left. He clearly misses you like nobody's business."

"He misses me? Tell him I miss him too. Give him an extra rub behind his big old ears. Is he eating okay?"

"You want to ask him yourself?"

"Sure, hold the phone up to him." On the other end of the line, he heard the familiar whining bay of his old hound dog. "Hey, Boo! How's my boy? Mom treating you okay? Daddy loves you!"

A loud bark, and then Nancy must have brought the phone back to her own mouth because she said, "I better go, Frank, I've got our Christmas Eve pie in the oven."

"Oh, okay," he said. "Well, goodbye, then." But he wasn't quite ready for the call to end. "Hey, Nancy, if anything were to happen to me, I just want to be sure you know that I love you." No reply. "Nancy? Hello? Nancy, are you there?"

Nothing. She was gone.

"I guess she hung up." He followed suit, the phone like a hundred-pound weight he could finally set down. "Well, she knows." He looked around at the empty room. "I wish Mom was here. She'd know what to do."

As if in answer, the door buzzer rang, and Frank started. He looked around in a panic and scrambled to pick up his failed attempts at a suicide note. He stumbled over to the intercom on the wall and fumbled at the button with shaking fingers. "Hell—hello?"

"Frank, it's Liz," Elizabeth said. "Open the door."

"Just a minute, I'm coming." He grabbed the notes and stuffed them in the wastepaper basket, then made his way to the front door downstairs.

He opened it and Elizabeth strode in carrying a grease-stained bag of fish and chips and shaking a light layer of snow off her coat. "You can use the buzzer to let me in from upstairs, you know," she said. "Are Tess and Dawn back too?"

Frank stared at her blankly. "No. It's just me."

"Oh, were you on the phone then?" She started up the stairs and Frank followed reluctantly.

"You could hear me all the way outside?"

"You don't seem to notice how loud your voice is." She laughed. "But don't worry, I couldn't make out anything you were saying. Was that Nancy?"

"Yeah," Frank said. He felt no need to mention his first call.

"Did you tell her?"

Elizabeth's question threw him for a moment. Tell Nancy about calling Jim? Why would she ask about that? But then he realized she was talking about their earlier conversation about money. "No, I didn't tell her."

Elizabeth sighed. "You're going to need to tell her eventually."

"So, I'll tell her eventually."

Elizabeth eyed him dubiously. "I thought you were going to meet Tess and Dawn at the hospital."

"I was, but I had to take care of a few things here first."

"Yes, I see." Elizabeth picked up the empty whiskey bottle. "Frank, listen, we need to talk about Mom. Are you sure you want to put her into private care? It's so expensive. You know, I don't need my share of Mom's money." She paused, looked him right in the eyes. "You could have it. That'd be one hundred thirty thousand dollars you'd be inheriting. That's enough to pay off the debt and get you back on your feet."

But Frank barely heard her. He hadn't been thinking about their mom's life all afternoon, he'd been thinking about his own. "Maybe I'm wrong," he blurted out.

Elizabeth twisted her eyes at him. "What?"

"Just, maybe I'm wrong about all lives having value. Maybe some don't, you know?"

Elizabeth looked at him with a combination of pity and self-doubt. "Frank, if this is about your problems, we can figure something out. I could help you get into a treatment program. Maybe you could get your license back."

"You know about return on investment, Liz," Frank said. "That's what your life is all about, return on investment. You spend ten, twelve hours a day doing calculations of return on investment. Some investments have a positive return, they generate more good than they cost. Some investments kind of break even. And then there are the turkeys, the losers, the investments that suck you dry. The goal is to focus on the investments with a positive return on investment and to avoid the turkeys. Isn't that how it works?"

"Well, sure, that's what I do with companies," Elizabeth said. "But those rules don't apply to people. They don't apply to real, living human beings. They're abstractions, not stuff from the real world."

"But, Liz," Frank continued. "When you work on your spreadsheets and decide to close a factory because it doesn't have a positive return on investment, that *does* apply to real people. Hundreds, maybe thousands of them. Sometimes an entire town lives or dies based on that equation."

"It's different, Frank," Elizabeth said. She had lost the matter-of-fact determination she normally spoke with.

"No, no." Frank had to get through to her. "You think it's different because you don't have to deal with the results. But it's all the same. Lives are lives. They're either important or they're not. Financial equations, risk and return, profit and loss, they either apply or they don't apply. If they apply when you're old, if an old life is worth saving at any cost, then they should apply when you're young.

If they apply to a person, they should apply to a group of people. To a factory, a town, a company."

"This isn't about Mom, is it?" Elizabeth asked, and he found he couldn't look her in the eye anymore.

"It's about value," he said, softly. "It's about value, those who have it and those who don't. Mom had value, no question about that. But now, lying there in a coma, she doesn't. The doctors are right, it's better to just end it quickly and painlessly." He gathered his coat. "I'm going out."

"Where, Frank?" Elizabeth's voice was still steady, but also quiet and uncertain. "Where are you going? Are you going to visit Mom?"

Frank shook his head. "To a bar," he said. "That's who I am, Elizabeth. It's what I do. That's my contribution to the world."

29

The strange conversation Jim had had with his father still bothered him as he readied himself for his shift. His dad was drunk,
obviously. Nothing new there. But Jim thought he had picked
up . . . something else. Some deeper problem floating in the background somewhere. An issue a bit more pressing than his dad's love
of drinking or even his grandma's stroke. Why had he chosen to
reach out to Jim after all this time? And while his words hadn't exactly been complimentary, he hadn't put Jim down either. It had to
mean something, Jim just wasn't sure what.

"Wilson!" Major Udall's voice greeted him the moment he
stepped into the drone trailer. "Get over here."

Great. Just what he needed, going from talking to one difficult
man to another. At least there was never any mystery with what
Udall wanted, since he was always shouting it directly in your face.

Jim marched up to the CO's desk, where an unfamiliar but
equally cold face regarded him from Udall's computer screen.

"Lieutenant Wilson, this is Colonel McNair," Udall introduced,
and the man on the screen glared even harder, his fierce eagle eyes
seeming to penetrate straight through Jim. Jim wasn't sure which of
his superiors to look at, so he shifted back and forth between the two
men as Udall continued. "Colonel McNair has sent me the authorization details picked up by our intelligence officers. Based on all

the hard work and time you've put in with your reconnaissance, our officers have identified your professor and learned that his brother is Muhammad Nari Massoud. That name may not mean much to you, but based on our intelligence reports, Massoud is one of the highest-ranking Taliban leaders in the whole of Nangarhar Province. Maybe the highest. He will be attending a wedding today. Suffice to say, you take this bastard out, it'll be the most significant strike of your career."

Jim nodded, saying nothing. His eyes had grown tired from bouncing back and forth between Udall and the colonel, so he focused on a blank spot on the wall in between the two. Neither appeared to notice.

"Now, one additional point I want to make." The fact he was speaking in a much more formal tone than his usual string of profanities and insults wasn't lost on Jim. Every few seconds Udall glanced over at Colonel McNair, like he was trying to see if his performance was impressing his superior. Nothing about McNair's expression suggested it was. "We normally have protocols for visual confirmation of the target, as you are aware. However, given the higher profile and significance of this target, we have added additional layers of confirmation. Given how rare it is for such a high-profile target to be exposed in this manner, we want to take particular care that he does not escape alive. We have no idea if we'll ever get a chance like this again."

"Yes, sir," Jim said. "Confirmed, sir."

"Based on our most comprehensive intelligence profile of Massoud, we know he has a long, graying-white beard, down to his chest. I know, I know, what else is new. But we also have indications that he deals with chronic knee and joint issues, due to arthritis. As such, he walks with a cane. This cane is one of the more significant visual confirmations you will have. Based upon our reconnaissance photos, the design is distinctive." Major Udall produced a number of blown-up images of an Afghan man wearing the traditional robes and sporting the long beard common among the Taliban types. He held a wooden cane carved in intricate, twisting patterns that resembled calligraphy. "You're not to take the shot until you get visual confirmation of Massoud himself. Do you understand?"

Jim responded with his most obedient demeanor. "Yes, sir. I understand, sir."

"You know, son," Colonel McNair said, drawing Jim's attention. The colonel's cold stare had been replaced by a more analytical, thoughtful gaze, his eagle eyes still penetrating but in a way that no longer made Jim feel like prey. "I've seen your file. You've been one of the more effective pilots at this base thus far. Your neutralization rate is quite impressive. If you can successfully neutralize this target, I can tell you it will not go unnoticed higher up the chain of command. By myself or my superiors. It will be a significant feather in your service jacket." His voice carried a kind of machine-like efficiency through the computer's cheap speakers.

Jim nodded with as much seriousness as he could manage. "Yes, sir," he repeated. "I understand. Thank you, sir."

"Based on our intelligence reports," Major Udall continued, "the wedding should be starting in a few hours, at dawn Afghan time. You'll be getting visuals there soon enough."

"Good luck, son," Colonel McNair said through Udall's computer. Then the screen went blank.

Jim retreated to his station. Flipping the camera on, he saw that the drone was capturing a wide-angle shot of Khewa. In a now-familiar corner of the city, Jim could picture Uzuri sound asleep in bed or awake early, sitting on her balcony, hair and skin exposed to the air, writing in her gold-edged, leather-bound diary.

He couldn't believe he'd told his dad about her.

30

Frank hadn't watched snow fall—really watched it—since he was a kid. He had dim memories of gazing out his window at night, watching the flakes come down, wondering if they would get enough snow to cancel school. But those innocent memories also brought back the picture of his dad drunkenly barking at him to shovel the driveway if he was going to stay home all day.

He'd learned to hate snow, and as an adult, his only relationship with it was his angry grumbles at Nancy that he'd have to be hauling his truck through that shit when the useless governor couldn't even bother to plow the roads.

He stopped in the middle of the sidewalk—he'd left Tess's apartment on foot and was wandering her neighborhood in search of a bar that wasn't the Happy Hangman—and watched the snow as it fell in gentle, consistent spirals through the foggy air. Every few seconds he focused on a single flake as it twirled in the light cones coming off the streetlamps until it disappeared in the mass of all the others. Frank craned his neck until it hurt but didn't stop watching.

Man, those snowflakes sure loved twirling around in the air. So carefree. So *free*.

Sue used to twirl like that. Frank recalled that cheerleading practice Nancy dragged him to, where he saw his daughter, in her red and white cheerleading outfit, doing backflips off the raised hands of her fellow cheerleaders. She nailed the landing and gave him and

Nancy an enthusiastic wave when she spotted them in the bleachers. Her wide smile that day was the only real smile Frank remembered her giving her parents after she became a teenager.

Watching the London snow, Frank suddenly smiled back.

Then he remembered his eyes drifting from his daughter to the naked legs of her teammates underneath their short cheerleading skirts. He remembered turning away from his daughter's smiling face to check sports scores on his phone. He remembered wondering how long he had to stay there before he could head for the bar.

His smile dropped, but the snow continued spiraling around him all the same. A thin film of white had built up on the sidewalk and road around him. He glanced behind him. The few smudged and disordered footprints he had left were already getting filled in. In a few minutes, there'd be nothing left of them. No trace that he had ever been there.

He was alone. Utterly alone.

Everyone else was inside, with their families. It was Christmas Eve.

And then, without anything to prompt it:

Did I ever build a snowman with Jim when he was a kid?

He blinked a few times, trying to focus on his only son. Sitting somewhere in the Nevada desert, blasting some asswipe Arabs all the way to hell in a desert on the other side of the world. He remembered seeing Jim off to Air Force basic training two years ago. He remembered his curt "Well, good luck," while he grumbled in his head about why his son had to get the laziest job in the military, why he couldn't even put on some boots and go over to bumfuckistan himself, rifle in hand, to give those towelheads a taste of America in person.

The same attitude Frank had learned at an early age from his own father.

"I'll be sure to call when I get the chance," Jim had said as goodbye, cringing at the tremor in his father's handshake. They hadn't talked again until that call a few hours ago.

Frank walked another block, rounded a corner. This new street was decorated with gold and silver Christmas lights that hung from light poles and store windows. The thousands of points of light caught the twirling snowflakes and cast the entire street into a living, breathing display of stars and crystals dancing as part of something too big and imposing for him to comprehend. His gaze softened, lost its focus, as the lights blurred into one massive glow, its comforting warmth summoning him forward.

He stumbled, one step then two, and slumped against a stone wall for support. As he let his eyes close, for just a moment, an image of Jim popped into his head. Jim was just a kid, no more than seven or eight. His face was lit up in a bright smile that stretched to his eyes and showed the gap where his latest baby tooth had fallen out. He stood in the yard of their home in Iowa, stretched out in the snow, hands extended to the gentle snowfall that circled around him, next to the snowman he had built. It was tiny, two pitiful mounds of snow stacked no more than a foot high. A baby could have made it. It didn't even have a face or arms or a scarf.

Dad, I made a snowman, Jim had said as he pointed proudly at the clumps of snow next to him. *Do you like it?*

And then Frank heard his own voice, gruff from complaining to Nancy that the schools had closed for nothing more than an inch or two of snow, and now he was stuck with the kids all day. The voice that was slightly slurred from the Jack Daniel's he had slipped into his coffee.

The voice that said: "That's not a snowman, it's pathetic. Don't be a loser, son."

31

"Are you sure about this?" Roseline asked.

Angie gulped. "Unless you have a gun—or, really, a tank—this seems to be our only option."

Just fake it till you make it, she told herself. *Just go through the motions. You have no other choice. That's what love is.*

Angie and Roseline emerged from their hiding place among the shrubs and slowly crept toward the orphanage. The gang members who had been standing guard out front had abandoned their post. They were now sitting off near an alleyway, drinking what Angie assumed was stolen liquor, smoking pot, and engaging in some kind of makeshift dice game. One of them looked ridiculous with a Santa hat perched atop his head, though it reminded Angie of the season. She had no idea what day it was. Had Christmas already arrived?

Despite every rational part of her mind screaming at her to turn and run, Angie puffed up her chest, gathered what remained of her courage, and forced her feet one in front of the other until she found herself at the orphanage door. The soft, high-paced breathing she heard behind her told her that Roseline had followed.

The guards, dulled by drugs and boredom, only gave them a passing glance as they approached. Until a lanky, heavily tattooed man with greasy hair let his gaze linger on Angie, his eyes working up and down her figure.

"Hey there, sexy lady!" he said with a crude laugh. "You looking for something here? I got all that you need." The man grabbed his crotch while his comrades let out a wave of laughter. Angie swallowed the burst of fear that was clogging her throat.

Just go through the motions, she told herself again. *That's all the faith you need. That's all the love that Lovelie needs.*

She took a deep breath and met the man's gaze. "I want to see who's in charge here," she heard herself say. She was surprised by how official her voice sounded, more like a dissatisfied customer demanding to see a manager than a scared and unequipped woman staring down her potential murderers.

He laughed again, the boastful laugh of a man who was covering up insecurity with bravado. "'In charge.'" He snorted. "Who you want to talk to? The mayor? The police? I call up the president and get him on the line for you, huh, sexy?"

Angie folded her lips in what she hoped was an intimidating scowl. "I meant, the man who is in charge of your little group here."

The man sucked down a drag of his joint and stood up. Only then did Angie realize he was much taller than she had initially assumed. "What, am I not important enough for a sexy lady like yourself? You want the big meat?"

Angie glared directly into the man's eyes. "I have an offer for him."

"An offer?" he laughed. "What're you offering?"

"I said, I have an offer for your boss," she said. She was surprised at how steady and in control her voice sounded. "Not for underlings. Bring me to him, and we can talk business."

The man took a swig from his paper bag–wrapped bottle and sized her up with his eyes. "You want to see Junior?"

Just hearing the name spoken aloud made Angie's blood boil. "Yes, Junior."

"Wait, you know him?" The man eyed Angie suspiciously, his brow crinkled in thought. Then he erupted in cruel laughter. "Ah,

I remember! You're the one traded your kids for a gallon of Junior's finest water! Ha!"

Next to her, Angie felt Roseline's breath tighten. "What's this?" she asked, looking at Angie with a mixture of surprise and dismay.

"No, no," Angie said, "it wasn't like that. They kidnapped—"

"You do good business here," the man interrupted. "You got more kids to sell? Junior got more water for you. The best in all of Haiti, fresh from Iceland glaciers or some shit like that."

"No!" Angie barked. "I didn't sell any kids to Junior, and I'm not selling any now. I want to buy"—she couldn't believe she was saying she wanted to buy a child—"something from him. Just take me to him, so I can talk to him directly!"

The man took another drag of his joint and blew the smoke into Angie's face. Her eyes and throat burned, but she managed to avoid coughing. The man took a few steps toward her, brandishing his machete in a slow, phallic manner. Angie stood her ground.

"You know what I think, sexy lady?" He was close enough that she could smell the noxious stench of halitosis and whatever disgusting affair he had eaten for lunch wafting from his smoky breath. She held her breath and suppressed the urge to gag. "I think you got the hots for Little Frankie here. But you're too shy to come out and ask. But don't you worry, I'm easy to approach. I got everything you need right here, and I'll give it away for free."

Little Frankie dropped the hilt of his machete to his crotch and swung the blade forward in a not-so-subtle imitation while he thrust his hips and made kissing lips with his mouth. The rest of his crew responded in a fit of juvenile laughter. Angie fought the urge to flee.

"Yo! Frankie!" a voice called from inside the orphanage. It bore a strange combination of high-pitch shrillness and deep, booming command. A combination that Angie immediately recognized.

"What is it?" Little Frankie yelled back, temporarily abandoning his threats of sexual assault. Angie thought she heard traces of nervousness creep into his tone. Almost like a schoolyard bully who talks nothing but tough until his much bigger and much scarier father suddenly comes to deal with his shit.

"The hell you talking to?" Junior called out. "We got buyers coming by. We don't got time to deal with your shit!"

"Some lady." Little Frankie's machete dropped flaccidly to his side. Angie felt his power dissipate. "Says she wants to talk to you."

"Talk to me?"

"Says she wants to buy a kid or something."

Junior's pointed face appeared from the shadows of the orphanage and walked out into the hot daylight. "Someone wants to buy a kid?" he barked. "We got buyers lined up already, who the hell's coming off the street here?"

Little Frankie shrugged. "She said she wants to buy a kid. It's that lady from earlier."

"What lady from earlier?" Junior glared at Little Frankie, then turned his attention to Angie. "Who the hell are you?" His sneer showed no sign of recognition. "You want to waste Junior's time?"

"You don't remember me?" Angie tried to sneak a look around Junior into the inside of the orphanage to check for any sign of Lovelie, but his short frame was blocking the entrance.

"Remember you?" Junior spat on the curb, as if to show off how moist his own mouth was. "I can get any bitch I want, and you think I'm going to remember some dumb whore who walks off the streets? I'm busy now, and you better believe I can get better ass than you!"

"The water!" Angie shouted suddenly. "You gave me the water, earlier."

Junior paused, looking her up and down. "Water? I sell a lot of water. But . . ." He took a few steps closer and tightened his eyes as he stared into her, through her. Angie suddenly felt violated, but she stood her ground. "Yes, yes," he said, a gleam of familiarity lighting his features. He smirked. "I do remember. You gave me those five kids. All for a few gallons of water. Ha!" His laugh was reedy and acidic, and his men mimicked it. "We got buyers lined up already, paying good money. I guess I should be thanking you."

"No!" Angie said. "I didn't—"

"Oh, I see!" Junior snapped at her, his face souring. "You want a cut of my profits, huh? Well, screw off! You got your payment when you handed them over for just a gallon of water each—"

"How much?" Angie had no idea what price tag this cretin would put on a child's life.

"How much?" Junior repeated, as though it was the last question he expected.

"How much do you want for a kid? One kid."

Junior brought his tongue against his exposed teeth and made a snake-like hiss. "One kid? You want to buy *one* kid?"

"A little girl," Angie said. "Young, about six or seven. Her hair is tied in pigtails. She answers to Lovelie. I know she's in there. How much do you want for her?"

Junior's serpentine smirk morphed into a sinister grin.

"A little girl?" he said. "A Lovelie? Ha! There's no way you could match the kind of offers I'm getting for any of those kids, let alone a cute little girl. You know the kind of money rich Americans will pay for a cute little Haitian bitch like that? You're walking off the street. What, you think I'm gonna take my gallon of water back?"

Angie felt a tidal wave of despair threaten to surge in her heart, but she fought it back. "I asked you a question," she said with as much authority as she could manifest. "How much do you want for her?"

Junior made a sound that was like laughter, though his eyes remained cold and spiteful. "How much you got?"

"What?" Angie said.

"You got hearing problems, lady?" Junior took another step toward Angie. This time, Angie couldn't stop herself from taking a reflexive step away. "I said, how much you got?"

"I have an American bank account," she said, struggling to find a better answer. Nothing else in her thoughts seemed particularly helpful now. "I have American money. How much do you want?"

Junior tilted his head, like an apex predator playfully regarding its prey just before the kill. "You make me angry, making me repeat myself. But I'm a sucker for a pretty face, even if I've seen prettier. I'll ask you again, how much money you got?"

Angie's thoughts spun. "A-a few thousand. It's my savings. If I could find a bank—"

Junior's merciless laughter interrupted her. "A few thousand?" He sneered. "American or not, you gonna have to add a few zeros there to match the kind of offers I'm getting."

"Wait!" Angie was desperate. "I can mortgage my house, take out a loan. I have options."

But Junior was already turning back into the orphanage. "Man, this little girl mean so much to you? Tell you what, I'll do you a favor and try to sell her to someone nice. If the price is right, of course. No, you go off now and stop bothering me. But you find any more kids out there, you bring them back here. I got lots more gallons of water. Hell, I'll even make you a special deal. You bring me more kids, next time I'll give you *two* gallons of water each!"

His laughter carried on the hot, dry wind as he disappeared into the orphanage and shut the door behind him.

32

Somewhere in the back of his mind, Frank recalled hearing that it was legal to drink in public in London. Did Alex Meter mention that? *"The one good thing about jolly ol' England is they let you drink in public. But I still don't think that's worth being a subject of a 'queen,' right folks?"*

He'd decided to hit up a liquor store instead of a bar. He wasn't in the mood to deal with people. As he shot back another gulp of Jack Daniel's, his thoughts howled against the howl of the wind. *This is who I am. This is my contribution to the world. Pathetic.*

As he walked past a deserted corner, he heard a familiar Christmas carol playing from the open door of a storefront. His hands were trembling. He hadn't remembered to bring his gloves when he stormed out of Tess's apartment. But he knew his tremors didn't really have anything to do with the cold. He had a sinking feeling he was stuck with this condition for however long his life lasted.

However long, indeed.

Where the hell was Tess's place? The past few minutes he had stumbled up and down streets that twisted and turned less like city blocks and more like the corn mazes he used to get lost in as a kid. Just as well. Not like he was planning on going back there.

He took another swig of whiskey, relishing the burning as it traveled down his throat and into his insides. It didn't feel much different from the burning cold that was blasting his exposed skin, like he was coming undone and being pummeled inside and out.

He turned another corner and saw a bridge in front of him. With nowhere else to go, his dizzy legs pushed forward, leaving smeared footprints in the snow. That must be the . . . what the hell was the name of that river again? The Thang? The Tim? Stepping forward, he placed a naked hand on the cold metal running along the side of the pedestrian walkway. The bridge was decorated with a long chain of wreaths and imitation holly, as well as lights that reflected in a shimmering glow in the water flowing below him.

To my wife and children . . .

"I have a few things to say." He didn't realize he was speaking out loud until he saw his foggy breath puff out in front of his face. "I just wanted . . . all I ever wanted . . . uh . . ." His mind was numb. The chill of the bridge's metal railing blended with the chill of his skin and insides as if there were no difference between the cold metal and himself. His hands, at last, were still, the tremor chased away by his grip on the only tangible thing he could find.

"Ah, screw it." He took a final gulp of Jack and hurled the rest of the bottle into the river. It landed in a blunt splash and sank out of sight.

The water won't be much colder than the air, he thought. He leaned over the side of the railing, looking for his reflection, but only saw the dark, swirling water and the outline of the city lights against the gray night sky.

Frank paused, one final time.

"If anyone out there is listening . . ." He wasn't sure who he was even talking to. "I need help. Please."

33

Angie stayed slumped on her knees for what felt like an eternity after Junior and his men disappeared back into the orphanage. At some point—she didn't know when—Roseline knelt beside her. "So what are we going to do now?"

Angie looked up. "I don't know," she said flatly. "A mother is supposed to 'go through the motions,' like you said. But I'm at a loss for what 'motions' we've got left."

"I know it may sound stupid to your American ears, but in the worst of times, the best option is sometimes just to pray."

"Pray?" Angie said. "To whom? Or what?"

Roseline shrugged. "My mama would always say Jesus. I had some great aunties who followed the old Vodou practices—or at least tried to—and would sometimes make offerings to the lwa when times got tough. For me, it was all kind of the same. Jesus, Allah, Bondye. And whenever I prayed, I always felt like someone was listening. Out there in the universe."

Angie looked back up to the sky. Her eyes narrowed and burned in the glare of the sun that was beginning its descent toward the horizon. "I've never really prayed much. I had a difficult situation with some of the more traditional religions growing up. I never conformed to their notions of . . . sexual morality, if you catch my drift."

Roseline nodded without saying anything.

"But," Angie continued, "there have been times throughout my life, when things were going wrong or when I was feeling lost and alone. I would . . . not pray, exactly. What's the word I'm looking for? Talk? Ask? Beseech? I don't know. But I called out to something, out there, in the beyond. Asking for help. Or comfort. Or just, you know, someone to talk to so I didn't feel so alone."

"And was anyone listening?" Roseline's face was soft and open, and Angie thought if God was as nonjudgmental as Roseline, she would have been happy to pray all these years.

She sighed. "Who knows? But I'm still here, aren't I?"

"Yes," Roseline said. "You're still here. And so are the children."

Thin, lazy strands of clouds passed in front of the sun, and a faint moon had appeared in anticipation of evening.

"Please," Angie called out, and Roseline gripped her hand. "Please, Jesus, Allah, whoever's listening. Please help me save Lovelie."

The wind suddenly picked up, blowing warm and soft. It felt the same as always, yet also different. More alive, carrying a pulse of something deeper and more fundamental to the universe as it stirred in a gentle embrace around Angie. It blew across her skin, drying and cooling the sweat that had drenched her. It blew *through* her, pacifying her raging heart and washing comforting hands across her frantic, despairing thoughts.

Angie was on her feet. Not only on her feet, but moving, striding confidently toward the orphanage. She didn't remember getting up or starting to walk. She wasn't even aware of consciously placing one foot in front of the other. But that didn't matter. No thoughts streamed through her mind save for the single, determined prayer that she offered up: "Please, Lord, help me save Lovelie."

She pushed open the door and entered the orphanage with a strength of purpose surging through her muscles. It took a moment for her eyes to adjust to the low light. When they did, she saw a large group of children crammed together in one corner so tightly their shoulders crushed against each other. Angie couldn't count how many there were. Five dozen? Six dozen?

"Hey! Hey, what the hell!" a man's voice shouted. It wasn't Junior, though, so Angie ignored it. She scanned the room and found him standing to one side, rummaging through piles of money and guns on a folding table, several of his lieutenants gathered around him.

"Junior!" Angie demanded.

He whipped his head up and looked around, clearly thrown off his game. For once, he looked unsettled. "What? What the hell is going on?"

Junior's thugs quickly had Angie surrounded. But she felt no fear. Her heart rate stayed steady and calm, her breathing even. Her fingers didn't twitch. It was suddenly clear to her that Junior's threats were all an illusion, a waking dream, something she could blink out of existence as she rose from a cozy nap on a warm, sunny afternoon.

"Junior!" Her voice was no longer the parched, raspy voice of a terrified woman. It was booming and authoritative, echoing off the walls and ceiling. Junior cringed, his hands clenching the table.

"Lady!" he shouted. "You don't listen, do you! You don't got the money for your precious little girl, so you getting nothing! Now get the hell out of here before I forget my promise and have some of my boys here teach you a lesson in manners!"

Despite his posturing, Angie heard a shift in his voice. A warble? A slight choke? A hint of unease? That same uncertainty seemed to have sapped the resolve of the gang members clustered around her. They kept a distance, not sure what to do next.

"I told you; I want Lovelie. You don't want my money? You can just hand her over for free. But I'm not leaving here without her."

Junior glared at her malevolently, muttering curses. He whispered something to the man to his left, tapping his skinny fingers against the folding table in a staccato, nervous rhythm. The gang member nodded, then set off for the crowd of children. Junior came around the table and approached Angie. She felt no impulse to cower as she had earlier. She held her ground with power and authority. She even took a step forward to meet him.

Junior's thug returned, dragging Lovelie by one arm. The little girl was crying softly, and the sound tugged at Angie's heart. Junior, not breaking eye contact with Angie, grabbed Lovelie's shoulder and pulled her close in a sharp motion that elicited a yelp from Lovelie.

"So, water lady," Junior said. "This the girl you looking for? This your Lovelie?"

"Hand her over."

Junior scowled. "You hypocrite. I remember when five of these kids were worth less to you than a gallon of water each. Now you looking to get yourself killed for just one. Crazy water lady needs to make up her mind."

Angie met Lovelie's pleading gaze and felt something pass between them, a silent exchange that harkened to that first day when Lovelie gripped Angie's hand, never letting go, trusting that Angie would save her. And Angie had, just as she was going to now. A deep, profound well of peace settled through her mind and body, telling her that she was in control, that Junior and his men had no power, despite their weapons, muscles, and threats. Something— the hand of God? The power of love? The mysterious forces of the universe beyond human comprehension?—sparked between Angie and Lovelie. Despite everything, Angie smiled. And across the room, Lovelie smiled too.

When Angie stepped forward, Junior flinched.

"You're going to hand her over," Angie said.

"You got a death wish, talking to me like that?" Junior was nothing but a scared little boy now, caught misbehaving and trying—and failing—to make himself sound like much more than he was.

"You know, I think I see why they call you Junior." Angie was the one doing the smirking now.

"The hell you say, bitch?" Junior shouted, but his shoulders had tensed up in a defensive position, and his eyes made a quick dart to either side of him to see if any of his gang were coming to his defense. But it was as if they'd all melted into the walls and shadows of the orphanage. For the moment, Junior was alone.

"They call you Junior because you're the smallest man there is," Angie said. The voice that came out of her throat had her familiar timbre and cadence, but it also bore a deeper, more profound weight that seemed to come from somewhere else. "You can only live off fear because you're too small to stand out to anyone else otherwise. Unless you make people fear you, you have no chance. You're just a pathetic, weak man-child who's stuck in this room, scared of a lesbian and a little girl."

Junior muttered an incoherent string of grunts, threats, and profanities. Angie allowed her smile to grow as she took another step forward. This time, Junior stumbled back. Lovelie was now out in front of him, with just Junior's hand on her shoulder connecting them.

"I taught you better than this, Tyrone," Angie heard herself say, though the voice didn't sound like hers and she had no idea who Tyrone was. "You stop messing with these children. You know what you need to do, so do it. Make me proud of you again."

"Mama?" Junior's face curdled in sick confusion. Around the room, mutters passed between his gang members as they faced this strange new vulnerability from their boss.

Angie gestured to Lovelie. Junior's hand fell from her shoulder with a pathetic flap.

Lovelie, unsure at first, looked back toward Angie. Angie smiled and nodded, the deep, cosmic spark still connecting the two and sending the warmest waves of comfort in her direction. Then Lovelie began to walk. Slowly at first. Then faster, more confident. Angie dropped to her knees and took the girl in an embrace as strong and warm as the sun or whatever burned deeper and longer beyond it.

"There, you got your girl," Junior hissed. "Now get the hell out of here."

But his spell was broken.

"What the hell's the matter with you?" one of his thugs suddenly shouted. "You gonna let some lady push you around?"

"Hell with this shit!" another voice said. "I'm taking my money and getting out of here. Hand it over!"

And they were upon him. Angie was still clasping Lovelie, eyes closed, when she heard the table get overturned and the money flutter to the floor. She opened her eyes to see the escaped prisoners all fling themselves into a chaotic pile to claim whatever they could. The ones who got there too late turned on their previous comrades with their machetes and clubs. Screams and curses rained throughout the room and blood began to pool across the floor.

Angie felt one last breath of the divine building in her lungs. "Kids!" she shouted.

The cluster of children burst from their invisible prison by the corner and ran across the room, around Angie's side, and out the door into the freedom of the fresh air. Behind them, the shouts and screams and threats continued to rise as the gang tore itself apart.

Angie rushed outside after them with Lovelie by her side, feeling the Caribbean sun reborn as something once again nourishing and life-affirming. Lovelie was in her arms, hugging her with an embrace that Angie hoped would last forever.

Her eyes found an ocean previously lost, and tears burst in thick, joyful waves down her cheeks and onto Lovelie's soft and loving face.

34

Tess didn't get back home with Dawn until well after dark. The lights were still on in the living room, and she could see a silhouette pacing behind the curtains. She rubbed snow out of her eyes and unlocked the front door. Despite all that had happened that day, her eyes were dry. She smiled as she leaned her shoulder against Dawn's.

"How are you holding up?" she asked.

Dawn smiled back. "Pretty good," she said. "I actually feel more at peace than I thought after . . . you know."

Tess pushed the antique door open. "Yeah," she said. "I do—"

She was interrupted by Elizabeth's frantic voice echoing down the stairwell. "Shit! Shit! Shit!"

"What the bloody hell?" Tess muttered. Just then, a muted ringtone began playing close by. Tess checked her purse and pockets before remembering she didn't even own a cellphone. She finally noticed Dawn's jacket pocket was glowing.

"Erm, Dawn," she said. "I think your phone is ringing."

"What's that?" Dawn's gaze was distant, but then surprise overtook her features. "Oh! Oh, yes, of course." She pulled her phone out just as the sound stopped.

From upstairs, Elizabeth's voice was frantic. "Shit, listen Dawn, when you get this message call me right away. I'm really worried about Frank. I think we need to talk to him. He's closer to you than he is to me, and I'm thinking you might be able to get through to him. I'll fill you in on what's going on after you call me. So call me!"

"Hello?" Tess called as she rushed up the stairs. "Elizabeth?"

"Tess?" Elizabeth poked her head out from the entryway above, phone in hand. Her hair was in disarray and her normally impeccable appearance was rumpled and frayed. "Thank goodness you two are back! I need to talk to you."

"Us too," Tess said, figuring it was best to break the news straightforwardly. "Mum is gone."

The skin around Elizabeth's mouth pinched into a frown. "No. She can't be. I didn't even . . ."

"It was wonderful," Dawn said, lower lip quivering just a little.

"She was so peaceful," Tess added. "Serene."

"And listen." Dawn's eyes filled with tears, but she was smiling. "She looked at me! I told her I loved her, and she looked right at me."

Tess hadn't told Dawn about her own final exchange with Mum; she was keeping that all for herself. Maybe Dawn was right, anyway, and there was a final surge of being right at the end.

"And then she was gone," Tess told Elizabeth. "It was over."

"I can't believe I missed it," Elizabeth said, tears glistening the corners of her eyes. "I should have been there. I came all the way over here and I never even said goodbye."

"She's at peace now, Liz," Dawn said.

"I can't do anything right!" Elizabeth's voice was hoarse, drained of its usual efficiency and strength. Though Tess had never quite cared for her half-sister's businesswoman demeanor, the stark change was almost unbearable to watch. "My life is one emergency after another, and instead of being a hero, pulling people from the wreckage of their cars just before they erupt in flames, I get there just a little too late, so all I can do is stand there and listen to them scream."

"It's not like that, Liz," Tess said. "You've been here for all of us. We needed you."

"Wait," Dawn suddenly interrupted. "What's this?" Tess turned to her. She was standing over the wastebasket, reading a crumpled-up piece of paper that she had picked up and unfolded.

"Oh, hell!" Elizabeth exclaimed. "Yes, that's what I was trying to call you about, before all this. It's from Frank."

"What?" Dawn said. "Frank wrote this?"

Tess's head spun. "Can somebody please tell me what's going on?"

"Here." Dawn shoved the paper into Tess's hand. Tess strained her eyes and tried to decipher the crude and disorganized handwriting and smeared ink.

"'To my wife and children' . . . What is this?"

"What does it look like? I'm really worried about him," Elizabeth said.

"Where is he?" Tess asked.

"That's the thing." Elizabeth scrubbed her hands through her unkempt hair, a very un-Elizabeth motion. "He left a little while ago. He'd been going on about return on investment and whether all lives have value, and then he just stormed off in search of a bar."

"Why on earth didn't you stop him?" Tess nearly shouted, remembering all his tirades and the empty bottle of antacids. She'd thought it was just regular stress, but clearly there was something bigger brewing under the surface.

Elizabeth's face collapsed in dismay. "I hadn't seen the note yet, and . . . Oh, crap, I should have realized!" She frantically starting shoving her arms into her coat sleeves.

"What are we going to do now?" Dawn asked.

"I'm going to look for him," Elizabeth said, already heading toward the door. "With Mom gone, my collection of family members is rapidly dwindling. I've learned a bit too late that it was never that big to begin with, and I'm not going to let Frank go as well."

Tess began searching for her own coat before realizing she hadn't even taken it off yet. "Okay, wait for me. Dawn, are you coming?

Dawn?" She stopped at the top of the stairwell, one half-sister at the door downstairs and the other standing stock-still in the kitchen, a faraway look in her eyes.

"On that mountain," Dawn said softly, "back when we were kids, Frank saved my life. But he couldn't accept our help to save him. Not really. All his life he tried to live up to these rigid rules that people placed on him. Black or white, sin or not, right or wrong. He never really understood that life isn't a sound bite or a sermon. Real life is more complicated, with no easy answers, but real life accepts imperfection. It lets you struggle along."

Tess didn't know what to do. The urgency of Elizabeth's shouting compelled her toward the door, but Dawn's voice, sweet and low, held her attention, and for a moment Tess was aware of something else in the space with them. Something deeper. Someone listening and answering their prayers, even if they didn't know they were making them. Replacing the web of panic that had blossomed in her chest was a burgeoning sense of peace and calm. The same peace that Mum had shown her at her very last moment on earth.

Downstairs, Elizabeth threw open the door and Tess heard her gasp. She looked down to see a wild and disheveled Frank standing on her doorstep, alive, his hands gripping his coat close to his chest.

"Frank!" Elizabeth shouted. "I just found the note you threw in the trash! We were all so worried about you! We were about to run out to try and find you! What happened?"

Frank opened and closed his mouth a few times, then sighed.

"I heard an answer," he said.

Tess stared blankly at her half-brother. "What?"

"I asked for help. On the bridge. And I got an answer."

"From whom?" Dawn asked. Tess hadn't realized she'd joined her on the upstairs landing.

Frank looked up, not toward the ceiling, but beyond it. "Mom, I think."

At that, Tess raced down the stairs and embraced Frank in a deep hug. Without any words or resistance, he wrapped his arms around her and returned it. Then Elizabeth joined in. And Dawn. The four of them held one another, ignoring the open door letting the cold, winter air blow in.

35

"Pilot authorized for visual confirmation, copy," the voice in Jim's headset said in a robotic tone. Jim gulped.

"Pilot copies," he responded. Jim had the HD daylight camera trained on Uzuri's house as he awaited the final authorization to pilot his drone to a remote location outside the city where the wedding would be held.

"Heads up, Wilson," Major Udall said from behind him. "We've received word from the ground that convoys are en route to the wedding, a few of them dinged for ID from previous targets. This is the big one."

Jim nodded. "Yes, sir." His words sounded distant and machine-like.

"Hey, Jim?" Jason said from a few stations down. "No pressure or anything, but we got an over-under running on how many of those towelheads you nail here, and I put money on the over. So, uh, try to keep that in mind."

"Shut the hell up!" Udall barked. "You wanna spare him your bullshit while he's working? If you were half as good as he was, you'd be getting the high-profile strikes instead of pissing away your money like some asshole!"

Jim ignored them. He gripped the joystick in one hand, rubbing the unease out of his eyes with the other. It was just another strike. No big deal. He'd done it dozens of times.

But before he could fully reassure himself, a flicker of motion caught his eye. The front door of the house was opening, and, with sinking dread, he saw Uzuri's father emerge. Then Uzuri herself. Her father sported a few bruises across his face, obvious even from 15,000 feet. He walked with a noticeable limp. Jim could picture the interrogation he had caused for Uzuri's father, that night he was kidnapped. Uzuri followed him a bit hesitantly, as if the trauma of the past few days had given her a deep fear of the world outside her house. Or even inside. But she still followed.

In the morning sunlight Jim could see Uzuri's features more clearly than ever. She wore fine silk robes and an ornate gold and silver headscarf framing her oval face. Jim could even see a few wispy strands of hair falling out from behind her headscarf, dancing in the slight mountain breeze. Without thinking, he trained the screen's target directly on Uzuri and zoomed the camera in as far as it would go. As if sensing his presence, she lifted her face from the ground and looked up into the clear blue sky above her, right at his camera. For a second, their eyes met.

Hers glowed like emeralds.

Shit, shit.

Jim glanced around. Major Udall was still chewing out Jason, while the rest of his unit watched with the same kind of glee kids have when one of their classmates gets called to the principal's office. No one was paying attention to Jim's screen. He turned back to his monitor and watched as the father and daughter climbed into their beige coupe and pulled out of the driveway, heading off in the general direction of the mountains beyond the city.

Don't panic yet, Jim told himself. They could be going anywhere. This may just be a coincidence.

"Wilson!" Udall barked. "Get the drone into position. We have word that people are starting to arrive at the wedding. You got the coordinates, right?"

"Yes, sir." Jim gulped the fear that had formed in the back of his throat and slowly began to move his drone eastward along the rural highway to the coordinates where intel placed the wedding. Jim's less-than-helpful thoughts noted that Uzuri and her father were driving in that exact direction, along that exact road.

He followed the projected line on the 2D map on his right monitor. The coordinates carried his drone over some mountains and a few low-lying clouds while Jim tried to ignore the dread churning his stomach. Within a few moments, he had his camera focused at the point where the coordinates converged. The wedding was taking place in the village square, which was right next to a soon-to-be bustling marketplace. He set the drone into a holding pattern above the location and scanned the site.

Sure enough, the setup for a wedding ceremony was well underway, with several ornate Afghan rugs and seats being placed in the square by men dressed in traditional formal wear. Relatives of the groom, no doubt. Already a few cars were beginning to show up, and the people getting out hugged one another in greeting. Jim pursed his lips and looked for Massoud. He saw several older men with the standard beard of Afghan tribesmen, but none of them leaned on an intricate cane.

"Any visual confirmation on Massoud yet, Wilson?" the major asked. Though he kept his eyes focused on the screen in front of him, Jim sensed his CO and the rest of his unit once again crowding around the space surrounding his console, winding themselves up in the anticipation and excitement that went along with a major strike.

Jim swallowed. "Not yet, sir."

"Well, keep your eyes open. Pray this asshole shows up. Though I'm sure we'll ID some secondary targets as well, so keep your trigger finger ready regardless."

"Yes, sir," Jim said, an autopilot response. He was imagining Uzuri happily greeting friends and relatives, exchanging hugs and kind words. Before he could stop himself, he envisioned her body lying on the ground, twisted and burned, buried under rubble. His mind drifted to the dozens, hundreds, of dead bodies he had mostly ignored after successful strikes. He saw the dismembered torsos lying at unnatural angles under piles of dirt and rubble, each with Uzuri's face. They stared up lifelessly with Uzuri's green eyes.

Get a grip, he told himself. She wasn't there yet. Maybe she and her dad were just out running errands.

On the screen, more and more people streamed into the village square, and he suddenly realized he didn't only care about not hurting Uzuri, he didn't want to hurt any of these people. Not wedding guests or market shoppers. He began to pray that no one of any significance showed up, that he wouldn't have to launch a missile at all.

And for a few moments, his prayer held firm. Jim scanned the wedding scene as the ground tilted with the slow shifting of his camera. The village was at the edge of a meadow next to the mountains. In addition to the formal seating being set up in the village square, across the open meadow—thick patches of green grass dotted with specks of purple and white flowers—attendees were laying out rugs in floral patterns of reds, greens, yellows, and purples, which mingled in rainbow harmony with the multicolored robes they all wore. The wedding guests were clustered in groups, chatting. A few glanced up at the sky, as if they sensed the threat to the festivities from above. But they were probably just admiring the beautiful winter day. They continued to chat and laugh and dance to music that Jim couldn't hear.

More and more cars arrived, more and more wedding guests joining the crowd. But none of the people on his screen raised any flags, and none were Uzuri or her father. Jim felt the tight wad of anxiety in his chest loosen, and along with it his grip on the joystick. For a second, he allowed himself to hope that he could end the day without having killed anyone, original target or no.

"There!" Udall's bark tore Jim from his state of calm. In his peripheral vision, he saw the CO's arm extend past his head and point to a space in the upper left of the screen. "Zoom in on that black car.

It matches the description of the car Massoud was last seen in," Udall said. "Keep a focus on it, and we'll see if he gets out. Hopefully, he doesn't get too close to that market. Air Force Command wouldn't authorize that much collateral damage. This many civilians would make the news somewhere, and if that happens, I'm the one getting chewed out. So keep alert!"

Udall's tone suggested he himself didn't care too much about anyone in the marketplace.

"Copy, sir," Jim said.

Udall leaned closer to the screen. "There!" He pointed to a table off to the side of the screen. "That's where the VIP guests will sit, including Massoud. And it's far enough away from the market. With the Hellfire kill radius, you hit over there and the collateral damage will be at acceptable levels. And intel suggests other VIP guests will be high-profile targets as well, so you hit there and we'll take out several birds with one stone."

Jim grunted out another emotionless "Yes, sir" and steadied his shoulders as best he could. But as he followed the vehicle, something else caught his eye.

No.

Behind the black car was another one, a beige two-door coupe. Uzuri's car.

Son of a bitch.

Both cars pulled to a stop in the parking area, and for a brief few seconds, nobody exited either car. Jim allowed himself a final moment of hope that this could all be one big misidentification, that the black car transported anyone but Massoud, that the beige coupe wasn't the one he'd grown familiar with, that Uzuri was somehow far away, and safe. Then, as if the universe had heard his thoughts and was mocking him, the passenger door of the beige car opened and Uzuri stepped out. She glanced around until her eyes fell upon someone she seemed to know, and her previously dour face broke into a smile. She called across the crowd, waving and moving to embrace another young woman dressed in similar garb.

"Zoom in on that car," Udall commanded, and unable to think straight, Jim mutely closed in on Uzuri's car. "No, not that one," Udall barked impatiently. "The black one."

Idiot! Of course. Jim scanned the drone camera to the other car in time to see a young, bearded man in a black and brown robe emerge from the back seat. He opened the front passenger door, letting out an older man sporting a long, gray beard, a white and black turban, and the detailed robes that denoted an elder in the community.

As he rose from his seat, he supported himself with an intricately carved wooden cane.

Jim watched helplessly as Massoud walked toward the VIP table at the head of the wedding ceremony. Uzuri and her father followed him.

"Positive ID," Major Udall said, pumping his fist in the air. "Massoud. Hell yeah! Once he's at the VIP table, Command will give you authorization to strike. Be ready."

"Um, sir?" Jim had no idea what he was going to say, but he had to try to stop this.

"What?"

"There . . . there's a problem."

Udall's hand fell onto his shoulder, gripping it a few notches tighter than what would have been comfortable.

"A problem?" he said. "What is it?"

Jim's mind brainstormed too fast for his words to form. The images of all those bodies lying twisted and broken under rubble poured across his imagination. More bodies than he could even picture at once. Uzuri's face, and then all the rest. Everyone that was crowded together in that village square.

"Uzuri—" he began, then stopped.

"What?" Udall grunted into his ear.

"It's just that . . . there are too many civilians," he said. "Between the wedding and the marketplace. There'll be too much collateral damage, won't there? Too many people killed."

From behind him came a few seconds of confused silence. Then the CO's hand gripped his shoulder even tighter.

"Too much collateral damage?" Jim could hear a jarring mix of confusion and irritation in Udall's voice. "What the hell are you talking about, Wilson? His table's far enough away from the market! Any shoppers are out of the blast radius. And intel believes most people at that table are legitimate targets as well. It's not like Massoud would be eating with the village plumber. Anyone else who gets caught in the blast is well within the acceptable collateral damage limit, for associating with terrorists, if nothing else."

"But . . ." Jim was at a loss. He said the first thing that popped into his head. "It's a wedding."

"I know it's a wedding!" Udall shouted. "I have eyes! Did you forget we have algorithms to determine acceptable levels of collateral damage relative to the value of the target? This whole thing more than falls into the 'acceptable' category! Hell, one dead Massoud is worth more than the lives of everyone else there put together! Now will you shut the hell up about all that and get Command on the line!"

Udall released his painful grip on Jim's shoulder. Jim's eyes burned and suddenly blurred with tears, and he realized he had been staring into the bright screen without blinking. Massoud was still walking toward the VIP table, flanked on both sides by his entourage, including Uzuri and her father. But Jim wasn't looking at Massoud. His eyes were trained on Uzuri.

As she made her way to the head table, she mingled with other young men and women, all dressed in beautiful formal wear, all smiling and laughing in the bright mountain air. Uzuri's eyes seemed to shine, and her face broke into a warm, carefree expression. The same smile she had worn the first night he had seen her, sitting on her windowsill, diary in hand, writing by moonlight.

A voice cracked into life on his headset. "Pilot, confirm ID."

"ID confirmed," he heard himself say. "Pilot copies."

"Pilot, confirm visual," the robotic voice continued.

Massoud slowly made his way through the crowd, delicately balancing his husky frame on his cane. From time to time, he lifted his hand and offered a brief, stoic smile or nod to someone he recognized, occasionally opening his mouth in what seemed like a greeting or blessing. Behind him, Uzuri chatted and laughed with other young women. Jim could imagine she had nearly succeeded in forgetting the horrors of the past few days.

The electronic whine on his headphones clicked to life again. "Pilot, confirm visual," it repeated.

"Pilot . . . pilot confirms," Jim sputtered.

Please, let her leave. Please just let Uzuri leave before the missile hits. He didn't know who—or what—he was praying to, but he prayed nonetheless.

"Copy," Command said through his headphones. "Pilot authorized to fire rifle. Confirm launch."

Massoud arrived at the VIP table and pulled out a chair next to a young man who wore the brightest and most ornate green robe of the entire table, stylized with the intricate native patterns of the Pasto culture. The groom. As Massoud sat down, the young man lifted his head in a look of respect and deference. Massoud whispered something into his ear, perhaps some kind of paternal advice or an official Islamic blessing that Massoud had taken upon himself to give. They spoke like that for a moment or two, Massoud whispering into the groom's ear with the good-natured affection of an elder, the groom smiling and nodding.

Jim's finger remained still on his joystick. He said nothing.

The voice in his headphones came to life again. "Pilot," it repeated, "confirm rifle launch."

"Launch the missile, Wilson," Udall ordered from behind him. "You have a clear shot at Massoud."

Jim's eyes shot back to the old man. Massoud gave the groom a double-shoulder pat as he offered a few last words of encouragement. Then he set his cane down on the ground and looked expectantly at the table with the familiar posture of someone waiting for the food to be served.

At that moment, Uzuri and her father arrived at the table. Her father sat down across from Massoud. Uzuri took a seat only a few feet away.

Well within the Hellfire's kill radius.

"Wilson!" Udall's patience was all but gone. "Just take the shot already!"

Jim's lungs seized, purging the air from his chest. He felt like he was drowning. At the table, Uzuri wrapped her arms around a young woman sitting next to her and laughed as one does when they find an old friend they haven't seen in a while. Gripping the young woman's arms, Uzuri smiled brightly.

"Wilson . . ." Udall warned, but Jim barely heard him. He couldn't take his eyes off Uzuri's upturned lips.

"Does pilot confirm rifle launch?" the voice from Command asked in a reedy, annoyed authority.

"Wilson!" Udall shouted again.

Everyone else in the trailer had gone silent. Jim could hear the radio, always set to Alex Meter's talk radio program, airing a commercial. ". . . *act now to get the secret to true health that big pharma and the liberal elites don't want you to know!*" He thought of his dad and that bizarre phone call and felt even more at sea. "Pilot . . ." Jim attempted. His voice was low and weak. "Pilot . . . Pilot . . ." He repeated the word over and over, as if saying it enough times would call the universe to give him some way out of the situation. But all he got was Udall's hand grabbing his shoulder again.

"Wilson, you idiot! Fire! The! Missile!"

The commercial break ended, but instead of Meter's booming voice, a softer, gentler one spoke. It was female, determined and forceful, carrying the weight of an Old Testament prophet in a woman's matter-of-fact tone.

"*Howdy there, folks,*" the voice said. "*This is Monique speaking. You may know me better as 'Monika' or the 'fat, black intern.' You're probably wondering what I'm doing on air right now. Mr. Meter has been working so hard this holiday season, I've decided to give him a bit of a break. In fact, he's just outside the studio right now, telling me to tell you how much you all mean to him.*" In the background of the broadcast, barely picked up by the studio's microphone, was a loud banging that sounded like someone pounding against a locked door. Underneath that, a string of shouts and curses in a familiar male voice. "*Okay, I locked him out of the studio, to be honest.*"

On Jim's screen, Uzuri turned her gaze up, into what for her had to look like a nondescript patch of sky. But at that moment, her eyes looked directly into those of the man watching her from a hot, sweaty trailer in the middle of the Nevada desert on the other side of the world.

Jim's shoulder flared in sharp pain as Udall dug his nails in even deeper. "FIRE THE MISSILE!!!" Udall practically screamed.

From the radio: "*I wanted to take this opportunity to tell you all about the true spirit of Christmas.*"

"FIRE THE DAMN MISSILE!!!!"

Jim was suddenly possessed by a calm he had never experienced before. His mind found something like peace in its single-minded focus.

"*Despite what my boss has been telling you,*" Monique continued, "*the true spirit of Christmas does not come from waging war on 'the other' or being the loudest one in the room. It comes from compassion. It comes from love.*"

"No!" Jim shouted.

"It comes from the deepest place in our hearts, deeper than the air in our lungs or the bile in our stomachs."

"Screw this!" Jim was suddenly thrown out of his chair. He went tumbling onto the floor of the trailer, shocked by Udall's action and dismayed to lose sight of Uzuri. "Cooper!" Udall shouted. "Get over here! Wilson's checked out for whatever reason, and we need this asshole dead! Fire the shot NOW!"

"Yes, sir!" Cooper cried as he jumped halfway across the trailer in a few strides and lumbered into Jim's chair.

Jim pulled himself up. There was nothing he could do now but watch.

"Firing rifle in three, two, one . . ." Cooper hit the trigger, and on the screen the impact countdown began to flash in bright red numbers. "Impact in thirty seconds." His tone was void of emotion. Just like Jim's had been only a few weeks ago.

Uzuri was still sitting at the table, chatting and laughing with her friends and family, carefree and happy. Her face, with its soft curves and bright green eyes, was framed on the screen by the countdown to the missile strike that was heading in brutal efficiency directly for her.

Please, please, please, Jim called out in his head. Who or what he was calling to he didn't know. All he could feel was the sheer urgency of his plea, sent without postage or conditions into the sky above him. *Please, just leave. Get out of there. Now.*

Uzuri looked up again. Her face tightened in a sudden realization of . . . something. Her eyes seemed to focus somewhere on the middle distance of the sky. Right into the camera once more.

Please . . .

"Impact in twenty seconds," Cooper said. The young men gathered around the room drew in their breaths in a familiar anticipation.

In the background Monique's voice continued its soothing message about Christmas miracles. *"True miracles occur in our hearts."*

Without any word or gesture to her friends, Uzuri got up from

the table and began to walk away. Away from the group, away from
the epicenter of the coming impact, back toward an empty expanse
of the rural village where they had gathered in what was supposed to
be a celebration. Jim didn't breathe.

"Impact in ten seconds."

"Because God lives in our hearts."

Uzuri, now at the outer expanse of the crowd, picked up her
pace. Her shoulders were raised and her back arched, as if some
invisible hand had placed itself upon the small of her back and was
hurrying her away from the crowd with an elemental force neither
she nor Jim could understand.

*"When God melts a cold and icy heart, that's a greater miracle than
turning water into wine."*

"Impact in three . . ."

Jim's chest burned, and every muscle in his body tightened to the
point of screaming.

". . . or healing the sick . . ."

". . . two . . ."

Uzuri broke into a run.

". . . one . . ."

Please.

". . . or even raising the dead."

On screen, the celebratory wedding scene was replaced by an
apocalyptic fury of destruction. In barely a second, the fireball had
enveloped the entirety of the screen. The seats, the altar, the beauti-
fully patterned rugs were instantaneously transformed into a chaos
of debris flying in every direction. Though he had seen it dozens of
times before, Jim's stomach burned to know that much of the debris
took the form of shattered human limbs and viscera, whichever pieces hadn't been rendered completely into dust, indistinguishable from
the dirt and crushed rocks.

"Target confirmed," Cooper said.

No one in the room spoke or cheered. Or breathed.

The screen now showed a haze of brown dust and gray smoke that obscured whatever was left of the impact site.

Jim's lungs were screaming for oxygen, but his brain could no longer remember how to breathe.

After a moment, the mountain winds carried enough of the smoke and haze away to reveal what was left of the wedding party. In the spot where the VIP table once sat, the impact crater had burned a hideous scar into the ground. There wasn't anything recognizable left in the center, not flowers, tables, or chairs, and certainly not people.

Farther away, the guests who had been sitting close to the main table were strewn in contorted positions. Many were maimed in hideous ways, missing limbs or heads or with their torsos torn open by debris turned shrapnel. Others had dark pools of blood streaming from their eyes and ears from the force of the shock wave. No one moved or showed any sign of life.

As he stared, unblinking, at the pile of bodies on the screen, Jim thought of the countless hours of video games he'd played, the pixelated gore and realistic "battle modes." Part of him wanted to force his mindset back to that safe video game logic. Bodies, blood, gore, all just pixels on his screen. Nothing more real than Call of Duty. He imagined he could just go back to the last save point, put the bodies back together, gather the smoke and debris back into its missile cell, and reset the wedding to the happiness and joy it had displayed only a minute ago.

But then Uzuri's face flashed to the fore of his thoughts. And the bodies on his screen came crashing back to the real world. The world that was on the other side of his own, but just as real.

And just as irreversible.

Then, off on the upper left-hand side of the screen, he picked up movement. A single figure, far away from the dead bodies and vaporized human remains, was slowly getting to its feet. Jim's eyes widened, sucking in every pixel of light from the screen. Uzuri. She was shaky from the force of the impact, and bloodied, covered with dirt and debris, shivering.

But she was alive.

On the radio, Monique continued: "*So this Christmas season, I want you to look for true miracles. Look for the strength that God has given you.*"

The dam in Jim's lungs burst, and a deep, guttural sob poured out of his mouth and echoed across the walls of the trailer.

"*Not to fight against external enemies, but to fight against the hate and anger that chokes the love in your heart.*"

Uzuri lifted her face from the ground and looked up. The same hand that had pushed her away from the missile strike—the hand of God, the hand of fate, the hand of the universe, whatever—seemed to lift her eyes up across the empty space to where Jim's drone hovered out of sight. Her green eyes, still wide with shock, terror, pain, and trauma, reached through thousands of miles of space and looked directly into Jim's.

"*Realize that the true gift of Christmas is the fact that your life—yes, yours!—has value. More value than you can imagine. And that, my friends, is the greatest miracle of all. Merry Christmas, everyone!*"

Jim sank to his knees and sobbed. Tears poured from his eyes and streamed down his face in heavy, leaden chunks. He heard himself cry out primally for the mercy that had spared Uzuri's life. Not a prayer or thanks, just an unformed wail of emotion sent storming out into the expanse of the universe.

She was alive. And just like Monique had said, every life had value. Uzuri, Jim, his grandmother. Even his dad.

EPILOGUE

Jim sat at his command station, as he had hundreds of times before. He wore his headset and gripped his joystick, watching his screen with determined focus. "Approaching target," he intoned while his steady hands guided his drone with expert precision.

The drone descended through cloud cover, revealing the land below: a lush tropical forest, encircled by warm, blue ocean waters. The drone descended farther and farther, its camera picking up dense clusters of buildings and houses piled onto hillsides and across the bay.

"Approaching target," Jim said again.

The screen showed an airport runway, with rows upon rows of planes and helicopters gathered from all around the world.

"Landing in three . . . two . . . one . . ."

Jim's drone touched down on the runway at the Port-au-Prince airport. Within moments, a group of rescue workers gathered around to pick up the boxes of supplies—food, clothing, medical supplies—that it had aboard. Jim, his mission achieved, leaned back into his seat and smiled.

Angie eyed the US Air Force plane that waited expectantly on the runway with its cargo door open to receive the long line of American citizens and Haitian refugees heading to the United States. Behind her, her parents were bickering good-naturedly, Mama supporting Papa by the arm while they bandied back and forth in Creole. Angie smiled and pulled out her cellphone, which thankfully had a strong signal at the airport.

"Hey, babe," Angie said when Dawn picked up. "I'm just calling to let you know we're about to board the plane. I can't wait to see you when you get back from London."

"I'll be there tomorrow." Dawn's soft, melodious voice made Angie weak in the knees. They'd been texting about their return home, but hadn't yet talked. "I've missed you more than you can imagine. It's been a . . . surprising time here with Frank, Elizabeth, and Tess. I have so much to tell you." She paused and hummed a moment. "We had a Christmas miracle here in London town."

Angie looked down. At her side was Lovelie, gripping her hand as tightly as ever, but smiling broadly and fiddling in child-like excitement as they embarked on their new adventure. Together.

"We had one of our own here too. And you'll be meeting her very soon."

Other books by
REBEKAH PACE

The Red Thread
When a 90-year-old Holocaust survivor reconnects with his childhood
sweetheart in a strange world of shared dreams, he must venture out
of the safety of his lonely life and go on a mission to rescue his lost
soulmate from impending tragedy.

All I Want For Christmas
When a young girl prays for God to heal her disintegrating family, a
fire suddenly destroys everything they own, forcing them to rediscover
each other and their faith.

Stay up to date:
Follow Rebekah on Amazon

https://www.amazon.com/author/rebekahpace